"You made the ru~~~~ follow them."

Adrienne's eyes widened, then narrowed as she frowned, trying to figure out what motivated him. "Why?" she demanded bluntly.

"Because I respect people who have the courage to make a stand about what they feel is right," he said calmly, his eyes holding hers. "I may not particularly like it when the firmness works to my disadvantage, but that doesn't stop me from respecting that person."

"You . . . respect me?" she questioned doubtfully, not really sure that was what she wanted from him.

Jared nodded, completely serious. "Yes, but I'll make no secret of this, Adrienne—I also want you. I'll go along with your terms, but that won't stop me from needing to touch and kiss you while you get to know me."

"Okay by me," she said huskily.

Dear Reader:

Romance readers have been enthusiastic about the Silhouette Special Editions for years. And that's not by accident: Special Editions were the first of their kind and continue to feature realistic stories with heightened romantic tension.

The longer stories, sophisticated style, greater sensual detail and variety that made Special Editions popular are the same elements that will make you want to read book after book.

We hope that you enjoy this Special Edition today, and will enjoy many more.

Please write to us:

Jane Nicholls
Silhouette Books
PO Box 236
Thornton Road
Croydon
Surrey CR9 3RU

ROSLYN MacDONALD
Transfer of Loyalties

Silhouette Special Edition

Originally Published by Silhouette Books
division of
Harlequin Enterprises Ltd.

To a special group of friends—
Dianne, Maureen, Rosemary, Tricia and
Veronica

All the characters in this book have no existence outside the imagination of the Author, and have no relation whatsoever to anyone bearing the same name or names. They are not even distantly inspired by any individual known or unknown to the Author, and all the incidents are pure invention.

The text of this publication or any part thereof may not be reproduced or transmitted in any form or by any means, electronic or mechanical, including photocopying, recording, storage in an information retrieval system, or otherwise, without the written permission of the publisher.

This book is sold subject to the condition that it shall not, by way of trade or otherwise, be lent, resold, hired out or otherwise circulated without the prior consent of the publisher in any form of binding or cover other than that in which it is published and without a similar condition including this condition being imposed on the subsequent purchaser.

*First published in Great Britain 1986
by Silhouette Books, 15–16 Brook's Mews, London W1A 1DR*

© Roslyn MacDonald 1986

Silhouette, Silhouette Special Edition and Colophon are
Trade Marks of Harlequin Enterprises B.V.

ISBN 0 373 09293 8

23-0686

*Printed and bound in Great Britain by
Cox & Wyman Ltd, Reading*

ROSLYN MacDONALD

moved to the West Coast with her husband several years ago and was quickly won over by the friendly people and casual life-style. Now living within the sight of the mountains and sea, she skis in the winter and braves the cold of the Pacific Ocean in the summer. An enthusiastic traveler, she enjoys exploring the challenging landscape of the West and northwestern states in rambling, unstructured vacations. Her writing, which began as a pleasure, has now become a career that pulls together the many varied interests in her life.

Another Silhouette Book by Roslyn MacDonald

Silhouette Special Edition
Second Generation

For further information about
Silhouette Books please write to:

Jane Nicholls
Silhouette Books
PO Box 236
Thornton Road
Croydon
Surrey CR9 3RU

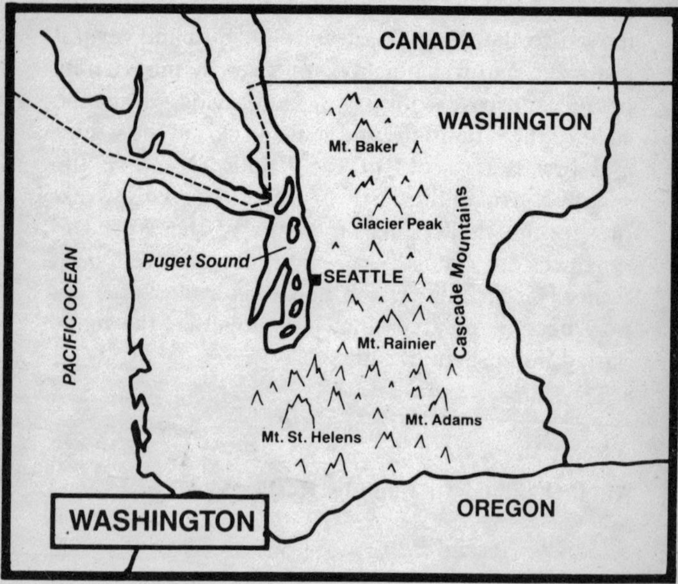
CANADA
WASHINGTON
Mt. Baker
Glacier Peak
Cascade Mountains
Puget Sound
SEATTLE
PACIFIC OCEAN
Mt. Rainier
Mt. Adams
Mt. St. Helens
OREGON
WASHINGTON

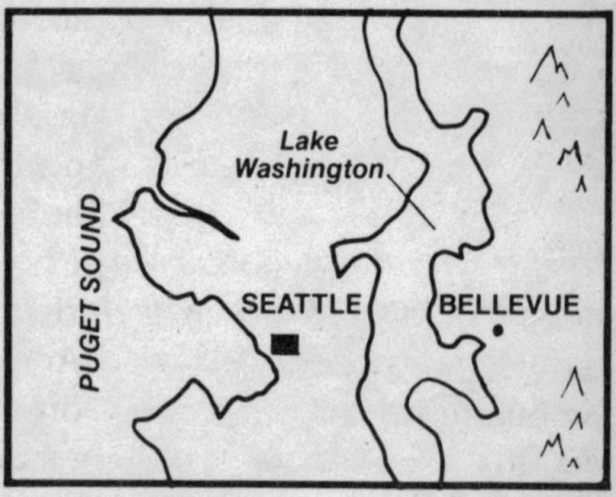
Lake
Washington
PUGET SOUND
SEATTLE
BELLEVUE

Prologue

Are you serious?"

As soon as the words were out of her mouth Adrienne Denton regretted them. They smacked of insubordination and that was no way to approach Emery Thorpe. He was glaring at her now, his small shifty eyes boring into her. Hastily she added, "I mean, Emery, this is such a shock! I had no idea!" Her apology soothed him and he subsided, blinking rapidly as he always did when he felt events were moving in the direction he preferred.

"This is a great opportunity, Adrienne," he said in lush, honeyed tones. Leaning forward, he rested his elbows on the surface of the big mahogany desk and clasped the short fingers of his rather pudgy hands together.

Adrienne swallowed her shock and managed to smile. "I believe you, Emery." She hesitated, marshaling her chaotic thoughts. For months rumors about the Seattle branch had been drifting around the New York office of APP, the large multifaceted corporation that Adrienne was employed by, getting worse and worse as time wore on. To be the one chosen to wrestle the branch back to peak performance was both a high compliment and tremendously exciting. After years of hard work, her loyalty to the company was finally paying off. Her feet itched to move but she subdued the urge. In her six years with APP, Adrienne had learned that it didn't do to show too much emotion; emotion was considered feminine and a weakness. So instead of jumping up from her seat and doing a little jig of delight, she smiled aloofly. "The word on the current Seattle administration isn't complimentary."

The satisfied blinking stopped and Emery's gaze fastened on hers. "Rumors!" he barked. "Since when do you waste your time listening to malicious gossip?"

"If it's true I want to know, Emery. I'm not flying all the way across the country without the facts—every one of them!"

"Fair enough," agreed Thorpe grudgingly. "You know that Seattle is an important branch. As well as providing the necessary backup for sales, the manager also liaises with some of our biggest suppliers of raw materials. It is a position of considerable responsibility—which the current manager has proved he doesn't have. His staff is lax, the district sales manager, Noel Granger, can't get any support from him, his expenses are way over budget and this is only the first half of our fiscal year. The problems grow with every passing day. Over the next few weeks you'll hear all about them, in detail. By the time you leave for Seattle you may wish you'd never heard of the branch."

Adrienne raised her eyebrows and said calmly, "It sounds like this will be a tough assignment."

Thorpe studied her for a moment, trying to interpret her response and mentally cursing her smooth, expressionless features. It always annoyed him when he couldn't read his subordinates because he prided himself on his ability to know just what a man was thinking, even though he might be mouthing entirely different sentiments. But that was the problem, wasn't it? Adrienne Denton was a woman, very much a woman, despite the severely tailored suits and blouses she wore.

Always pleasant, rarely angry and never snappish, she kept a tangible wall of reserve between herself and her co-workers. Adrienne had learned the hard way never to let her colleagues penetrate her defenses. Even Emery, with his people sense and excellent manipulative skills, couldn't break through the barrier to discover what she was really thinking.

He leaned back in his chair, expecting a show of excitement from her, even though it would be out of character. This was a plum appointment for a woman with her limited experience, although the branch was a seething caldron of potential problems. He could give it to her straight or he could gloss over the worst of the difficulties. Either way, it didn't matter. She was taking the assignment. She had no choice.

He decided to mix a little judicious flattery with the bad news. "This will be the worst mess you've ever faced. You're good at troubleshooting, Adrienne. I have confidence you can work things out. I'm not expecting any miracles. No overnight turnarounds. It will take two or three years at least to put Seattle back on stream."

Adrienne's mind seized on the length of the assignment. Three years! It sounded scary. It sounded fun. She'd never been out of New York before, except on family vacations to Cape Cod. Seattle was a world away and she had no idea what to expect. She forced herself to remember that this would not be an extended holiday, but one more step in her steady advancement through APP's ranks. She could never let herself forget that her career came first. "And after Seattle, Emery?" she asked coolly. "Then what?"

Thorpe blinked several times. "Well, Adrienne, you know that we think very highly of you here in the logistics department. Head office needs talent like yours."

That was exactly what Adrienne wanted to hear. For her, administering a branch office was only an interim position on her path to the executive, no matter how important that branch might be. She curled her lips into a faint, apparently amused, smile to hide her excitement. "You can be so persuasive, Emery. I'll have to start reading up on Seattle, if it's going to be my home for the next few years."

Chapter One

The insistent ringing of a telephone dragged Adrienne out of a deep sleep. Groggily she reached for the receiver and automatically raised it to her ear.

"Good morning," said a soft, husky female voice. "This is your six o'clock wake-up call." Adrienne blinked in confusion before memory rushed in. She was in Seattle, lodged in a comfortable, but uninspiring, downtown hotel. Her flight from New York had arrived last evening. Between the three hour time change and the long hours cooped up on the jet, she had been so exhausted she hadn't bothered to do more than check into her room and tumble into bed.

"Oh," she muttered into the mouthpiece, her voice still thick with sleep. "Thanks."

"You're welcome," replied the voice pleasantly. "Have a nice day."

The line clicked then went dead as the operator broke the connection. Adrienne slowly sat up as she gradually came awake. Today was Monday, her first day in her new job and she wanted to get to the office before eight o'clock. By being early she hoped to make a good impression on her new staff and to meet them individually as they arrived.

She sighed and rubbed her eyes with the back of her hands. Still drowsy, she contemplated curling up and letting herself drift back to sleep, but she quickly dismissed the idea. If she didn't get up now she would never make it to the office on time, which would create the wrong impression.

Resolutely throwing off the covers she slid from the bed, reaching for her old, familiar and comforting quilted robe before crossing to the bathroom to prepare for her day.

An hour later she was staring critically at her appearance in the mirror. Her face was subtly made up to look natural but sophisticated, there was not a strand out of place in her sleek, swept-back hairstyle and her tailored slate gray suit of fine woven wool gave just the right touch of severity to her image. The most difficult part of this morning, she knew, would be to make her new staff see her in the same light as they would a man—as an authority figure in the office, someone to be respected and obeyed, the equal of any male manager they'd ever worked for.

A wry smile marred the reflection in the mirror. First impressions could help, or hinder, the process to a remarkable degree. That was why it was so important for her appearance to be perfect this morning.

Well, there was nothing out of place that Adrienne could see. She flicked off the light over the mirror and went into the bedroom, walking slowly to counter rising excitement and apprehension. So much was at stake! She stopped to pick up her purse, checking the contents to be sure she had everything she needed. By the time she was through, the fluttering butterflies in her stomach had calmed.

After a light breakfast and two cups of hot steaming coffee she was ready to face anything her new staff thrust at her. Returning to her room to pick up a raincoat, she looked around at the impersonal decor and decided that she would have to find an apartment and get settled in as soon as possible. The room was pleasant enough, but if she stayed too long it could easily become depressing. Despite its elegance the hotel was a place to be used as a stopover between here and there. It had not been designed to accommodate a semipermanent guest.

Since she had no idea where the office was located, she took a taxi. The Seattle sky was a dreary iron-gray, casting a pall over the thrusting towers of the city. What an introduction to her new home, Adrienne thought, as she shivered in the damp January air. Unless she was sadly mistaken it was soon going to rain.

After a short ride, the cab pulled up in front of a steel-and-glass office complex. Adrienne paid the driver, gave him a generous tip and asked for a receipt.

Her heels clicked a light tattoo as she made her way through the revolving doors and crossed the lobby floor to the elevators. Though still early, there was a crowd waiting for the next car to arrive. Adrienne looked thoughtfully at their faces. Were some of these her new staff? The steel doors slid open and she followed the others inside. People moved, shifting as they reached to press the controls for their floor. Adrienne waited to see if anyone would choose ten, the level she wanted, but no one did. A little disappointed, she pushed the button herself as the car began to glide upward.

As there were only four businesses housed on the tenth floor she had no difficulty finding the door labeled APP, but when she tried the handle she found it locked. Frowning, she glanced at her watch. Twenty to eight. Company hours were eight to four-thirty, but in New York some staff members always arrived before seven-thirty. She glanced once more at the engraved name plate to make sure she was in the right place. She was.

For the next few minutes she clock-watched and tried to suppress growing annoyance. There was nothing in the company rules that said you had to come in early or leave late, but doing so always gratified those above you. Just as she had wanted to make a good impression on APP's Seattle employees, Adrienne expected them to feel the same way about her.

The elevator doors slid open with a well-oiled thump. Adrienne straightened, mentally warning herself to be alert and prepared. This was probably one of her new staff; in a moment she would be facing her first test. Her nerves tightened, adrenaline pumping through her veins.

What emerged was a tall, broad-shouldered man, standing well over six feet, with thick black hair, dark-gray eyes and hard, angular features. He was wearing a navy-blue suit that was beautifully tailored to his muscular body. The suit was expensive, as was the crisp white shirt of the finest cotton, the dark-blue silk tie shot through with gold pinstripes and the soft, black leather boots. Absurdly, this good-looking man was carrying an enormous pink teddy bear in his arms, fully half as long as he.

Adrienne watched him with detached interest. She was quite sure that this man didn't belong in APP's offices. The district sales manager, she knew, was about forty-five years of age, much older than this man, whom she estimated to be in his midthirties. That made him too old to be one of the company sales reps. Undoubtedly he belonged behind one of the other three doors on the floor.

As she watched, he shifted the burden in his arms and came toward her. That didn't surprise Adrienne because one of the other doors was past her at the end of the hall. As he strode closer he began to smile, softening the hard features and warming his gray eyes.

He stopped in front of her, plopped the bear on the floor and said happily, "Boy, am I glad you're here! You're new, aren't you?"

Adrienne looked at the stuffed animal, then up at him. "Yes," she said repressively.

The gray eyes smiled down at her. "Too bad," he murmured, a hint of promise in his voice. "I would have enjoyed working with you." His gaze swept down her slender form. Fleshed and lean in all the right spots, Adrienne knew she had a nicely curved figure. Her legs were long and slim, but she kept them well hidden by demure, knee-length skirts. She was not the type of woman to advance in the business world because of her feminine charms.

The black-haired man's scrutiny was making her uncomfortable. She fought down the desire to close her raincoat and wrap her arms around her breasts to protect herself from his eyes. His gaze roved upward, to her face with its high cheekbones, thin, straight nose and deep-set blue-gray eyes. He smiled again, this time with sure male appreciation. Adrienne set her teeth over rising anger and waited for his next comment, which she was sure would be suggestive, and to her, offensive. She didn't like men of his sort. She'd been used by them before and never would be again.

To her surprise he patted the teddy bear on the head, almost as if it were a familiar pet, and said, "Give this to Noel, would you?"

It took Adrienne a moment to catch up to this sudden switch in mood. "You've got to be kidding!" she blurted in disgust.

He looked surprised. "No. Why would I be?" He grinned mockingly, the gray eyes glinting with amusement.

"I'm not going to stand here holding that stupid bear until someone comes to open the office!" Adrienne cried, thoroughly indignant.

He said annoyingly, "You don't have to hold it. Sitting down is what this little fellow does best." He thumped the bear again.

Adrienne glanced at the oversize pink teddy bear with its plastic mask of brown features and thought about first impressions. "Forget it," she said firmly, a thread of anger coloring her tone.

The glint disappeared from his eyes and the black brows met in a frown. "Look, what's the problem?" Suddenly he was smiling again, a warm, provocative, charming smile that probably melted women's hearts. Not this woman, thought Adrienne, staring back stonily. "I'd like to stick around and talk, Miss..."

"Denton," Adrienne supplied coolly, deliberately leaving out her first name.

He continued smoothly, "...but I've got an appointment that I can't be late for. You'll be doing me a tremendous favor—"

"Not a prayer," Adrienne said firmly, trying to cover the insidious weakening effect his rich, velvet-smooth voice was having on her. His appointment might be important to him, she argued silently, but so was her first meeting with her staff. He could wait, just as she was, and hand over his stuffed bear to whoever arrived first.

He lifted his arm and flicked up one white cuff to check a handsome silver digital watch. His sensual mouth firmed into a thin line and he cast a speculative look at Adrienne. "My name," he announced crisply, "is Jared Hawkes. This bear is for Noel Granger. Tell him I'll call him later." He turned and began to walk away.

"Now just a minute—" Adrienne began, calling after his retreating form. She launched herself into motion, planning to grab him and force him to stop. What she would do after that she hadn't figured out. Not watching where she was going, her feet tangled in the fat legs of the pink teddy bear and she stumbled to her knees with a little cry that was a mixture of surprise and frustration.

At the elevator Jared Hawkes turned to see what had happened. He was back to her in a few lithe strides. His strong fingers closed over her upper arms as he helped her to her feet. "Are you okay?" he demanded, concern in his eyes and voice.

"Yes!" Adrienne all but snarled, wrenching herself away. Nothing had been hurt but her dignity and pride. Under his thoughtful gaze she felt herself color with embarrassment. "Take your damned bear and go!" she shouted, glaring at him.

"Come on, be a sport," he coaxed, backing away. The hateful mocking grin was now back on his face.

Adrienne was sure he thought this whole stupid fiasco very amusing. "Look, I told you—" she began impatiently.

The elevator doors opened and he stepped inside. For one horrified moment Adrienne thought some APP employees might be on that car, but blessedly no one emerged before the steel doors snapped shut. She sighed with relief until she realized that Jared Hawkes was gone, leaving her to mind a gigantic stuffed animal with a silly expression and a tag tied to one round, fluffy ear.

With nothing else to do she looked at the card. It read *To the newest addition to the Trent family, Elaine or Jon Junior.*

Who on earth are they, she wondered indignantly. This was just terrific. The wretched toy didn't even belong to Noel Granger; it was destined for a friend. That made Jared Hawkes's insistence on leaving the bear here a hundred times worse. She glared at the bear who smiled brightly back. What a way to start a new job. First the rain, now this. Was it an omen? She shivered, pushing the thought aside. She didn't believe in omens.

When the first of the office team arrived at five to eight, Adrienne was standing on one side of the door while the bear guarded the other. She'd assumed a deliberately detached attitude, hoping that it would look as if some prankster had left the stuffed toy long before Adrienne's arrival. The thin middle-aged woman who emerged from the elevator halted in surprise when she saw Adrienne and her companion, then smiled blandly and came forward.

"I hope you haven't been waiting long," she said formally, her oblique glance at the pink monstrosity expressive of the questions she was too polite to ask. As she unlocked the office door, she added, "I'm Lilith Page, by the way. And you are?"

Adrienne said her name, eyeing the bear with resentment as she did so. Lilith was opening the door and flicking on the light switches. It looked as if Adrienne got to bring teddy into the office. She hefted the pink bundle, which all but obscured her vision. Peeking around one fluffy ear, she moved carefully forward. Even with her vision obscured, she noticed Lilith suppress a smile and her temper flared.

"You're the new manager," said Lilith, her voice carefully neutral. "Noel, my boss, has been looking forward to meeting you."

"Good," Adrienne said curtly, restraining her temper with difficulty. She refused to make the situation worse by taking out her anger on Lilith. This could all be blamed on that black-haired scoundrel, Jared Hawkes, and if she ever saw him again... Well, he was the one she should be exercising her temper on. She thrust the bear at the older woman. "This belongs to your boss. Would you put it in his office?"

"Certainly," Lilith agreed diplomatically, gathering up the soft giant without any qualms. "I wish my kids had had toys like this when they were small. Is it for Elaine Trent's baby?"

"I guess so," Adrienne replied coldly. "A man by the name of Jared Hawkes left it outside the door about ten minutes ago."

"Of course," said Lilith, enlightenment brightening her eyes. "Jared! He's a super man. Give me a minute to put this in Noel's office, then I'll show you around."

Super was not how Adrienne would describe Jared Hawkes. Good looking, sexy, a deceiver and probably a dangerous predator would be closer to the mark. Men like him used their charm to manipulate women. Definitely not a wonderful man.

Forcing herself to forget Jared and his wretched stuffed bear, she looked around at her new domain and was taking note of the general air of careless disorder when Lilith reappeared. As she followed the secretary into the main part of the suite, she decided the entrance area needed attention. Even the potted plant beside the reception desk was wilting.

"Shouldn't our receptionist open up the office?" Adrienne demanded, determined to create a businesslike atmosphere, as she and Lilith entered the staff lunchroom.

The older woman's expression was unreadable as she said neutrally, "I don't mind doing it. Really, it's whoever gets in first. Sometimes Melissa, that's the receptionist, is the last to arrive, sometimes one of the first."

Adrienne slowly stripped off her raincoat, thinking deeply as she made the familiar movements. Though Lilith wasn't saying much, it sounded as if this was a staff problem she would have to sort out.

Lilith flicked the Start button on the small automatic coffeemaker, then turned and smiled at Adrienne. "Shall I show you around? All those dull, necessary details like where the light switches are, whose desk is whose, how the files are organized?"

Adrienne smiled in agreement, following her out of the rather sterile lunchroom. They were standing by a large gray metal filing cabinet when a young girl, her beautiful figure clad in skintight jeans and sweater, strolled in. At the sight of Adrienne her undistinguished face registered surprise, which was quickly replaced by wary hostility.

"Good morning, Avril," Lilith said firmly. "This is Adrienne Denton. She's replacing Grant Booth."

"Hi," Adrienne said, calmly ignoring the expression in the girl's eyes. "Why don't you tell me a bit about yourself, Avril?"

The girl looked uncomfortable, then blurted out defiantly, "Grant hired me."

"I see," Adrienne said slowly, realizing she had another problem on her hands. This must be Avril's first job after high school, and she hadn't learned yet that loyalty was owed to the company, not an individual manager.

Laughing voices were heard in the hall and two more staff members wandered into the office. Adrienne quickly identified one of them as the receptionist, Melissa. She was a beautiful, well-groomed blonde with a perfect figure, but rather vacant features. The other was a vivacious young woman of about Adrienne's age, with dark-brown hair, lively brown eyes and a heart-shaped face. It was her laughter that Adrienne had heard before the two girls stepped into the suite.

The dark-haired girl smiled and said brightly, "You must be our new boss! Welcome to the West Coast. I'm Carol Tynan, your secretary, and this is Melissa Lyons, our receptionist and switchboard operator. I'm sure Lilith has already given you a tour, she's terribly organized, even on Monday morning!''

Though Carol appeared to be willing to continue indefinitely, Adrienne smiled and stemmed the flow of words. Too much talk while the teddy bear incident was fresh in Lilith's mind and she might mention something to the others while Adrienne was talking casually with them. Adrienne hoped Lilith, as the sale manager's secretary, would have the tact not to gossip about the incident later on.

Melissa smiled vaguely, murmured something about coffee and opening up the switchboard, then disappeared. Lilith also left, with a cool comment about Adrienne being in safe hands. Adrienne sent her a sharp glance and asked that she be notified when Noel Granger arrived.

The branch soon settled into its normal routine. Adrienne went into her office to acquaint herself with the manager's personal files—ongoing problems, potential disasters, routine tasks, staff background. Grant Booth's records were lamentably poor, except for the personnel files. These were models of efficiency. Their contents ran from the ordinary statistics required by the company's bookkeepers, to surprisingly personal information—a woman's favorite flowers, candies and foods, even the names of husbands or current boyfriends.

Adrienne felt her stomach clench. She carefully closed the folder and replaced it in the desk drawer. She knew very clearly what kind of man Grant Booth, the Seattle branch's former manager, was because she had personal, painful, experience of a man who used the same smooth tactics. Booth hid behind his doting female staff, letting them do all the work while he took the credit. Only Grant had misread the situation. He'd gotten lazy and eventually he'd been found out. Not all of them were. Ted Conrad never was.

She swiveled in her chair to look out the plate-glass windows. Fog had crept over the city, softening the contours of the downtown office towers in a woolly haze that found an echo in her mind. Ted Conrad was part of the past, and today of all days she should be looking toward the future. But she was sitting in Grant Booth's chair, in Grant Booth's office, and he was cast in exactly the same mold as Ted. How could she help but think of the past?

She'd met Ted Conrad in her first year at APP. Fresh out of college and eager to put all her newly learned skills to use, she had pranced into the New York headquarters like an excited puppy. Her expectations for her future were high. Brought up to be career oriented, she had applied to APP because of the company's excellent reputation and its policy of promoting capable young managers to senior positions rather than hiring from the outside. Adrienne knew she was intelligent, quick to learn and decisive. In her opinion her career in business would be as successful as her father's was.

Morgan Denton was a vice president in a large company that he'd joined more than thirty years before as a management trainee. At the time, his firm had been small but prosperous. It and Morgan had grown together; as business flourished, Morgan was promoted to increasingly responsible positions. He was happy in his job and had brought up his four children with deep-rooted beliefs about conduct and company loyalty. According to Adrienne's father, if you worked hard and showed ability, you couldn't help but progress up the corporate ladder. No one was just an employee, they were all part of a team. To function at the peak of his potential, each member of the team had to put his loyalty to the company first.

Adrienne had joined APP's team with these starry-eyed expectations. It never occurred to her that the seasoned pros would see her enthusiasm as naive and exploitable, or that her father's utopian doctrines were not universally held. Even after the whole messy affair with Ted was over she couldn't let her cherished convictions slide away. She hugged them to her like a talisman for better times. And these were the better times, she told herself resolutely.

Her intercom buzzed and Carol Tynan announced that Noel Granger was in and could see her any time. Adrienne ruthlessly dragged herself back to the present and told her secretary to inform Noel she would be there in five minutes. By the time she reached Granger's office her memories were safely tucked away in the back of her mind where they belonged.

Monday set the tone for the week, and for the one that followed. The confusion left by the previous manager forced Adrienne to do everything the hard way, feeling out the direction she should take, testing each idea before she implemented it. As she began to make her presence felt, more and more problems were brought to her attention, leaving her with the wry suspicion that she and a drowning victim had much in common. But there was no one to rescue her here—she had to swim to safety all alone.

The long days often spilled over into the evening, hampering her search for an apartment. Though she was anxious to locate a place, she had trouble finding her way around Seattle during the dark January nights. After a weekend of nonstop rain she still hadn't had any luck. She was beginning to worry about the length of time it was taking to find suitable accommodations.

Adding to her disquiet was the determined way Jared Hawkes hovered in her mind. There hadn't been a day since she'd met the man that she hadn't thought about him. Why she should picture him as he looked stepping off the elevator—his strongly defined features softened by his smile, the gray eyes warmly appreciative as he walked toward her—she didn't know. But her heart would beat a little faster and her mouth would suddenly become dry.

It occurred to her that he didn't look like the type of man who preyed on women. He seemed tough and very self-confident. Perhaps she was responding to his innate strength, despite his actions that first morning. Irritated that she would be silly enough to be taken in by a handsome exterior, she threw even more of her energies into sorting through the mess created by Grant Booth.

Few people, if any, were aware of the drains her job was making on her. She continued to dress crisply in a businesslike fashion and her hair was always neatly drawn back from her face. Even on those days when everything seemed to go wrong and Emery Thorpe used his daily phone call to give her a tongue-lashing, she kept her cool facade intact, refuting his accusations with mocking efficiency or accepting them with calm grace. To her staff she never allowed the depth of her tension to show, but by Friday of the second week she was a seething caldron of fatigue, disappointment and frustration.

She didn't hear from Emery until four o'clock New York time, which made it 1:00 P.M. in Seattle. He phoned, she discovered, not on some business-related problem, but because of her. He thought she was milking the company's expense policy so she could have a nice vacation in a cushy hotel.

He began his attack innocently enough. "Adrienne! How's the weather out there on the coast? I hear you've finally got some sun!"

She turned her chair to face the windows and leaned her head back wearily. It was indeed a beautiful day, the clouds of the previous two weeks gone as if they had never been, the sky an intense cerulean blue, the sun sparkling off the glass of nearby high rises. To the east the pristine white snowcaps on the Cascade Mountains gleamed, to the west the waters of Puget Sound rippled and danced. "Yes, we have," she agreed hollowly. "They're forecasting an equally fine weekend."

"Great!" said Emery. "Then I'll expect some good news on Monday morning."

Adrienne sat up straight and searched her tired brain frantically for his meaning. "Good news?" she repeated doubtfully.

His voice hardened. "Sure. You can spend this weekend looking for an apartment. It's time you got serious about it."

"Serious!" She heard her voice rise in anger and ruthlessly leveled it. "For your information, Emery, I have spent every evening and all of last weekend looking for a place to live. I resent your implication!"

There was a pause, then Thorpe said coldly, "Look, Adrienne, I've been there, remember? I was transferred three times and I've never spent two weeks apartment or house-hunting. Now, I know things have been hectic out there—" his voice softened "—but questions are being asked and I'm running out of excuses."

Adrienne wanted desperately to tell her boss exactly what he could do with his questions and excuses, just before she slammed down the phone and stalked out of this office for good. Emery Thorpe was a lucky man, blessed with a wife who helped smooth her husband's path. Emery had never had problems finding a place to live because Mrs. Thorpe saw to all the details of each move. There was a long silence while Adrienne struggled with her boiling anger and wrestled it back under control.

"Are you still there, Adrienne?" demanded Thorpe's incredulous voice.

"Yes." Her tone was a miracle of cool control. Emery would have no idea of the searing rage that surged beneath. "Who's asking the questions?"

"The accounting people, of course," he replied querulously. "They think you're being overly generous with the company's money."

"That's odd," she retorted amicably. "I only send in an expense statement once a week, and this week's won't reach New York until Monday. It goes to you first, then to accounting, so—"

"All right, Denton, you want straight goods? This is it. Your nice little fling is over. The company won't subsidize you any longer. Have an apartment by the end of the week or you start paying your own hotel bills! Do I make myself clear?"

She managed to say, "Very," in a cool, detached voice before the line went dead. She held the receiver away from her ear, staring at it with a stormy gleam in her blue eyes. Damn Emery Thorpe, he hadn't even given her the chance to hang up on him.

She slammed the phone back in its cradle and stood up, calling for her secretary. When the girl appeared in the doorway, her brows raised in surprised inquiry at her boss's unusual behavior, Adrienne said curtly, "Carol. I'm going out to lunch. If there are any problems while I'm away sort them out as best you can. I don't want to hear about them. Oh, yes, I'm leaving on time today. If anyone wants something done tell them to wait until Monday. I've already got a stack of things on my desk that take priority."

Carol swallowed, nodded and said, "Right, boss."

Adrienne didn't hear her. She swept out of the office, her mind still seething with fury over Thorpe's unwarranted attack.

It was close to two-thirty before she returned to the office, her temper much restored by a tasty lunch and a walk in the sun. She had decided that Emery was being pressured by those above him and was passing the heat along to her. The rationalization didn't make her feel any better about the criticisms he leveled, but she could understand why he'd spoken as he did and the understanding soothed her flaming anger. It didn't lessen her determination to leave on time or the rather jaded way she felt about her work, the company or Emery Thorpe.

She was back at her desk, plodding through a minor problem, when Noel Granger wandered through her open doorway and stood leaning his stocky body against the wall, his arms crossed casually over his chest. His dark eyes surveyed her interestedly. She looked up, smiled coolly and raised her brows in query. "This is a surprise, Noel. If you've got a problem I'm afraid I won't be able to get on to it until next week."

"Even if it's urgent?" demanded Granger, with a slight frown.

Responsibility fought a war with jadedness in her conscience and won. She suppressed a sigh and said, "What is it?"

Noel launched himself away from the wall, sauntered over to one of the visitor chairs and sprawled in it. "Tomorrow," he said, a mischievous smile playing at his thin lips, "my wife, Wendy, and I are having a few people over for a barbecue. I thought you might like to join us."

"A barbecue!" she burst out, her eyes widening in surprise. "At this time of year? It's January!"

Granger laughed. "You'll find that we do things differently out here, Adrienne. It's supposed to be warm and sunny on Saturday, a perfect day for a cookout. Now, what do you say? Are you ready to try some western hospitality?"

Adrienne thought wistfully about his invitation. She liked the sound of a barbecue in January. It appealed to the sense of humor she kept hidden from her colleagues, and the idea of meeting some new people was tempting. But Emery's ultimatum nagged at the back of her mind. Finally she shook her head decisively.

"Noel, it sounds lovely, but I can't. I've got to find a place to live this weekend and I need every minute to look. I'm sorry. Perhaps another time."

He studied her a moment, his dark eyes shrewd, his expression somber. Then he said carefully, "After you've been here awhile you'll discover that we take it a little easier on the west coast. Things that seem vital

to New York don't necessarily affect us the same way."
He slapped his knees with open palms and stood up.
"Drop by if you change your mind, Adrienne. There'll be plenty of food for all. Someone always brings an extra guest or two, anyway." At the doorway he paused and grinned. "You never know. You might get lucky and find the perfect place tomorrow afternoon."

"Thanks, Noel," she said to his retreating back. "I'll keep it in mind."

He raised a hand in silent acknowledgment as he ambled toward his own office.

Adrienne was left feeling like the only girl in her class who hadn't been invited to the prom. The more she thought about the barbecue the more she longed to go. Her distraught senses told her she needed a break, but with Thorpe's nasty suspicions still fresh in her mind she was reluctant to make any move that might be misconstrued. After several abortive attempts to work she gave up, put her stack of papers safely in a drawer and spent what remained of the afternoon reading the want ads and calling potential landlords.

By late Saturday afternoon she still hadn't found a place. Exhausted, she thought about another lonely evening followed by a depressing day apartment-hunting and suddenly made the decision that had been hovering at the back of her mind all along. She would go to Noel Granger's party and enjoy herself!

Not sure how formal a western cookout in January would be, she decided to wear a velvet pantsuit and a silky white blouse with a draped neckline. If they spent most of the time indoors she could easily slip the jacket off and if they were outside it would be all she needed for warmth. Over the past few days she'd discovered that when the sun shone in Seattle the temperature quickly shot up. Today had been as warm as a spring day would be back east.

Noel Granger lived in one of the city's suburbs, Bellevue, across Lake Washington from Seattle. Adrienne drove there in the car she'd rented for the weekend. Once she found the street, it was easy to figure out which was the Granger house. Cars clustered in the sloping drive and clogged the road in either direction. Every light in the low, ranch-style home seemed to be on and as she rang the bell, she could hear a babble of voices inside.

Noel himself answered the door, his expression delighted when he saw who it was. "Adrienne, I'm glad you're here. Come on inside and meet my wife." He ushered her into the house with one hand resting lightly between her shoulder blades.

If it hadn't been for that, Adrienne thought, she might well have slunk away in embarrassment. Everyone she saw was much more casually dressed than she, wearing jeans or slacks and sweaters or informal shirts or blouses. A few people were wearing jackets or blazers but that was mainly for warmth as they wandered through the sliding glass doors from the family room to the red-tiled patio where dinner was cooking on the barbecue.

Noel didn't seem to notice her chagrin as he led her over to a petite woman dressed in jeans. Beside her stood a tall man with broad shoulders and thick black hair, wearing a silver V-necked sweater and faded jeans that hugged his lean hips. He was staring down at the woman with amused affection in his face, the smile on his lips warming dark gray eyes and softening hard, angular features.

"Wendy!" Noel said imperiously. "Look who's come! Adrienne Denton, my wife, Wendy, and an old friend of ours, Jared Hawkes."

Adrienne fought a dreadful clawing panic that threatened to choke her as she shook hands with the warmly smiling Wendy. It had never occurred to her that Jared Hawkes might be here tonight, but of course, it should have. In a moment he would remark that they had met before, there would be questions and the whole humiliating story of their meeting would come out. She turned mechanically to face him, preparing for the inevitable embarrassment that must follow.

Chapter Two

He smiled and shook her hand as if he'd never seen her before. Drawing on all her sources of composure she was able to respond with her usual cool calm, despite the confusion that swirled in her brain. Had he forgotten their meeting two weeks before? It certainly seemed that way. Noel was droning on about Adrienne's dedication and the long hours she was putting in to rectify the chaos left by the former manager. Jared listened to this litany with surprising concentration while his intelligent gray eyes studied Adrienne thoughtfully. She could feel a blush creeping up her throat and cursed herself, Jared and Noel for putting her in this position.

Coming to Noel's party had been a mistake. With Jared Hawkes here she would never be able to relax and enjoy herself. Except for occasional slips, she'd pushed Jared out of her mind. But at times when her thoughts roamed freely, he had an annoying way of popping into them. It was bad enough that she was thinking of him. What was worse though, was the path her imaginings were taking. She remembered the way his gaze had sensually raked her body, the smile of male approval on his lips, when he'd met her eyes and the warm flush of pleasure she'd felt, not the indignation she knew she ought to.

Now his presence was affecting her equally strongly. Soon he would say in his deep velvet voice, "Yes, of course, we've met.... I left her a present...a great big pink teddy bear...." Noel would laugh and Adrienne's credibility would sink to zero. Managers with APP did not get stuck with giant teddy bears on their first day in a new position. It showed a certain lack of professionalism.

The expression in Jared's gray eyes became mocking as he took note of Adrienne's tense features. Noel's monologue had dwindled into pithy comments about Adrienne's predecessor, and she felt her spine stiffen instinctively. Her panicky brain told her that this was it. Any moment now Jared would strike. Noel was winding down, his list of complaints completed. She shot Jared an icy glance that would freeze melting butter in seconds and received a calmly raised eyebrow in return. Whatever Jared Hawkes planned to do, he'd do. She couldn't stop him.

"How do you like Seattle, Adrienne?" he asked moments later, his deep tones sending shivers down her spine. Those she attributed to her uncertainty. There had to be some reason Jared's voice would shake her composure when Noel's didn't even register.

"Fine," she replied formally. "Seattle seems to be a beautiful city. I'm sure I'll be happy here." Even to her ears the words sounded stilted. Adrienne cursed her lack of control. Where was her poise when she needed it?

He smiled down at her, the gray eyes mocking. "You've been here, what—two weeks? Not a lot of time to make a decision."

He knew exactly how long she'd been in Seattle. He'd met her on her first day here. Why was she letting him play these cat-and-mouse games with her? She glared at him, telling him without words that she knew what he was up to and she wasn't going to play, while her lips smiled sweetly. "It doesn't take long to assess a situation and know how you will respond."

His lips twitched and the black brows rose in a question. "Do you often make snap decisions, Adrienne? That's not always wise—in business."

They weren't referring to business and both of them knew it. They were talking about each other. Adrienne had lashed out and he'd responded, not in anger but with a subtle hint that she'd misjudged him. Shaken, Adrienne began to wonder if her initial impression of his character had indeed been wrong.

"Well, now," Noel said cheerfully, "since you two are getting along so well I'll just leave you to it. I have to go mind my barbecue. Help yourself to anything you'd like, Adrienne. The bar's over in the corner." He wandered off toward the sliding glass doors that gave access to the patio, pausing to speak briefly to his wife, who had slipped quietly away when he began his monologue.

"Would you like a drink?" Jared asked, taking over Noel's hosting duties.

Adrienne thought about that. She was reluctant to continue talking to Jared Hawkes. Although she was willing to admit she might have misjudged him, for her opinions of people had been known to be wrong, she was still wary of him. If she wandered away while he was off pouring her something from the well-stocked bar, he would most likely follow her and that could be embarrassing. Also, running would tip her hand, giving him hard evidence that she was afraid of him.

"I'm not the monster you think I am," he said softly, his deep voice wrapping sensuously around her.

That little shiver crawled up her spine again. This time she couldn't attribute it to uncertainty. It was definitely because of Jared Hawkes and the effect he had on her equilibrium. Six years ago another attractive man had slipped under her guard and hurt her badly. She wouldn't let that happen again. She stiffened and said curtly, "I wasn't thinking anything like that."

"No?" he derided. "Then why were you looking at me as if I might pounce on you any minute?"

"Won't you?" she snapped. "And when can I expect you to enliven the party with a humorous recounting of the teddy-bear incident. During dinner, when we're all clustered together? Or will you tell only a select few who might be expected to enjoy a good laugh?"

"Wait just a minute!" he said forcefully. "Before we go any further let's get a few things straight." Anger had lightened the gray eyes to silver, but he had himself well under control. His voice remained level, if not quite calm. "I don't know where you got the idea that I was planning to make fun of you tonight. Hell, I didn't even know you'd be here."

His words had a strong ring of truth to them, but Adrienne refused to be placated. She said coldly, "I've already seen how adaptable you are. You twist a situation to suit yourself."

Laughter darkened his gray eyes and his lips quirked. "Why, thank you."

Adrienne gaped at him.

"I think that drink is called for now," he murmured unrepentantly. "What would you like?"

"A glass of white wine," she replied mechanically. Once again he had neatly turned the tables on her, this time by accepting her insult as a compliment.

Fortifying herself with a mushroom smothered in cucumber-flavored dip, she watched him at the bar. He really was a disturbingly good-looking man, she mused dispassionately. In the close-fitting jeans his hips were lean, his legs long and muscular. When she felt a warm flush just under her skin she realized her thoughts hadn't been so cool and detached after all. He turned around, holding a glass in each hand. Beneath the silver sweater she could see the swell of well-developed muscles. A good-looking man, she thought again as she raised her eyes to his face.

Across the room he smiled quizzically at her, and Adrienne realized that he had been aware of her blatant visual examination of his body. She bit her bottom lip in consternation and saw his mouth twitch with amusement.

He was back at her side a few moments later, handing her the wineglass while he kept a pottery tankard of beer for himself.

"Thank you," she said frostily, deciding somewhat belatedly that her only defense against this man was to turn and run. "If you'll excuse me..."

"Not yet," he replied pleasantly, a hint of determination in his voice. "We haven't finished our conversation."

"Mr. Hawkes," she said quietly, "I don't want to continue the discussion."

He ignored her feeble attempt at formality. "Adrienne, for some reason you think I've got it in for you. Well, I don't. The day we met I was in a rush. I arrived at APP's offices early, hoping someone would have already opened up and I'd be able to dump the damned teddy bear right in Noel's office. When I saw you, you were the next best thing."

"It was my first day," she said bitterly. "I was left to face my staff for the first time with that pink bear branding me. Luckily, it was Noel's secretary, Lilith Page, who arrived first and she has the sense not to gossip. If it had been one of the others I would have been a laughing stock and my position undermined from the beginning."

He frowned. "I think you're making too big a deal of this," he said judiciously. "Nobody expects perfection of you."

Except me, Adrienne thought with sudden insight. In her own mind she had made a fool of herself at a crucial point in her career, and instead of turning her anger inward she had directed it at the absent Jared Hawkes who wasn't there to defend himself.

"Perhaps not," she agreed weakly.

He continued seriously, "If I'd known it was your first day I would never have left the wretched bear. I'm not totally without feelings, you know."

Adrienne felt a little shiver of relief as he smiled at her, coaxing an answering smile from her stiff lips. She said cautiously, "I may have reacted too strongly. I was tense and on edge."

"From what Noel said earlier you had reason to be." He shrugged away the references to APP and held out his hand. "So, shall we start again?"

Adrienne laughed. "Sure, why not?"

They shook hands like two strangers meeting for the first time. After that Adrienne took refuge in sipping her drink. She wasn't sure if she was doing the right thing, but her instincts told her that Jared Hawkes was not the self-centered cutthroat that Ted Conrad had been. She could trust Jared not to make a fool of her. Whether that realization was based on her surprisingly intense physical reaction to him she wasn't sure, so she added a liberal splash of wariness to her intuitive response.

"Have you known Noel long?" she asked idly.

"About ten years," Jared replied easily, his gray eyes studying her.

"How did you meet him?" she asked curiously, trying to find the appropriate niche in which to pigeonhole Jared Hawkes so that she knew what to expect from him.

"I worked for Noel while I was with APP. I have a lot of respect for him."

She smiled warmly. "You and most of the company. Noel has an excellent reputation."

Jared nodded, his lips curling in the faintest of smiles. "And he's a shrewd judge of character."

Now what was that supposed to mean? She eyed him warily and Jared chuckled. As his eyes mocked her lightly she realized he'd paid her a compliment, referring back to Noel's enthusiastic comments earlier. She blushed, not sure how to respond.

He rescued her by asking, "How long have you been with APP, Adrienne?"

"Six years," she said uneasily.

"A year after I left the company," he observed thoughtfully. "No wonder I hadn't heard of you."

The relief she felt at his words was out of proportion to how she should react. That first year at APP, when she'd made a fool of herself with Ted Conrad, was still a sore point for her, though it had been forgotten by everyone else. Even if Jared had been working for APP at that time, there would be no reason for him to remember the gossip that had flown through the company for months afterward. Despite this logical reasoning she was glad that he'd never heard of that part of her past. She wanted to deal with Jared Hawkes as an equal, an adult, as a sensible businesswoman he could respect as well as desire.

The last thought made her stumble mentally. So far the only indication she'd had of a physical response between them was all on her side. Jared had been polite, amused, angry, but he hadn't given her any sign that he felt the attraction she'd been fighting all evening. Something she should be glad of, she told herself sternly. She was only in Seattle for a three-year assignment. She couldn't afford to let herself become involved with a man, no matter how attractive he was.

Embarrassed by the turn her thoughts had taken, she was relieved when Noel sauntered in through the patio doors to proclaim that the ribs were done and could be served any time. Jared made a light comment and the dangerous moment slipped away.

After her husband's announcement, Wendy vanished into the kitchen, reappearing a moment later to tell her guests that supper was being served buffet-style and all was ready in the dining room. The hungry crowd trooped eagerly toward the food and in the rush Adrienne and Jared were separated.

Adrienne filled her plate, then found a seat on a small sofa, beside a diminutive blond woman who was concentrating on demolishing an enormous mound of ribs. Balancing her plate on her lap, Adrienne began to eat, enjoying the tangy flavor of the barbecued ribs, accented by a light rice pilaf and delicious buttered vegetables. The hubbub of conversation, so evident before, was subdued as everyone ate with keen enjoyment, stopping now and then to compliment the chef.

"Umm, that was good," the woman beside Adrienne said, licking her fingers. She grinned at Adrienne. "The only way to eat ribs is with your fingers. Do I have any sauce smeared on my cheeks?"

Adrienne blinked, amazed at the openness of this complete stranger, but she scrutinized the woman's face as asked, then grinned and said, "A little bit just below your lower lip on the right side."

"Here?" asked the woman, pointing.

"Right."

She dabbed energetically with a napkin and succeeded in obliterating the spot. "Thanks. You know, I don't think we've met. I'm Elaine Trent. That's my husband, Jon, over there talking to Jared Hawkes." She broke off, frowning at Adrienne's suddenly pale complexion. "Is something wrong?" she asked with spontaneous concern.

"No." Before she had time to think or to censure her words, Adrienne heard herself blurt out, "Did you like the teddy bear?"

Elaine's eyes widened. "How did you know about that? Oh, but you must be with Jared! How stupid of me. I'll bet he made you pick it out. Isn't that just like a man—"

"No, I..."

Elaine looked doubtful. "Really? Well, that's even kinder of him then. A busy man like Jared taking time to buy a baby's toy."

"Hardly a baby's gift," said Adrienne dryly. "It should last your child until he or she is a full adult."

Elaine threw back her head, laughing delightedly. "Huge, isn't it?"

"It certainly is," Adrienne agreed with feeling.

"But—I still don't understand how you knew the teddy bear came from Jared."

Adrienne hesitated. "I work with Noel. When Jared dropped the bear off at the office, I, er, took delivery, you might say."

Elaine's warm brown eyes sparkled with amusement. "Reluctantly?"

Again Adrienne hesitated before admitting, "Very reluctantly. It was my first day."

Elaine looked blank for a minute, then she bit her lip to stifle giggles. "Oh, you poor thing. What a rotten trick!"

Adrienne felt her skin prickle. She glanced cautiously at Jared. He was watching her, a mocking quirk to his lips as he listened blatantly to her conversation with Elaine. Ironically, despite her earlier fears it had not been Jared who exposed her involvement with the teddy bear, but Adrienne herself. At least he was appreciating the humor of the situation, instead of getting angry at her irrational behavior. She smiled tentatively back at him.

Elaine watched this interplay with interested, discerning eyes. Adrienne said hastily, "I'm Adrienne Denton. I don't think Noel or Wendy introduced us."

Elaine laughed. "Probably not. Wendy never bothers with that sort of thing and Noel always forgets."

There wasn't much more to be gained from that conversational gambit. Afraid that Elaine might ask more questions about Jared, and painfully aware he could hear their words, Adrienne tried again. "When is your baby due? You still look so slim. If I hadn't known about the teddy bear I wouldn't have realized you're pregnant."

"I only found out a couple of weeks ago," Elaine confided blithely. She added comically, "I don't know if this is all in my head or not, but I seem to have acquired the most gargantuan appetite since I was given the good news!"

Adrienne laughed. "Why don't you go for a second helping? A lot of other people seem to be doing it."

"Nope," said Elaine decisively. "I don't want to have to lose weight after the baby's born. I hate dieting," she said with a sigh, "so I'm exercising restraint now."

Adrienne laughed again and decided for Elaine's sake to steer the conversation off the subject of food. "How long have you known Noel and Wendy?" There was a trick to that question. She wanted to know if Jon Trent was a business associate of Noel's or perhaps a member of the APP sales force. There were a number of people here tonight whom she had noticed at the office, but she was by no means clear on everyone who worked for the company.

"Two years," Elaine replied promptly. "We live three houses down and we met the Grangers when we moved in. Wendy was really kind. I was a new bride, could hardly cook, and I knew nothing about keeping a house beyond making the beds and vacuuming. I was swamped! Wendy took me under her wing and showed me the ropes. She was great. Noel and Jon play golf together every Saturday, rain or shine, and it rains more often than not—"

"In the summer," said Adrienne, thinking she hadn't heard correctly.

Elaine opened her eyes wide. "Oh, no, all year round. It gets a little nippy in the winter months, but Jon just wears a heavier sweater."

It was Adrienne's turn to appear startled. "All year round? Can't be!" Then she thought of a barbecue in January and suddenly golf in every season made sense.

Elaine confirmed her silent thought. "Sure. Look at today. Perfect weather for golf. Say, are you new to Seattle, Adrienne? You must be, or you'd know we try to do everything year round here."

"Even ski?" Adrienne asked humorously.

"Well, we try. We don't quite succeed, but we try." Her warm brown eyes dancing, she continued, "So. Where are you from, Adrienne?"

"New York."

"Wow. That's a long way. I bet you find Seattle pretty small stuff after New York."

Adrienne grimaced. "I haven't been in the city long enough to really know. I was only transferred here a short while ago." She looked at Elaine's open features and found herself revealing the frustration of her unsuccessful apartment hunt to the woman. "I have spent every spare moment of the past two weeks trying to find a place to live. I'm certainly getting to know Seattle—the hard way!" She wrinkled her nose and laughed in a deprecating manner. "I've been lost more times than I can count and I've ended up in some of the strangest places."

Elaine listened sympathetically, thought a moment, then said, "Where have you been looking? What kind of place do you want? Maybe I can help, suggest neighborhoods that might suit you."

Adrienne, involved in the conversation, didn't notice the sharp-eyed, curious expression on Jared's face as he listened to their discussion. "Would you?" she replied, relief in her voice. "I'm nearly at my wit's end and my boss in New York has given me a deadline to find a place by next week." She laughed shakily and looked down at her plate. "He thinks I'm trying to soak the company for a free stay at the hotel."

"Good grief!" Elaine said. "Sounds like you've got a real tartar of a boss. I'd be happy to help, though offhand I don't know of any places that are vacant."

"Just a few hints from someone who's familiar with Seattle would be great," Adrienne replied frankly. "So I'll know what to avoid in the future, as well as what to pounce on."

"Okay," Elaine said efficiently. "Let's start with what you're looking for."

Adrienne gathered her thoughts, then said slowly, "I don't care if the apartment building is old or new, as long as it's well maintained. I only need one bedroom, and the kitchen doesn't have to be large because I eat out a lot. I'd like a balcony, but it's not necessary. What else?" She laughed then added, "Oh yes, plumbing that works!"

Elaine chuckled. "I know what you mean. I lived in a dreary little place when I went to college and there was never enough hot water to wash my hair. It was awful. My next apartment seemed like Buckingham Palace in comparison!"

Adrienne laughed. "I'm not looking for anything that grand! Just a place where I can feel comfortable. I'd prefer to live in Seattle rather than one of the suburbs—"

"You mean like out here," Elaine interjected, amusement in her eyes.

Adrienne shrugged. "I may have no choice. I've spent most of my time searching in the city and getting nowhere. I've noticed that there are a lot of complexes renting in the suburbs, and I guess I'll have to start looking at those, even though I hate to be so far from my work."

"Lots of people commute regularly, especially here in Seattle. The city is so spread out," Elaine pointed out matter-of-factly.

"I know," Adrienne agreed, "but I don't have a car and I'm not really used to being so far from work. Of course, I don't have much of a choice if I'm to find a place by next weekend."

"Sure you do," said Elaine firmly. "You keep looking where you want to live. Don't give up. You'll find something."

Adrienne laughed. "You do my flagging morale a world of good."

Elaine waved a hand and said magnanimously, "It's nothing. Now, whereabouts have you looked? I can at least tell you what areas to steer clear of."

Elaine's information gave Adrienne a better understanding of the city and replenished her dwindling store of optimism. By the time they got up to return their plates to the kitchen she was feeling hopeful that tomorrow, Sunday, would see an end to her demoralizing hunt.

With dinner out of the way, the party shifted gear. Noel put on the stereo while Wendy chose a record that could be listened to, as well as danced to. An area was cleared, and soon couples were swaying to the soft music.

Adrienne was a good dancer and ordinarily she would have enjoyed this conclusion to the evening, but tonight she was tired from her long day fighting Seattle's traffic and losing her way on the hilly streets. She found a spot in a corner and made herself comfortable, planning to listen to the music, have a cup of coffee and relax. Noel had other ideas. He brought over a thin, very young, sales rep whom he introduced as Guy Denby and left them together.

Denby was the first of a series of partners. Adrienne was rarely off her feet for the rest of the evening. It was a good thing she enjoyed dancing, she reflected ruefully as the hour grew late, because her skill had certainly been called into practice tonight.

It was sometime after midnight when Jared Hawkes came to claim her for the next dance. The tune was a slow one, a sensual love ballad meant to be danced to with bodies fused and cheeks touching. He gathered her into his arms, holding her lightly. Her skin tingled under the warm touch of his hand, and she felt a wicked, unaccustomed urge to snuggle sensuously close to his muscular length.

Caution and good sense won out over instinct and desire and she decided that Jared was dancing with her simply to be polite. At different moments through the evening she had noticed him talking to other men, dancing with Wendy Granger and Elaine Trent, completely uninterested in what Adrienne was doing. It reinforced the thought she'd had earlier, that he was not as affected by her as she was by him. Though she might have wished otherwise in different circumstances, she knew she didn't have the time to indulge in an emotional relationship while she was here in Seattle. Her assignment was only for three years and APP had to be first on her list of priorities.

The music wove its sensual web and imperceptibly Jared's hold tightened. "I've been waiting all evening for this," he whispered, his breath ruffling her hair.

Adrienne was tall, five-foot-eight in her stocking feet, and in the two-inch heels she was wearing tonight she usually faced a man eye-to-eye. At least, she did with Boyd Sykes, the man she'd been seeing before she left New York, and Ted used to complain if she wore shoes with high heels. But Jared Hawkes was a different matter. He was well over six feet, and she had to look up at him. It produced a warm, feminine feeling in the pit of her stomach. "I've been here all night," she parried, in a husky voice at odds with her usual clear tones.

"And surrounded by every male in the room," he retorted briskly, smiling with his lips, but not his eyes.

Fatigue had relaxed some of Adrienne's stern rules of conduct. She laughed flirtatiously, taunting, "It has been fun."

The arm at her waist tightened. "Tease," he growled, his eyes roving over her face and lingering on her lips. Smoky with emotion, his gaze rose to meet hers and very slowly he smiled.

His look was charged with messages and invitations. Adrienne sank painlessly into the sensual net he had spread for her, luxuriating in feelings no one had ever roused in her before. She had a wild desire to slide her hand which rested on his shoulder, across to his neck, then tangle it in his thick black hair. She wanted to touch him, to feel him, to taste him.

The song ended and another began. Neither Jared nor Adrienne noticed. They continued to dance close together, lost in each other. If Jared had bent his head a few inches to kiss her, Adrienne would have melted against him, responding with needs she'd never known she possessed, forgetting that she was at a party given by a co-worker, throwing all her normal scruples to the four winds. All she could think of was the touch of his hand on hers, the warmth of his long legs against her body and the promise in those far-too-expressive gray eyes.

The music changed, becoming faster, the tempo more rhythmic. It was the steady hammer of the drums that broke Adrienne out of the sensual spell Jared had cast around them. She blinked hazily, then remembered where they were and laughed shakily. "I think I'd better sit down. I'm too tired for anything energetic."

He gave her a lopsided smile and released her, guiding her over to a sofa with a hand in the small of her back. This time, Adrienne decided with primitive feminine satisfaction, she wasn't the only one affected.

They sat on the sofa, a decorous distance between them, each aware of their surroundings now with painful clarity. Keep it light, Adrienne told herself sternly as she searched her barely functioning brain for something to say. If she remained silent she would be in danger of sinking under the spell of those dark eyes once more and making a complete fool of herself in front of Noel and the other employees of APP who were at the party. She said inanely, "Does it always rain so much here?"

For a moment he looked astounded. Then his expression became quizzical and he laughed. "In the winter it does. You come to cherish days like today, when the sun is warm and there's not a cloud in the sky. A good day is one where it's merely overcast, but it doesn't rain."

"How do you stand it?" she asked doggedly, determined to keep the conversation going.

"You get used to it. In fact, before long you'll find you like the rain and miss it if it's sunny too long."

"Really?" she said, with spurious interest.

"Yes, really," he replied, grinning.

She felt her lips twitch and gave in to a chuckle. "I suppose when that happens I'll be fully acclimatized. How long does it take?"

"How long have you got?" he asked lazily, his eyes scrutinizing her face and belying his casual attitude.

Smiling, she answered smoothly, "Two to three years. My boss in New York figures it will take a year or so to bring the Seattle operation back in line and then another six months to a year to ensure it's working smoothly."

"Then what?"

"Back to New York and my next promotion," she said, making no effort to hide her satisfaction.

"You sound very certain of that," he remarked, his eyes narrowing.

"I am. I've got guarantees."

"Really?" He challenged huskily, "I'll make you a bet, Adrienne Denton."

Her brows rose in cool hauteur, but her eyes sparkled with excitement. "What's that?"

He laughed softly. "By the time your boss back East issues the order to return to New York, you'll be fully settled in Seattle and won't want to leave."

She grinned at him. "I accept. That's a sucker's bet."

He smiled mockingly and raised black eyebrows. "But who's the sucker?"

She chuckled. "I'm not going to fall into that trap. What are the stakes?"

"Dinner and a night on the town."

She laughed outright at that. "Okay. But what if you're married at that point?"

He replied sardonically, "I might ask the same of you."

"Not me." She shook her head. "I'm a career girl. No strings."

"My God!" he said derisively. "You should hear yourself."

She laughed again, thinking that she hadn't behaved so freely with a man since her college days. She looked up into his intent gray eyes, grinning mischievously, "I know. Cold, relentless career woman."

"Are you?" he demanded huskily.

The directness of his question threw her into confusion. With any other man she wouldn't hesitate to say yes. With Jared she wanted to forget caution and deny everything she had built over the past few years. Her survival instincts screamed that he was dangerous, that he would overturn her world if she wasn't careful. She hesitated, then said abruptly, "Yes."

He leaned close to her, reaching out to cup her chin with long shapely fingers. "Don't sell yourself short, Adrienne," he murmured hypnotically. "I can see far more important traits in you than those."

His eyes held hers and Adrienne almost felt as if she were drowning in their gray depths. She swallowed nervously, lowering her lids protectively. A second later his hand dropped, leaving her curiously shaken. She glanced at her watch, but couldn't focus on it. Still, she said breathlessly, "It's late. I've got to go." She jumped nervously to her feet and stuck out her hand. "It's been nice meeting you, Jared."

He slowly stood up and caught her fingers in a warm clasp. His smile wrapped her once more in a cocoon of his own special magic. "My pleasure," he murmured.

She waited for him to suggest that they meet again. When he remained silent she turned away, vaguely disappointed. Once again she'd misread the man. He wasn't really interested in her, despite his rather provocative words. But as she drove back to her hotel through the dark streets, she discovered he filled her thoughts in a most disconcerting way.

Chapter Three

The bubbling water in the superheated Jacuzzi soothed the knots in Adrienne's tense muscles. She stretched languidly on the tiled bench, her eyes closed, her thoughts drifting. This, her weary mind told her, was the first real relaxation she'd had in days. She didn't count the party of the previous day because part of her had always been aware of Noel and all the others who worked for APP. Not to mention Jared Hawkes. It wasn't fair of the man to make such an impression on her.

She'd arrived back at the hotel last night so preoccupied by thoughts of him that she'd forgotten to request a wake-up call so she could get an early start. After a night of vaguely remembered dreams full of Jared's overwhelming presence, she'd woken up late. She rushed through her morning routine, sparing time only for a cup of coffee, before she was off diligently searching for the perfect apartment.

A splash of hot water on her nose brought Adrienne out of her near-doze. A group of boisterous conventioneers had invaded her peaceful spot. Suddenly, the small, circular tub was uncomfortably crowded. She decided she had been in the hot water long enough. Her skin was pink and her brain was beginning to fog. She rose and moved gracefully to the stairs, grimly aware of the watching male eyes.

The water of the swimming pool, cold after the Jacuzzi, was an invigorating shock to her system. She swam two quick lengths before she ran out of energy. Grabbing hold of the edge she hung suspended at the deep end, letting her breathing return to normal. Now that her skin was getting used to it, the temperature was warming up. It had never been all that cold, it was only her imagination that made it seem so.

Had that been all there was between her and Jared last night? After a depressing day with no lunch, she'd hoped, almost expected, to find a message from him waiting for her at the hotel desk. Her disappointment when she was told there wasn't one was ridiculously sharp. If Jared had wanted to see her again he would have said something last night.

Her breathing restored, she let go of the side and floated on her back. Today had not been one of her better days. After a frustrating morning spent in a fruitless search in the city, she'd broken down and driven out to the suburbs. The apartments there had been available, but not what she wanted. Crossing her fingers, she hoped for better luck tomorrow.

She let herself drift in the cool water, enjoying the respite from her cares. Tomorrow she would have to return to the grind. For now, she could relax.

At precisely eight o'clock the next morning she was startled by the shrill jangle of her phone. As usual, she had been at her desk for a half an hour and was already immersed in a welter of paperwork. She paused briefly before answering, steeling herself for what was to come. It was probably Emery Thorpe and he wouldn't be pleased that she hadn't rented an apartment over the weekend.

She was right. He was furious. There was a cutting edge to his voice when he repeated his order that Adrienne find a place soon. She tried to make him understand her dilemma, but it was impossible. He seemed to think that finding accommodations with ease was a woman's natural skill, like giving birth, and couldn't be convinced differently. At the same time he made it clear that he wanted her to continue her intense work schedule. It was an impossible situation.

After she had quietly returned the receiver to its cradle she walked slowly over to the long plate-glass windows that made up one wall of her office. She realized that Emery was wary of her. He valued her work and her dedication, but he wasn't sure what to expect from a career woman.

She stared moodily out at the ships dotting Puget Sound. How could Emery do this to her? It wasn't as if she planned to stay in the hotel any longer than she had to. She wanted to find a place to live. Until she did she felt as if her life was on hold.

The telephone shrilled again, dragging her out of her gloomy thoughts. She eyed it suspiciously, wondering if she could get away with not answering it. But her conscience made her walk back to the desk and pick up the receiver. This was her office, not her home. Here she couldn't hide from problems, no matter how much she might want to.

"Adrienne Denton," she said briskly, pushing her reluctance aside.

"Adrienne! How's it going?"

"Boyd! Well, I'm glad you called. I was just feeling sorry for myself because I still haven't found an apartment."

Boyd Sykes, a manager in the shipping department of APP, laughed. "Sounds like a tough problem. Who wants to have to cook and clean for themselves when they can get someone else to do it for them?"

The gibe was uncomfortably close to Emery's attitude. Adrienne could feel anger building and fought it. Boyd could have no idea of Emery's high-handed tactics so his comment was just that; a careless remark made by one friend to another. Keeping this in mind she said lightly, "I can't believe how much energy it takes to find a place to live in a new city. I've spent the past two weekends in a rented car getting lost as I looked for roads and addresses."

"Why don't you get a map?" Boyd suggested reasonably.

"I have one! Maps are designed for passengers to read, not the driver. Have you ever noticed how tiny the lettering on one of those things is?" She tried to keep her voice light, but some of her disgruntlement must have come through.

"Seattle getting you down?" he asked, a hint of speculative interest in his tone.

"Some," she admitted, amending quickly, "not much, really. I'll be glad to get this apartment problem solved so I can concentrate on the chaos the previous manager left. I find it distracting to have to divide my time this way."

Boyd laughed. "Single-minded Adrienne. Dedicated to the point of blindness."

"Cut it out, Boyd," she said sharply. "APP comes first for both of us."

"Yeah," he agreed sullenly. Adrienne was struck by the petulant note in his voice. She'd never heard it before.

Boyd Sykes was the epitome of a rising young corporate executive. He wore well-cut three-piece suits, usually in charcoal or dark-blue shades, and the expression on his regular features was always smoothly noncommittal. He was dedicated to his career and determined to rise to the top of the company hierarchy.

That was what had drawn Adrienne to him in the first place. Boyd didn't have time for emotional entanglements and neither did she. They dated in an erratic way, when busy schedules and career commitments permitted it. Since they worked in separate departments and had different timetables, their relationship remained lukewarm. That was all Adrienne wanted. An occasional dinner out, the odd play or concert to enliven a dull weekend, a pleasant lunch companion to relieve a tension-filled day. No demands, no responsibilities.

So why was Boyd sounding so sulky? A warning bell went off in her head. Could it be that he was jealous of her success? Her promotion put her one level above Boyd and Emery's promise that she would be transferred back to head office at the end of her assignment implied a quick leap to far more prestigious positions. Boyd, on the other hand, was stuck in a department where promotion was slow.

Her eyes flashed as she grimly decided Boyd was overstepping the invisible but carefully drawn line she'd kept between them. After Ted Conrad she refused to let any man come too close, and she would never let one interfere with her career. Boyd had no right to start acting as though he should mean more to her than her career. He knew her rules.

They talked for another ten minutes about a problem with the Seattle warehouse before Boyd hung up. Even then Adrienne was still shaken by the rush of feeling Boyd's hint of possessiveness had generated. She believed she'd put the pain of her humiliation behind her, but obviously she had not. Even now an image of Ted's cynical, worldly wise features and laughing green eyes sprang vividly to mind. What a fool she had been to trust him, a naive, twenty-one-year-old innocent fascinated by the practiced charm of a human snake.

They began dating after Adrienne's six-month probation was over. Casual dinners quickly progressed to an emotionally charged love affair, and Adrienne found herself falling ever more deeply under Ted's subtle control. At the time it seemed like love, though later she realized it was merely infatuation.

Whatever the title, she'd plunged into the relationship with the same enthusiasm she showed at APP. It seemed appropriate that their conversations almost always centered around the department they both worked in. They discussed the current status of their particular jobs and even fell into long philosophical discussions about how APP could make better use of its manpower and resources.

They had been lovers for several months when Adrienne finally discovered that he was using her. A staff notice was passed around announcing that Ted was being promoted. With her usual generosity she was delighted for him, though a little surprised he hadn't mentioned it to her. She knew his career meant a lot to him and that he'd been working hard. Impulsively she hurried over to congratulate him.

He wasn't at his desk, but she spotted him not far away, talking to the department manager. Reluctant to interrupt them, she hovered indecisively. His back was toward her, but she could hear his voice. Gradually the full impact of his words hit her. Phrase for phrase he was repeating an idea she had been working on for several weeks. It was almost ready for submission, and the previous evening she had asked Ted what he thought of it. He had shaken his head and told her it needed work, and she believe him implicitly. Now he was offering it to their mutual boss as his own.

The department manager, Mr. Waite, boomed, "Excellent thinking, Conrad. You're more than confirming my faith in you. With a mind like yours, Ted, you are sure to rise quickly in APP." He clapped his hands paternally on Ted's shoulder, and as he did so his gaze shifted to where Adrienne stood rooted to the spot. Her eyes wide and horrified, she could only stare at the scene before her.

"Yes, miss?" Waite inquired coolly. His eyes narrowed. "Denton, isn't it?"

She nodded dumbly. Ted turned slowly until he faced her, but his eyes didn't meet hers.

Her silence, especially her white, vulnerable expression goaded the department head into contemptuous speech. "If you ever want to make anything of yourself, Denton, you would do well to take young Conrad here as your example. Instead of standing around gaping like a fish out of water, get to work! We don't have time for slackers at APP."

He walked away. So did Ted—without a word. Adrienne had stood watching him, astounded that he didn't even have the decency to try to explain.

Waite had turned, and seeing her standing there, had glared dangerously at her. Finally coming to her senses, Adrienne stumbled back to her desk.

She didn't think things could get any worse, but they did. She discovered that Ted hadn't been content to steal her ideas. He'd also let it be known that she was a sweet young thing who lacked ambition and had a distressing inability to make a decision. In an aggressive organization like APP this was the kiss of death on any aspiring career.

Adrienne was shattered. Ted had spread these rumors deliberately. Why? The answer was plain once she thought about it. To keep her in her lowly position, so she would continue to come up with ideas that he could use as his own. His cold, callous manipulation shocked her and his method of extracting the information tore her apart.

Even now, after she'd put the incident behind her, it hurt to remember how freely she'd given her trust and love to Ted. But five years ago it had smashed her into pieces. Somehow she'd managed to pull herself back together again. But in the rebuilding, some parts were missed, and the woman who emerged from the ordeal was not the happy, enthusiastic girl of before.

Though she retained her deeply ingrained views on the loyalty due an employer, she became wary of her co-workers. In an effort to eliminate the hateful appellation of being a weak female she modeled herself on the cool, arrogant Waite, donning an armor of expressionless reserve.

It took her a year and a transfer into her present department, logistics management, before she lived down the reputation of being unambitious and indecisive.

With a little shiver Adrienne wrenched her thoughts away from the past. What Ted had done was unforgivable. It was buried now, under the weight of her dedication and ability. Thinking about it wouldn't solve her immediate problems and it only wasted precious time.

She spent the rest of the morning working tirelessly to clear her desk, then took the afternoon off to look for an apartment. By dinner she was grimly aware that her chances of finding the perfect place before the end of the week were near zero.

The next morning she received another eight o'clock call from Emery and another growling ultimatum. It wasn't the best way to begin the day. When Elaine Trent phoned a couple of hours later and suggested they meet for lunch, Adrienne was ready for a break.

They met at a small restaurant recommended by Elaine. When Adrienne arrived a few minutes late her friend was already seated at a cozy table by a window. The view was of the busy street outside and beyond, through the tall buildings, to the gray waters of Puget Sound. The decor was white wicker with green linen tableclothes and dozens of plants. Not, Adrienne thought wryly, a particularly innovative interior, but an always pleasing one.

While she studied her menu, Elaine kept up a running commentary on each of the entrée items, recommending several. "It sounds like you're a regular customer," Adrienne remarked with amusement, when Elaine finished the recital.

"I am. The gang I work with often come here for lunch. The price is right and the food is well prepared. I'm opting for the chicken crepes. How about you?"

"The steak sandwich," Adrienne decided. "I feel like I need energy if I want to make it through the rest of the week."

Elaine cocked her head. Her brown eyes were sympathetic. "No luck on Sunday?"

Adrienne sighed. "No. Look, let's not talk about apartments or the lack of them. I just want to forget for an hour or so."

Elaine laughed. "Sounds good to me."

There was a pause while the waitress took their orders, then Adrienne said casually, "Elaine, I'm curious about something."

"Ask away," she replied breezily, as Adrienne hesitated.

"You'll probably think I'm crazy, but... Why on earth was Jared Hawkes giving you that enormous teddy bear? I mean, he doesn't seem like the, er, family type."

Elaine laughed. "If you're asking whether he's married—he's not." Adrienne flushed and opened her mouth to deny this suggestion. Elaine giggled and continued, "Though he's not a close friend, we often see him at the Grangers' or when we're up at one of the local resorts, skiing. Jared is an avid skier; in fact, he's into most sports."

That lets me out, Adrienne thought, before she pulled herself up short, shocked at the turn her thoughts were taking.

"In fact," Elaine continued blithely, "he and Evan Lucas own a firm that specializes in importing sporting goods."

"Evan Lucas?" Adrienne repeated blankly.

"You've never heard of Evan Lucas?" said Elaine, awed by her friend's ignorance.

"No. Should I?"

"Wow! Where did you spring from? The moon? Evan Lucas was one of the top quarterbacks in the country for years."

"Oh, football," Adrienne dismissed.

Elaine laughed. "If you ever meet Evan don't tell him you've never heard of him. He likes to think he's a hero to women."

"Wonderful," said Adrienne dryly. "I think I'll avoid him like the plague. So that's what Jared does? Imports sporting goods?" When Elaine nodded, she said doubtfully, "It doesn't sound very lucrative."

"Oh, but it is. There's been a steady growth of interest in sports of all kinds over the past few years. Evan and Jared's company has flourished. Evan concentrates on the promotional work while Jared does the organizing and the wheeling and dealing. They make a great team."

Salads were set down before the two women, interrupting their conversation. After she had finished hers, Adrienne said dryly, "You know, you still haven't explained about the teddy bear."

"I haven't?" Elaine pushed her empty plate aside as she mentally reviewed the earlier discussion. "No, you're right, I haven't. It's simple really. The day I found out I was pregnant I was delirious with happiness. I told Jon and he was so enthusiastic he wanted to announced it to the whole neighborhood. We went over to Wendy and Noel's, bursting into their house and babbling nonstop. Jared was over talking to Noel and couldn't help but hear. He knew how happy we were and I guess the teddy bear was his way of acknowledging that and sharing in it. He's a generous, giving man."

Adrienne smiled, thinking that Elaine was right. Her initial suspicions of Jared had already been proved false at the Grangers' party. He was not like Ted Conrad, a user of women. Jared made his own way in the world; he had the strength and courage to rely on himself. The thought intrigued her at the same time as she thrust it away. Like Elaine she would only know him as a casual acquaintance. It was better to remember that.

"Oh, good," Elaine remarked happily, "here's our main course. I'm starving."

"Me too," said Adrienne, eyeing the six-ounce steak, home fries and sautéed mushrooms on the platter. It looked delicious, and when she bit into the rare meat she decided the restaurant deserved its good reputation.

She and Elaine parted after coffee, promising to get together soon. Adrienne strolled back to her building feeling much less tense than she had before lunch. With her breezy vitality and inner joy, Elaine was a tonic to the spirit. Adrienne looked forward to their next meeting.

When her Tuesday evening apartment search was as unproductive as ever, Adrienne made a decision. Tomorrow she would take the bus out to the suburban complex she had seen on Sunday and rent one of the suites. She hated the idea but consoled herself with the thought that she could continue to look in a more leisurely way and move again when she finally discovered the perfect apartment. She had to find a place soon. The longer she dithered, searching out perfection, the lower she would fall in Emery's estimation. At present her reputation as a cool, decisive manager was solid, but Thorpe like many men had a reserve of hidden assumptions about women and their place in the business world. She was constantly fighting that stereotype, proving she was as good as—or better than—any man, and she didn't want to lose ground because she couldn't find a suitable apartment.

She slept badly that night, waking to a new day heavy with coming storms. The weather affected her mood, increasing her edginess. As the black clouds that hovered threateningly over the city grew thicker, Adrienne's spirits sank progressively lower. When her telephone buzzed just after one, she answered it in a dispirited voice.

"Hi. This is Jared Hawkes."

The clear, deep tones flowed like velvet over her body, dispelling some of her gloom and injecting her with much-needed energy. "Jared," she said slowly. "It's good to hear from you."

There was a slight pause. "But you didn't expect it."

"To be perfectly honest, no, I didn't." She laughed huskily, part of her mind astonished at the emotional rush she was getting from just hearing his voice. "But the surprise makes it all the more pleasant that you called."

There was another pause and irrationally she panicked. Was she coming on too strong? Did he think she was fishing for something? Why was she letting a near-stranger shatter her composure this way?

He sounded concerned as he asked, "Have you had any luck finding an apartment? I seem to remember you saying you were having trouble finding one."

Masking her confusion, she answered with a cool her co-workers and staff would have recognized. "I'm still searching. So far I haven't seen a place I would want to live in. I guess I'm just too picky." She forced a light laugh. "I'm not giving up, though. Somewhere there must be a decent apartment in this city."

"I think I might have found it," he said.

"Wh—what? I mean, I beg your pardon? I don't think I heard you right."

"I'm sure you did, Adrienne." There was open laughter in his voice and she could imagine the gray eyes gleaming and the sensual mouth quirked with amusement.

"Jared," she said lightly, "don't tease." She was working too hard to keep her facade of collected cool to consider that they hardly knew each other well enough to tease.

If Jared noticed he wasn't offended. He laughed and said, "I'm serious, honest. I have a friend who is moving from Seattle and has to sublet his suite. I overheard you describing what you wanted in an apartment to Elaine Trent and I thought Barry's place fit the bill."

Disappointment flattened her voice. "Oh. I see."

"You don't sound too interested," he remarked, an edge to his voice.

"I appreciate the thought, Jared, but I need an apartment that's vacant now. I've got to be able to move in immediately." Regret threaded her tones.

"I know that," he said impatiently. "Barry left town on the weekend. I decided to wait until the suite had been cleaned and was ready to view before calling you."

"Oh," she said again, feeling foolish and elated all at once. "In that case, thank you and yes, I'd like to see it. Where is it located?"

He named a street that meant nothing to her and an area that rang a warning bell. "What's the rent like?"

"Expensive, but not unrealistic."

She sat stiffly, thinking fast. "When can I see it? Do you have the landlord's phone number?"

"Why don't I pick you up after work, say about six o'clock, at your hotel and I'll take you over there."

Pleasure rippled along her nerve endings, but she said hesitantly, "That's very kind but I can't impose..."

"Adrienne," he interrupted quietly, "you aren't imposing. Barry left me with the key and asked me to watch the apartment. He's got three months left on his lease, and the landlord knows he's good for it so he's not looking hard for a new tenant."

"What happens if I decide to take it? I hate the idea of moving again in three months." She made no effort to hide the worry in her voice.

"If you take the apartment you'll have no problem with the lease, believe me. So," he continued, switching the topic abruptly, "is six o'clock okay?"

"Fine," she replied mechanically.

"Good. I'll see you then." The line went dead as he hung up. Adrienne slowly replaced her receiver, suddenly aware of the great weight she had been carrying, because now it wasn't there anymore. Unless the apartment had some totally unacceptable flaw she would take it. Jared Hawkes knew the city, knew what she was looking for and, she suspected, he knew and looked for quality. It was a revitalized Adrienne who turned back to her work.

At four-thirty when the office cleared, she muttered an absentminded good-night to Carol, thinking that she would work a while longer before going back to her hotel to change. Somehow, despite her diligent efforts the papers kept piling up on her desk. Half an hour in the quiet peace of the empty office should put a nice dent in the stack.

She worked quickly, her mind absorbed by what she was doing, and did not look up for some time. When she eventually glanced at her watch, a pretty feminine timepiece that had been a present from her parents this past Christmas, the hands read five forty-five. For a moment her mind blanked in horror, then she hastily chucked papers into her desk drawer, not worrying about the confusion she was producing. All she could think about was being late for her meeting with Jared Hawkes.

Chapter Four

She reached the hotel with a minute to spare, hoping that Jared was not the type to arrive early and wait impatiently. A sleek Mercedes was swinging into the short, curving drive as she hurried to the revolving doors, but she ignored it. Once inside the lobby her eyes anxiously scanned the large, open space until she was satisfied Jared wasn't there.

Drawing a deep breath she wondered what she should do. Go up to her room and change, risking being ten or fifteen minutes late? Or stay here and wait? She stepped politely away from the door as she felt the movement of cool air on her back, her mind on her decision, not on who had entered the lobby.

A dark voice from behind said in her ear, "Looking for me?"

She jumped and pivoted around to stare up into the amused eyes of the man she was to meet. "Jared! I didn't keep you waiting, did I? I just got here."

He shook his head, smiling faintly. "No. I only arrived a minute ago. I saw you rushing into the lobby; I gather you were held up."

"Yes. My own stupid fault," she said breathlessly. Standing in close proximity to his hard, masculine body was doing strange things to her equilibrium. Dressed in a beautifully cut gray suit, his black hair brushed severely away from the broad forehead, he looked very imposing and capable of mastering any situation.

He raised his shirt cuff to glance at an expensive digital watch on his wrist. "Would you like to take a moment to go up and change? We have plenty of time." His gaze traveled down her form, noting the tan raincoat thrown over a tailored clove-brown suit, her long slender legs and the fashionable, but restrained, leather shoes with the medium heels. On their return trip his eyes lingered a moment on her breasts beneath the creamy silk blouse, before they lifted to stare directly into hers.

The expression in his dark-gray eyes, the color of thunderclouds she thought whimsically, was telling her he saw nothing wrong with how she was dressed. She smiled, amazed she wasn't furiously angry at his blatant male appraisal. Had any of the men she knew at work surveyed her that way she would have been highly offended. But when Jared looked at her she felt only a warm glow of pleasure, liberally mixed with feminine satisfaction. "Thanks, but I won't bother," she said calmly, masking her quick response with a cool attitude. "I do want to thank you again for finding the apartment."

He sent her a mocking look and said, "Wait until you've seen it before you start thanking me. You may hate the place." He put a hand on the small of her back to usher her through the door.

"Maybe," she said smiling, as they went outside. She found she was enjoying the firm, light touch, despite the interference of several layers of cloth.

He led her over to the oyster-white Mercedes she had noticed as she rushed into the lobby, waiting until she settled herself on the leather-covered seat before slamming the door and swiftly crossing to the driver's side of the car. He maneuvered his tall frame into the seat with a fluid grace that fascinated Adrienne. With a quick practiced movement of long, attractive fingers he set the powerful engine purring, put the car into gear, then eased into traffic.

After a moment he said conversationally, "Looks like it's going to clear up tonight." Adrienne, who had been paying attention to Jared and little else, frowned, puzzled. "The weather," he said softly, pointing at the sky, his eyes full of amusement.

Adrienne blushed, ashamed to be caught staring. She quickly glanced up. Though it was completely dark she could see that the night sky was a patchwork of shades as the heavy cloud cover broke up, promising better weather to come. To hide her embarrassment she said enthusiastically, "Great! I get so tired of gray, gloomy days."

He laughed. "I think we've had this conversation before."

Adrienne glanced at him, noticing the way the skin crinkled around his eyes when he smiled and the length of his long black lashes. They stopped at a light and he turned his head to look at her, the amusement still there in his dark eyes. Adrienne smiled serenely and said, "The weather seems to be something everyone out here talks about. It dominates conversations."

The light switched to green and the car moved smoothly forward with the other traffic. Adrienne found herself admiring the ease with which Jared drove, so different from her own nervous, harried performance.

"There's a reason for it, of course," he said casually. "Seattle weather is unpredictable." He went on to point out a local landmark and tell her a bit about the area they were passing through.

It didn't take long to reach the apartment, probably the reason for his generous offer to drive her there. The building was situated on one of the hills that made Seattle such an inviting city. It was a low structure, only five stories high, set back from a tree-lined street. Only a dozen years old, the building looked well kept and attractive.

Jared drove into the underground garage and parked the powerful car. "Barry's spot," he explained, when she looked surprised.

Adrienne nodded, then slipped easily out of the car. "What kind of trees were those on the street?" she asked casually, as they walked toward the security door that led into the building. "Without their leaves I didn't recognize them."

"Flowering cherry," he responded, inserting a key in the door. "In a couple of months they'll be covered with blooms...."

"A couple of months!" she repeated, surprised.

The lock clicked and he pushed open the door, turning to smile teasingly at her. "February or March is when they usually flower, depending, of course, on the weather."

"You get spring that early?" she demanded suspiciously.

The skin around the dark-gray eyes crinkled attractively. "Not a real spring, like you have back East or on the plains." His hand on her arm urged her into the building. "But the vegetation starts to come back to life, leaves and flowers for the deciduous trees, new pale-green growth for the conifers. Even the grass brightens up. The temperature doesn't change much, though."

As they waited for the elevator Adrienne tried to decide if he was teasing her or not. He was watching her with an intent, amused expression, almost as if he was reading her thoughts. Which was, she told herself, quite absurd.

She remarked lightly, "It must be nice to live so close to nature. My apartment in New York was in a high rise, seventeen floors up. The view was of other high rises or someone else's roof. Nothing green in sight except my houseplants."

"This may surprise you," he said, as the doors opened and Adrienne stepped into the small paneled cubicle, "but the people on this street tend to complain about the mess the trees create when the flowers die and the petals fall to the ground. They say it makes the sidewalks and the roads dangerously slippery."

"Surely not!" said Adrienne indignantly, as he followed her inside and punched the button for the fifth floor.

He chuckled at her heated response. "When you've got something in abundance it's easy to be critical."

She raised her brows skeptically.

Jared laughed. "You'll see."

The elevator rose smoothly to the top floor. When the doors opened Adrienne stepped out into a long, well-lit passage, carpeted in dark brown, the walls covered by a textured paper of a muted cream color. She looked around curiously as she followed Jared down the hall, noting the light fixtures beside each door and the security locks above the doorknobs. There were only about half a dozen apartments on the floor, a big change from the twenty or more her building in New York had housed.

She waited until he had the door open and the lights turned on before entering the apartment. The floor covering here was a better grade of wall-to-wall carpeting than that in the hall outside, a thick pile in a soft mushroom color.

The kitchen was the first room she looked at, as it opened off the narrow entryway. It was a large, square room, fitted with a dishwasher as well as the necessary fridge and stove. She wandered around it opening the cupboards, while Jared leaned casually against the doorjamb watching her.

She smiled vaguely at him as she passed him to wander deeper into the suite, trying to hide her growing elation. She liked the kitchen with its cedar doors and butcher-block counter, and the broad breakfast bar that made up one wall and opened into the dining room. From what she'd seen through that wide aperture, the rest of the apartment would be equally pleasing.

After she had passed, Jared launched himself lazily away from the door frame to follow her into the living area. She stood in the center of the room, mentally decorating it with her furniture and feeling a little thrill of pleasure as she thought about it. Still with the vague, thoughtful expression, she opened the sliding balcony doors and stepped outside. She was not surprised when Jared followed her.

"I have a view," she said, pointing into the darkness. "What is it?"

"The Cascade Mountains." A smile flickered at the corner of his mouth as he registered her slip.

She didn't notice, being absorbed in inspecting her surroundings. "This is nice, having a covered balcony. It's almost like it's part of the apartment. It means I can sit out in any weather."

"A definite bonus in Seattle," he agreed mockingly.

She laughed. "Does the suite get much light?" She shot him a rueful look. "Since I've moved here I find I miss long spells of bright, cloudless skies."

"The morning sun. Barry used to complain about being woken early on weekends with the sun in his eyes."

She laughed and headed for the door.

"And Adrienne," he added softly. She paused, about to move inside. "The sunny days will come, believe me."

She blushed, smiled falteringly, then hastily stepped over the sill. By the time he followed her inside she was walking with precise determination toward the bedroom, which was at the end of a short hall off the living room.

The bedroom was smaller than she would have liked, but she saw she could easily fit her furniture in it and the closet space was more than adequate. It was only as she was leaving the room, her feet making no sound on the thick carpet, that she realized Jared hadn't followed her here as he had through the rest of the apartment. She paused, wondering why. Did he feel she needed privacy to view the bedroom, perhaps the most personal room in the apartment? Or did he think he had wounded her by that last softly voiced comment on the balcony? She didn't know, but either way his action showed a sensitivity she liked. She left the room with a smile on her full lips.

She found him standing by the balcony door, his jacket pushed back and his hands thrust firmly in his trouser pockets. The hard angular planes of his face looked set, almost tense. She grinned at him. "Okay. I'll take it. When can I move in?"

His face softened as he grinned back. "Tomorrow, if you want."

She shook her head decisively and for a moment her lips drooped with fatigue. "No, not tomorrow. It will have to be Saturday, I guess. I can't afford to take a day off right now."

His eyes narrowed for a minute, scrutinizing her face, then the eyelids slid down and the long lashes masked the expression in them. Adrienne had the distinct impression she had said something that annoyed him, but a moment later the expression was gone, his eyes open and friendly. "If you like I'll make the arrangements with the superintendent. He knew Barry wanted to sublet, so he won't be surprised."

Agreement hovered on her lips, then she shook her head firmly, tempering the refusal with a warm smile.

"Thanks, Jared, but no. I have to deal with the man eventually, so I might as well start now. Besides, I'll have to contact the moving company to find out when they can deliver my furniture. I'm sure Saturday will be fine, but I want to be positive."

He nodded evenly, apparently unaffected by her refusal, as he came toward her. "Want to look around one more time before we leave?" he asked, gesturing around the room.

"No. I've seen enough. Let's go."

After he locked the door he dropped the keys in her hand. "These are yours now. Door key, garage key, mail key." As he spoke he flicked the appropriate key to identify it. Adrienne felt a little shiver run along her spine as the tip of his index finger touched her palm, a feeling that intensified when she smiled up into his face. The smile withered and died at the expression in his gray eyes, smoky now with some indefinable emotion.

Their gazes held, locked together in unspoken communication, then Jared moved and the moment was gone. She didn't protest when he put his hand between her shoulder blades then slipped his arm over her shoulders as they walked slowly toward the elevator, but she did move to stand well away from him in the tiny box. She was attracted to Jared Hawkes, his hard good looks, that aura of controlled masculinity, but she wasn't prepared to get involved.

He seemed to take her action with the same equanimity with which he had accepted her rejection of his help with the superintendent. When he caught her staring at him in the small confines of the elevator, he raised his eyebrows mockingly, making Adrienne rush into speech.

"I was just trying to find the words to express my gratitude for your help. You know, I was at my wit's end. I hated the idea of taking some dump just to have a place to live, but that was what I was afraid I was going to have to do."

A smile glinted in his eyes. "I never realized good deeds were so much fun. I get praise all around for this one. Barry is pleased to have his apartment taken off his hands. The landlord is pleased because he's got a new tenant without the bother of showing the place. You're pleased because you've got an apartment you can enjoy, and I'm pleased because you can now have dinner with me tonight without worrying about your future." The elevator doors opened with a swish. He took her hand firmly in his larger one and led her out toward the garage.

"Dinner?" she said doubtfully as she settled in the padded leather seat of the Mercedes.

"Dinner," he confirmed, slamming the door.

"Jared, this is very kind," she began as he eased into the car, "but..."

"But. Adrienne, is it always 'but' with you?"

She sat silent, staring at her hands, not noticing as the car slid into motion, wheeling out of the garage back to the street. Why had she bothered to protest? She wanted to go to dinner with Jared Hawkes. But he had already done so much for her. "Why don't I buy you dinner instead?" she offered brightly.

He shot her a derisive look that told her very clearly that his women did not pay for meals. She subsided, looking at her hands again, amazed at how quickly a pleasant situation could dissolve into painful tension.

"I'd like that," she said finally, looking out the window at unfamiliar street scenes. "And thank you."

"Stop thanking me," he growled. He paused at an intersection, indicated a left turn and waited for a break in the traffic.

She looked idly around her, not at all sure of their location in the evening darkness. Soon she realized that they were nowhere near her hotel and that despite her half-voiced protest and his gruff reply he'd never intended to take her back there. Contrition gave way to indignation and she shot him a speaking glance in the dim light as he parked the car.

He caught her look and laughed. "I hope you like seafood," he said, guiding her toward a large building covered in gray weathered board and made to look like a huge fishing shack. She didn't get a chance to reply before they entered the elegant interior that belied the rough outside. He spoke to the hostess, confirming reservations he'd made earlier. It crossed Adrienne's mind that he was annoyingly certain of himself.

She followed the hostess to a table for two nestled in a corner with a view of the city and harbor, the rows of street lamps shining like welcoming beacons in the darkness. When the woman politely asked if they would like a cocktail, Jared looked over at Adrienne with a raised, questioning brow. "A margarita, please," she said wearily. Jared ordered Scotch and water.

After the woman left, he leaned forward, placing his elbows on the table and propping his chin on his linked fingers. "Mad at me?" he inquired whimsically.

Adrienne felt her irritation softening at the little-boy expression of mock contrition on his hard male features and said severely, "You are very sure of yourself."

He grinned and lounged back in his chair. "I planned to bring you here whether or not you took Barry's apartment. I hoped it would be in celebration, but if it wasn't I figured you might need cheering up."

She twisted her lips in a wry expression. "You're right, I would have."

He moved forward again, reaching out to touch her cheek with one long, lean finger. "So, does it really matter why we're here? Can't you just relax and enjoy it?"

She felt her lips curl in an intimate smile as her blue-gray eyes locked with his gray ones. "I can and will," she agreed softly, thawing under the caress of his eyes and hand.

The moment was interrupted by the return of the hostess with their drinks, but the tight feeling of tension between them was gone, replaced by a warm, faintly tantalizing attraction. After taking a sip of the cocktail and feeling the tangy liquid slide down her throat with pleasurable ease, Adrienne opened her menu. She was amazed to find that it listed a huge assortment of seafood, but little else. A single concession to meat eaters was an offering of roast prime rib served with baked potato.

"I did warn you," Jared murmured, watching her with amusement.

"So you did," she replied dryly, sipping her drink again.

"See anything you like?"

She shook her head, not in denial, but in confusion. "My mind boggles."

His black brows met in a quick frown and the gray eyes narrowed. "Look, if nothing appeals to you, or you're tired of seafood, just say so. Don't bother being polite.''

She looked up, met his gaze, her startled expression confirming her reply. ''Jared! I like seafood. I love shrimp. Do you have shrimp here? I haven't had a chance to find out yet.''

He was still frowning, but the lines of tension on his face were less pronounced now. He said lightly, ''Haven't you tried any of the local restaurants, or have you stuck to the hotel dining room?''

She said with a grimace of distaste, ''Room-service sandwiches and fast-food outlets mostly. I haven't had time to sit down in a good restaurant for a meal. The service is usually too leisurely.''

She was surprised to feel the full blast of his personality, emanating anger, and it shook her. She was sure that in the flickering light of the table candle the gray eyes had lightened to a hard silver. She waited for him to speak because she couldn't figure out what had ignited his temper.

''So this is the first decent meal you've had since you got here?''

''Well, I had lunch with Elaine Trent and there was Noel's barbecue.''

He drew in a deep breath. ''No wonder you look so drawn and dragged out!''

''Thanks a lot!'' she snapped back indignantly, her face flushing and her eyes sparkling.

''Loyalty to your company is an admirable trait,'' he said slowly, picking his words carefully, ''but it must be tempered by loyalty to yourself—''

''Jared,'' she interrupted coldly, ''I don't need a lecture.''

His lips clamped together in a firm thin line and his body tensed aggressively. Over the table they glared at each other. Adrienne realized it would be very easy for her to be overwhelmed by the dynamic man opposite her, but she refused to concede defeat. She had stood up to high-powered executives before, she would again. A cool reserve stole over her features and into her eyes, though she was unaware of it.

Jared took note of the expression, quickly interpreted its meaning and backed off. "Okay. Point taken. I'll lay off your attitude to your job." He paused to rest his hand halfway across the table, palm upward. "Friends again?"

Adrienne looked at his face, the quizzical lift to his black brows, the faint quirk to the firm lips, then to the symbolically outstretched hand. Her tension began to drain away. She reached out to clasp his warm fingers with her own, a smile on her lips. "Friends again," she agreed huskily.

He smiled back at her in warm satisfaction as the cool businesswoman dissolved into the beautiful creature who had captivated him earlier. Giving her fingers a little squeeze he removed his hand and indicated their open menus. "Have you made your selection yet?"

"Shrimp," she replied promptly, "served *a l'espagnol*. It's there under specialties of the house. With wild rice and a salad. What about you?"

"The squid," he said. "They do it nicely here." He laughed at her disgusted expression.

Two hours, a bottle of wine and a delicious meal later, they were strolling back to the car. Adrienne was feeling the weary contentment that comes after good conversation and good food. They'd talked steadily through the meal, mainly about Seattle and New York, where Jared admitted he had lived for a short time, and their tastes in theater, music and food. They stayed carefully away from their respective backgrounds, as well as their jobs, almost as if they might be dangerous fuses neither wanted lit.

At the car he stopped and didn't immediately bend to unlock it. In the muted light of a distant street lamp she could barely make out his features, but his intention was clear. His head dipped slowly toward her, giving her plenty of opportunity to move away. Adrienne felt her blood begin to pound and lifted her face to meet his kiss. One arm slid around her waist, pressing her against his hard thighs, while the other caught her head to hold it still.

His firm lips brushed feather-light across hers, awakening her senses so that she was vividly aware of the musky scent of his after-shave and the tantalizing touch of his flesh on hers. She lifted her hands to his shoulders, stroking the smooth skin of his neck above the crisp white collar, then raising them to rub the hard line of his jaw.

The kiss deepened, his lips hardening on hers and his tongue demanding entry. Adrienne reveled in the wash of tingling fire that made her legs weak as her body arched against his, pliant and giving. His lips moved, leaving hers to caress the corner of her mouth. She leaned against him, bewildered by the sudden rush of feeling the one kiss had generated.

"Adrienne," he muttered hoarsely, "the things you do to me. Come on, I'd best get you home." He loosened his hold on her and reluctantly she moved away. He unlocked the car, again waiting until she was comfortable before striding around the front of the vehicle.

It was nice to know that Jared had been as moved by that kiss as she had been, Adrienne decided mischievously, as he drove to her hotel through the sparse traffic. She'd thought about him many times since the party on Saturday, wondering if he would call, trying to convince herself that it didn't matter whether he did or not. But it did. It mattered a lot. Tonight would have told her that if she hadn't already known.

As they drew up in front of the hotel Jared turned to her, his gray eyes dark and smoldering. He leaned over and kissed her lightly on the lips. She kissed him back, amazed by the sensations his touch sparked in her. He reached out to draw her against him, his lips firm but gentle on hers, coaxing, not demanding, a response. She melted against him as her body caught fire. All too soon he gently pulled away from her, calmly leaving the car.

She sat spellbound until he opened her door and reached down to help her out. "Good night, Adrienne," he murmured huskily, kissing the tip of her nose. She only regained her senses when the motor roared and he was gone.

Chapter Five

The moving van arrived promptly at nine o'clock Saturday morning. Adrienne was already at the apartment waiting for it, dressed in jeans, a vivid blue sweater and well-worn running shoes. She had swept her hair up in a ponytail to keep it off her face and it swished gently on her shoulders whenever she moved her head. She looked ten years younger and surprisingly alluring.

The three men who accompanied the truck were an established team and they all, including Adrienne, worked hard throughout the morning. Adrienne rushed about nonstop, supervising the placing of her furniture and inspecting for damage, while the men carted and hauled it into place. When the truck was unloaded, her furniture settled in and the packing cases emptied, it was noon and the three were off to another job. Adrienne was left to fill cupboards and cabinets with her uncrated possessions, now spread haphazardly over the apartment.

Abandoning the task for a moment, she collapsed wearily onto her squashy sofa with its bold flower-patterned cover. As she sat breathing deeply, her mind went back to the phone call she'd made to New York two days before.

She'd expected Emery to be pleased about her success in finding an apartment at last. She had been totally unprepared for his curt denial of what was a very simple request.

"Saturday? I'm afraid that's impossible, Adrienne."

She had stared out the window, her brows puckered in confusion. "But why, Emery? I know it costs more to have a moving company deliver on Saturday, that's why I'm calling to get your consent. The difference isn't all that much, however—"

"Take a couple of hours off tomorrow, Adrienne. Saturday's out."

"Emery," she said with all the composure she could command. "I've already spoken to the representative of the van line and they're booked tomorrow. They can fit me in on Saturday because they have extra staff on, but if Saturday is not acceptable then Tuesday is the first possible alternative."

There was silence on the other end of the phone, then Emery's querulous voice demanded, "Why the hell did you put it off so long?"

Adrienne didn't pretend not to know what he meant. She said coldly, "Personally, I would prefer to spend the extra three nights in my own bed rather than the hotel's, but if you insist..." She let the implication hang between them. Damn Emery Thorpe and his nasty suspicious mind!

"No," he replied quickly. She was sure he was calculating the cost of the additional three days Adrienne would be on expenses and deciding that the carrier's fee was not out of line. "No, I'll okay the extra expense. You can move in on Saturday."

She had to be satisfied with that grudging acceptance.

Stretching languidly on her own sofa, in her own apartment, she had no regrets. It would have been extremely difficult to organize the move if it had to be done on a weekday. The men had been quick and obliging about placing her furniture where she wanted it, but it was a time-consuming task that would have taken a large chunk out of her workday. Stifling a yawn she went back to the chore of sorting and storing linens.

She was in the middle of making her double bed when there was a loud rapping on her door. She straightened slowly, wondering who would be calling on her today. As she passed through the living room her nose wrinkled with wry amusement. Whoever it was, they would certainly see the place at its worst.

When she opened the door her heart gave a little leap of pleasure. "Jared! Come on in." She hadn't heard from him since the night he'd shown her the apartment, and she'd wondered if the desire she'd felt in that kiss was merely the response of a healthy male to an attractive woman.

Now she had her answer as he smiled down at her and stepped through the door. "Hi," he said huskily. "Are the movers gone?"

She nodded, glanced at her watch and said, "They left an hour ago."

"Good," he stated firmly, heading into the kitchen to deposit the paper bag he was carrying onto a clear space on the counter.

She followed him in, her head cocked to one side in puzzlement, her chestnut hair spilling over one shoulder. He turned to look at her, the dark eyes changing to a smoky gray. He reached out, grasped her shoulders and pulled her gently against him. Adrienne put her hands on his chest, her fingers splaying over the soft cotton of the brown plaid shirt he was wearing under a leather bomber jacket.

For the space of a heartbeat they stood that way, poised, their eyes searching each other's faces, then his lips came down on hers while his hands gathered her closer. Her arms slid up, to wrap around his neck. It didn't occur to Adrienne that their actions were more those of lovers who had been separated for days than a man and a woman who had only met a few times. As soon as she had seen him at the door she'd felt a sudden flash of joy and she was expressing that feeling.

He kissed her with a curiously suppressed passion, like a man who was questioning his right to a response. Adrienne sensed that he wanted more from her than just kisses, but he wasn't sure what her reaction would be. His tongue was outlining the shape of her lips, driving out rational thought with a fiery pleasure that threatened to overwhelm her. She allowed her questioning thoughts to slip away and gave herself up into his keeping.

The kiss seemed to last a wonderful eternity, but it was only moments later that Jared was loosening his hold on her and moving away from their close embrace. Adrienne reluctantly let her arms fall from his neck, as reality slowly crept in.

He smiled crookedly at her, then delved into the paper bag and brought out a bottle of champagne. "I thought you might like a housewarming gift," he said gruffly, and Adrienne knew that although he might have brought the wine for that purpose, it was not the champagne he was talking about.

She took the bottle and smiled teasingly back. "Thank you. It was a lovely idea."

He grinned lightheartedly and she burst out laughing. "I'll put this in the fridge. What else do you have in that bag, or shouldn't I ask?" she added, as she stowed the first article in her new refrigerator.

"Go ahead and peek," he said indulgently, handing her the bag and leaning back against the counter, his hands casually thrust into the pockets of his jeans.

"Melba toast and... what's this?" She looked up, her eyes shining with excitement. "Pâté! Jared, how did you know I was hungry?"

He looked a little smug. "I thought you might be and I didn't want you starving before dinner tonight."

She said severely, though there was a smile in her eyes, "Don't you ever ask people out first, or do you always spring it on them this way?"

"Only you, luscious," he replied lightly, bending forward to kiss her lips. When he straightened he surveyed the counters and table, looking for another free spot and finding none. "Why don't we take the wine and pâté into the living room and eat there? It will take hours to clear off a space on your table."

Adrienne looked around her and silently agreed. She couldn't resist teasing, "I could always put you to work stacking dishes."

He surprised her by saying seriously, "Oh, I intend to do that, but later. I don't want you passing out from malnutrition." His gray eyes mocked her. "How would I know where to put things?"

Adrienne gasped, then laughed. "Okay. I'm willing. I've been at it since nine o'clock anyway. I could use a break."

He peeled off the leather jacket in a casual, controlled gesture while Adrienne pretended not to watch the fluid play of muscles under his shirt. "Any hangers in the closet yet?" he asked, holding the collar with one finger.

Adrienne looked doubtful. "I don't know. I suppose so. There was a garment box marked 'hall closet.' One of the moving men opened it and put everything it contained into this closet. I'm not sure if they brought the extra hangers." She sighed wearily. "I haven't had time to look."

He slung the jacket over his arm, handed her the paper bag and said, "You go over to the sofa and get started on lunch. Don't worry about it. If there aren't any hangers I'll toss it over a chair back."

Adrienne nodded, letting a kind of calm relief wash over her. It was thoughtful of Jared to bring her food and drink. If he hadn't, she would have worked all day without a break.

It wasn't until she had the box of melba toast and the pâté out of the bag that she realized there was no knife. By that time Jared had carefully stepped over her cluttered floor, juggling the champagne bottle, two wineglasses, two plates and a knife that he had somehow discovered in her chaotic kitchen.

She looked at him gratefully as she quickly took the plates and glasses from his hands. "I'm glad you're organized. I'm definitely not!"

He grinned. "My specialty." Setting the bottle down on the floor, he moved a low table in front of the sofa. Adrienne put the plates down and opened the brown paper wrapping the pâté, spreading it out on the table so they could each cut what they liked. The melba toast she arranged on each plate.

With that little task done she sat back to watch Jared's manipulations of the champagne bottle. It felt good to lean her head against the soft cushions and let some of the tension flood out of her body. It also felt good to be able to admire the play of muscles across Jared's shoulders and upper arms while his attention was elsewhere and he wouldn't be aware of her hungry gaze.

His head turned slightly and his eyes, that disturbing smoky gray, met her unmasked, open gaze. He held it for a meaning-charged second, then let his eyes drop to linger on her lips, her breasts, her long graceful body as she relaxed against the cushions. Adrienne didn't move, but in that short moment she felt as if she'd been undressed and caressed by hands sensitive to her every need. The impact of that look left her shaken, but curiously light-headed, as if she had drunk too much of the champagne his fingers were still expertly uncorking.

Be careful, she thought to herself as she watched the cork progress smoothly out of the narrow mouth of the bottle. She couldn't deny the fire that was building between them. When a man was able to arouse desire without saying a word, without lifting a finger, merely by a look, he was indeed dangerous. He could coax her into bed with the same smooth, capable precision that he was using to ease the stopper from the bottle.

And when they made love, she thought with wry detachment, watching the cork fly upward with a muffled bang to land innocuously a few feet away, it would be as explosive as releasing the cork from a champagne bottle. But would it be as harmless?

There was something about Jared Hawkes, something that transcended the tough good looks and the self-assured confidence. He was a man who knew what he wanted and went after it. She'd be willing to bet that he found it, too. He was independent, a renegade from her carefully controlled corporate world. And that was part of his attraction. With Jared she didn't have to hide behind her professional mask. She could let the passionate nature she kept sternly repressed flare forth, as it already had, precisely because he had no ties with APP.

Adrienne's career had always been important to her, but after Ted she'd pursued it with an unswerving concentration that left little room for outside affairs. She dated infrequently and her tepid relationship with Boyd Sykes was a fairly recent development. She always made sure that it never conflicted with her work schedule.

Jared, she was certain, would never be content with that kind of relationship. He would demand physical and emotional intimacy. Adrienne wasn't sure she was ready for that kind of intensity.

She watched as Jared poured the champagne into the glasses, feeling a sharp surge of desire in the pit of her stomach. Jared was watching her again, devouring her without apology. She kept her gaze firmly on his strong, capable hands as she sought for some measure of control.

It would be easy to let herself be absorbed by this strong, decisive man—to let herself go completely, to be loved by him until nothing else mattered. But how could she be sure of him? She had tumbled headlong into an emotional whirlwind once before and it had almost destroyed her. How could she risk going through that pain with Jared, a man she'd known only for a few short days? And yet, when he touched her she forgot everything but the sensations his hands and lips created. It was as if her body and her mind were at war with each other.

His long fingers closed over the stem of one of the wineglasses, and he handed it to her. Adrienne leaned forward, smiling slightly, trying to avoid his intense gray eyes. "To Seattle and the future," he toasted softly. Adrienne murmured acknowledgment. The glasses clinked.

As she sipped the wine her eyes rested on his sensual lips, moistened by the touch of the champagne. The desire that always seemed to lie just beneath the surface when she was with him stirred, making her heart beat faster. Almost as if she had communicated her needs verbally, he took the glass from her and set it down beside his on the table.

Adrienne raised her blue-gray eyes to his and saw a reflection of the burning desire that fueled her body. She met his lips eagerly as they came down on hers and lifted her hand to the thick tumbled black hair. His lips tasted of champagne as she trailed the tip of her tongue over them, tracing their shape and savoring their sweetness. His arm came around her, pulling her closer, binding her against him as he deepened the kiss, his lips hardening on hers. His free hand burrowed beneath her sweater to cup one breast, then smoothly dealt with the front opening of her bra. The palm of his hand cupped the soft skin while the long fingers teased the nipple into taut awareness. Adrienne moaned deep in her throat, lost in a cascade of sensation.

The loud militant rumble from her empty stomach slashed into their concentration like a shot from a gun. They jumped apart almost guiltily, confused and disoriented. As the sound came again Adrienne's eyes opened wide and she flushed with embarrassment. Jared began to laugh.

"Never let it be said that I starve my woman into submission." He leaned toward the table, the smile still twitching at the firm line of his mouth. Diplomatically focusing on the pâté and toast, he allowed Adrienne a moment to rearrange her clothes away from the devastating effect of his knowing look.

Their conversation during the makeshift lunch ranged over a variety of subjects, but carefully avoided discussing the white-hot cord of attraction that linked them. By the time they had finished the pâté and the champagne that moment of passion had cooled, and Adrienne was content to let it smolder for the time being. She got up hastily, claiming a need to wash her hands, and headed for the sanctuary of the bathroom. When she returned Jared had cleared the table, replaced it in its original position beside the sofa and stacked their dirty dishes in the sink.

They spent the rest of the afternoon working companionably. Jared shifted the heavier things while

Adrienne darted about doing lighter jobs and deciding what was to go where. It was a curiously intimate afternoon, though they rarely touched and their words were always related to the task at hand. It was as if his help in getting her settled in the apartment drew them more closely together.

At four o'clock, when Jared finally called a halt, they had the kitchen generally in order, books stashed in her bookcase and household necessities tucked away in the big utility closet. The dining-room table was free of its clutter and what debris remained in the living room was pushed against the walls, safely out of the way.

Adrienne felt hot, limp and grubby. She sighed wearily and rubbed the back of one hand over her forehead, leaving a streak of black. "I knew movers packed everything, but I didn't know they even brought the dust with them!" she mumbled tiredly. Her eyes followed Jared as he sauntered out of the kitchen where they stood, widening slightly when he returned with his leather jacket draped negligently over one arm.

He put his hands on his hips and surveyed her with rueful amusement. "Once you set yourself a task you go at it with steely-eyed determination, don't you?"

Adrienne managed a weary chuckle and nodded. "I like to see a job done properly."

He watched her for a minute, the caress in his eyes smoothing away her exhaustion, replacing it with building desire. Finally he said firmly, "Okay, you're finished for today. No more work. I'm leaving now, but I'll be back at six to pick you up." His eyes gleamed with mischief as he bent to kiss her lightly on the lips. His voice whispered softly in her ear, his breath tickling the sensitive skin. "I'll imagine you soaking in the tub, bubbles lightly touching your body, hiding but exposing..." He nibbled her earlobe and Adrienne felt once again that core of desire whiten with heat. Her eyelids drooped as languorous pleasure caught her in its grasp.

Jared chuckled softly with satisfied male appreciation, then moved away. She opened her eyes in time to see him framed in the apartment doorway. "See you later," he promised huskily, then was gone.

She almost did have that bubble bath he had so graphically described, but the bathroom was one room they hadn't tackled and her bottle of spicy perfumed bubble bath was lost somewhere in the unsorted confusion. Instead, she had a long, luxurious shower, letting the spray pound over her tense muscles in a hot massage.

Once out of the shower she toweled her hair dry roughly and forced herself to think of mundane things like the length of time it took to thoroughly dry long, thick hair like hers and figuring out where she had put her hairbrush. It was still in one of the suitcases she'd brought from the hotel that morning and not yet unpacked, but where exactly was the suitcase?

Somewhere in the bedroom, of course. She wandered out of the bathroom, a towel wrapped around her body, her hands still working the one around her hair. She found the suitcase without any problem and picked it up to sling it onto the bed so she could open it wide and rummage through it for the brush.

The bed was in total disarray. She'd started to make it up after the movers had left, but Jared's arrival had interrupted her and she'd never finished. The bottom sheet was neatly tucked in, but the top sheet was a swirl of bright, geometrically patterned percale. As Adrienne stood looking at the colorful display, it suddenly struck her that the untucked sheet on the half-made bed looked like the tousled result of passionate lovemaking by two people so lost in themselves that they were oblivious to all else. She moistened parched lips as her mind envisioned Jared's legs entwined with hers, their bodies touching, hands caressing, lips burning on responsive skin.

Heavens, she thought, flopping down on the bed, forgetting her wet hair, the brush, the suitcase, her still-damp skin. The image had shaken her to the core. She knew she wanted him, but she hadn't realized how badly. Jared was disrupting her life in a way she would never have dreamed possible.

Deep in thought she plumped a pillow, slipped it behind her back and leaned against the headboard. Jared's handsome features, his well-proportioned body, the rakish way a lock of that black hair tumbled on his forehead, would make any woman's heart beat faster, she mused. The expression in his smoky gray eyes could caress with a glance, and the intuitive way he used his hands and lips to stroke and arouse would break down the strongest defenses.

She nibbled the tip of one slender finger as she remembered his comment about not letting "my woman" starve. *My woman,* she thought with a little shiver of mingled apprehension and pleasure. He was moving too fast. She wasn't prepared for this—not now.

Shaking off the lingering effects of the powerful attraction she felt for Jared, she slid off the bed, found her brush and the hair dryer and closed the suitcase. Before working on her dark chestnut hair she carefully made the bed, not satisfied until the sheets were covered and smoothed beneath blankets and the spread.

The tangles in her long hair gave easily beneath the brush as she stood before the mirror on her dressing table. Plugging in the dryer she continued to brush the thick mane away from her face.

Ordinarily she would have arranged her hair into a chignon or a knot, allowing loose strands here and there to soften her normal daytime look, but after a moment's debate she left it down, brushing it back from her forehead to fall freely over her shoulders. The effect, she was pleased to note, enhanced the high-necked indigo dress she had chosen for the evening. She deliberately used more makeup than usual, accentuating her eyes, cheekbones and lips. When she had finished she stood back and surveyed herself with some pride, deciding that the blue dress, though not blatantly sexy, was subtly alluring.

When Jared arrived she was ready, opening the door with a warm welcoming smile. His eyes widened, then narrowed appreciatively. "Very nice," he murmured huskily, reaching out to catch a lock of her hair. He moved toward her almost as if he wanted to kiss her. His fingers tightened in the thick strands, then he stepped back and drew his hand away, his angular features twisting into a rueful smile.

"Would you like to come in for a drink?" she asked chokily, wondering if he did, whether they would ever leave for dinner.

"I think not," he replied gruffly, raising one black brow. "If you're ready we should be on our way."

She nodded agreement, took her coat from the closet and with some misgivings let him help her as she shrugged into it. His hands lingered for a moment on her shoulders, sending her temperature shooting up, then were withdrawn before the contact pushed either of them too far.

As they waited for the elevator she watched him covertly. He was wearing a navy-blue blazer teamed with cream-colored slacks. The fine fabric of the jacket was tailored to emphasize the muscular physique of the man who wore it, and Jared looked very handsome as he smiled down at her and helped her into the cubicle with a fleeting touch at her elbow. Even more so than before, if that was possible.

They dined at a small, intimate restaurant where the lighting was muted and the tables were graced with fine linen, heavy silver and flickering candlelight. The atmosphere was blatantly romantic, emphasizing Adrienne's sensual response to the man seated opposite her. The cuisine was French, the entrées a mixture of seafood and fine cuts of meat.

Adrienne was sipping a glass of wine while inspecting her menu when Jared asked huskily, "Will you let me order for you?"

Ordinarily she preferred to make her own selection, but tonight, caught up in the ambience of the restaurant and the potent spell Jared had been weaving around her all afternoon, she found herself nodding agreement. "That would be nice."

He smiled slowly at her, his gray eyes smoky. "Good," he said softly. Adrienne felt a warm heat under her skin as her body responded to the message in his eyes, and she had to swallow against the sudden dryness in her throat.

The whole evening was like that, the sexual awareness between them underlying every word, every move. Even Jared's choice of meal had subtle overtones—oysters on the half shell to start, prawns in a creamy sauce for Adrienne, steak Diane for himself.

They lingered over dinner, talking a great deal, enjoying each other's company. No one at the restaurant seemed in a hurry to see them leave, but as the clock crept slowly toward eleven Adrienne found herself hard-pressed to stifle a yawn.

"You're tired," Jared stated flatly. "It's been a long day for you."

"Yes, I am," she said slowly, her voice surprised, as if she'd only just realized the fact. Jared's presence had kept her mind and senses stimulated throughout the day. It was only now, responding to the note of concern in his voice, that she realized just how fatigued she was.

He pushed back his chair. "I'll take you home."

She shook off the moment of lethargy, smiling lightly. "There's no rush. I can sleep late tomorrow. No more pressures, no more deadlines to meet until Monday."

He grinned, observing with tender mockery, "What a hedonist," as he came over to her chair to help her to her feet.

Adrienne basked in the unaccustomed pampering and decided that the evening couldn't have been more perfect.

He took her directly back to the apartment. As they walked slowly to her door Adrienne let her head droop lightly against his shoulder, enjoying the firm pressure of his arm around her waist.

When they reached their destination, she turned in his embrace to face him. Even though she wore high-heeled evening sandals, he topped her by several inches and she had to look up to see his expression.

He was watching her intently, his eyes smoky gray, which she now knew meant he desired her. Her lips parted enticingly as his head dipped toward her. She slid her hands beneath the beautifully cut blazer and wrapped them around his body, feeling the heat from his skin through the fine fabric of his shirt.

His mouth covered hers gently in a light, fleeting kiss that momentarily threw her off balance. She had expected one of those hungry, passionate caresses that turned her blood to a hot boiling caldron.

"I want you, Adrienne," he whispered thickly, his lips nibbling temptingly at the corner of her mouth.

"I know," she groaned, wishing she could agree to his demands, but knowing that to allow herself to become more deeply involved with him was emotional madness. "Jared, I can't...."

He laughed huskily at that, "Sure you can, lady. All you have to do is relax and let it happen."

His lips were playing havoc with her senses, denying logic, persuading her to give in to her body's demands.

Very slowly, she removed her arms from his waist, lifting her hands to cup his face. Beneath her fingers she could feel the hard contours of bone and the faint bristle of beard. "Dear Jared," she murmured regretfully, "no."

Their eyes met and clashed. "Why?"

She sighed, her mind busy phrasing words and sentences. Almost of their own volition her thumbs caressed the taut line of his jaw. His arms tightened on her waist, drawing her against him, keeping her close when she knew she should be putting distance between them.

"I like you enormously, Jared. And—and you know how attracted I am to you." She broke off, blushing, as he made a soft mocking sound in his throat. His gray eyes watched her as she bent her head, letting the heavy chestnut strands fall forward to cover her expression.

When she looked up her lips were trembling. "Jared, we have met each other a total of four times and one of those was a complete disaster! I don't know you well enough to make love with you."

There was silence as he considered this. She could feel the pulse pounding in his neck as he worked to control the desire their caresses had aroused. When he finally spoke his voice was low and rasping. "How long does it take before you decide you know someone?"

"I'm not sure," she replied honestly. "I've never felt this way before."

His eyes gleamed. "That gives me hope then, doesn't it?"

She swallowed, knowing she was being unfair. She didn't go in for casual affairs and there was no time in her life for an emotional commitment right now. She'd been given a tremendous opportunity here in Seattle and she didn't want to blow it because she let her heart rule her head.

He gave her no time to protest before his mouth took hers with driving intensity. All the need, all the desire she'd rejected was in that kiss and Adrienne reeled from the force of it. She clung to his shoulders, needing his support because her legs felt weak and incapable of holding her up. Her head was bent back and he lifted one hand to cup it and keep it steady.

He moved slightly, shifting his stance to spread his legs more widely apart and lowered the hand that held her waist to press her forcefully against his hard thighs. Adrienne murmured low in her throat, her mind whirling, her eyes behind closed lids blinded by a fiery torrent of flame colors. She was past thinking, past rational action as his lips gentled on hers, his tongue delicately probling and evoking a hot yearning that made her previous furious desire seem like a cool lick of ice cream.

In the midst of this, while she still craved more, his hands fell away and he stepped back. "Key," he demanded, breathing hard, holding out his hand to take it.

Bemused, she handed it to him, not sure what he planned to do next.

He unlocked the door, pushing it open before gently placing the key in the middle of her palm and closing her fingers over it. His eyes mocked as he whispered seductively, "It's going to be a long, lonely night without you."

He strode away without a backward glance. Adrienne stood weakly, staring after him, her mind in turmoil. It wasn't until she heard the elevator doors slide open then close that she went into the apartment. Her body began to shake as she relived that last embrace, the passionate fire roaring back into life once more.

It would be a long, lonely night indeed.

Chapter Six

Adrienne slept surprisingly well, considering the emotional turmoil she'd been in when she went to bed. She woke an hour or so later than her usual time and lay drowsily thinking about the events of the day before.

Jared, she decided, was a difficult man to understand and so far she had read him wrongly at every turn. First she had assumed he was another Ted Conrad. Once she got to know him at Noel's party she'd realized her mistake, but had fallen into another misconception when she assumed he wouldn't call her again. Now she was speculating on what his actions last night meant and was probably going to stumble off in another wrong direction.

She thought he'd been frustrated. She knew he wanted her. She hoped he would contact her again. What did all that add up to? Confusion. With a little shake of her head she sat up and stretched, yawning as she climbed out of bed. Really, he was a fascinating man, a breath of fresh air in her stuffy career-dominated world. She hoped she would have a chance to get to know him better. Lazily, she brushed her hair, then wandered into the bathroom to shower.

Fifteen minutes later she was dressed and standing in the kitchen filling the coffeepot, her dark hair tumbling over her shoulders as she worked. Absently she flicked the heavy locks behind her ears and over her shoulders, making the red highlights flame in the overhead light. Once the coffee was percolating she opened the fridge sleepily, expecting to find breakfast and seeing instead only stark white emptiness.

Damn! she thought, putting her hands on her hips in an irritated movement. For a moment there, when she had reached for and found a can of coffee that had traveled all the way from New York, she'd forgotten that she hadn't gone shopping yesterday. That meant she would have to shop before she ate, and right now she was starving. She looked through the cupboard at the other canned goods that had come with her from New York, finding tomato paste, cream-style corn, pineapple chunks and beef bouillon cubes. She debated about the pineapple chunks, secretly wished they were eggs and bacon, then decided she couldn't afford to be choosy. She lifted down the can, quickly opened it and dumped the contents into a bowl.

When she finished the fruit, the coffee was done. She poured a cup, then wandered into the living room to drink it. As she relaxed in the easy chair, she looked around, mentally judging what remained to be done. Pictures had to be hung up, she decided, wrinkling her nose with distaste. That was a chore she'd always hated. It seemed to take hours to do each picture and then they never looked right.

Then there were the drapes. Jared had put them up yesterday, but they weren't really wide enough for this window, they made the room look odd. She'd have to get a new set, a rather bleak prospect since she had only purchased these a year ago and new drapes would be expensive. Her gaze wandered around the room and she realized that it looked odd, not because of the curtains, which could be left open most of the time anyway, but because of the couch. It was in the wrong place. It was too large to be across the room as it was, facing the wide bank of windows. It should actually be against the wall. The chair she was sitting on now would fit nicely on the spot where one end of the sofa presently rested and the table...

She sighed, finished her coffee and stood up. If she was going to move furniture this afternoon she had better get some groceries in first. She wandered back to the kitchen, rinsed the mug, then went in search of a telephone book to find out where the nearest supermarket was.

She stopped dead, standing in the hall with her hands on her hips in frustration. She didn't have a telephone book because she didn't have a phone yet. The apartment was wired with a system of jacks, eliminating the need for a service call each time the tenant changed. The line was to be activated next week and Adrienne had planned to pick up the phone and directories on Monday. Of all the stupid stunts, she castigated herself. How could she be so organized at work and so harebrained when it came to her own affairs?

With a little sigh she shook her head, went to the closet to pull soft black boots over the narrow legs of her jeans and throw a short buff jacket over her sweatshirt. She had vague recollections of passing an open-every-day supermarket in a small shopping plaza not far away when Jared was ferrying her back and forth. She only hoped she could find it again.

She could, and did. An hour later she was struggling under the weight of two grocery sacks as she headed away from the store toward her apartment. In the cart her purchases hadn't looked like much. In her arms they weighed a ton and were getting heavier by the minute.

Fortunately she didn't have too far to go. In twenty minutes, she told herself stoutly, she would be home and could safely dump the bags. Twenty minutes carrying the awkward burden stretched into an awfully long time. When she eventually turned on to her street she had decided she would have to invest in a car or some kind of carryall.

At the corner she stopped for a breather, leaning against the solid trunk of one of the cherry trees that lined the street. She debated putting the paper bags on the ground so she could rest her arms, but a quick glance at the damp sidewalk put an end to that idea. The sound of footsteps made her look up. Her face lit in a smile.

"Well, hello there," she said happily, feeling like a kid who has just been given a second helping of her favorite dessert.

"Let me take those," said Jared Hawkes, plucking first one then the other bag from her arms. "You look about done in."

She grinned. "Perceptive man."

His eyes flickered over her, lingering for a moment on the rise and fall of her breasts under the open jacket, then on her lips. A slow smile lit his eyes. "You could say that."

She blushed and her smile faded, but she held his gaze steadily, telling him with her eyes that nothing had changed from last night.

A strange, rather lopsided smile quirked his lips, then he set out in the direction of the apartment. Adrienne followed.

"How did you know where I'd be?" she asked, after a moment.

"When I buzzed you and there was no answer I assumed you were either still asleep or out somewhere so I tried a couple more times. When there was still no answer I guessed you were out."

"That doesn't explain why you were waiting for me here," she protested.

He grinned at her, amusement warming his eyes. "I know the state of your fridge, remember? I would have come to pick you up in the car, but I wasn't sure which route you'd taken and I was afraid I'd miss you. I knew you would have to come back this way so I hovered around the corner."

"Am I glad you did!" she remarked with heartfelt relief.

He laughed at her tone and asked, "What have you got in here?"

She told him, then said slowly, "I wasn't sure if I would see you again." She found that she was holding her breath as she waited for his reply. Deliberately she released it, forcing herself to breathe naturally.

His words were like soft velvet brushing gently over her skin. "You made the rules. I'm willing to follow them."

Her eyes widened then narrowed as she frowned, trying to figure out what motivated him now. "Why?" she demanded bluntly.

"Because I respect people who have the courage to take a stand about what they feel is right," he said calmly, his eyes holding hers. "I may not particularly like it when the firmness works to my disadvantage, but that doesn't stop me from respecting that person."

"You—respect me?" she questioned doubtfully, not really sure that was what she wanted from him.

He nodded, completely serious. "Yes, but I'll make no secret of this, Adrienne, I also want you. I'll go along with your terms for now, but that won't stop me from needing to touch and kiss you while you get to know me."

They had reached the apartment building and were climbing the concrete steps to the front door. She searched for the key in the big purse she had slung over her shoulder, found it and inserted it in the lock. Then she sent him a mischievous look. "Okay by me," she said huskily and opened the door.

She led him up to the apartment and asked him if he would like a cup of coffee. He nodded agreement, took the mug she handed him and wandered into the living room while she put away the food. He was standing in the middle of the room idly surveying it when she came up behind him carrying her own mug of coffee.

"I suppose you want to hang the pictures," he observed.

"Eventually," she replied, feeling the furniture arrangement grate on her nerves now she'd decided it wasn't properly placed. When he looked sharply at her she elaborated. "The couch doesn't work where it is. It makes the room seem small. When I told the movers to put it facing the window I thought it would do just the opposite. But now—" she shrugged, then concluded fiercely "—now I don't like it at all!"

He looked at the sofa, shot a wary glance at Adrienne, and took a gulp of coffee.

She didn't notice. Her mind was absorbed by the annoying problem at hand. "And until I get the furniture straightened out I can't hang the pictures."

"Okay," he said wearily, "where do you want it to go?"

She looked up at him in surprise. "Jared! I wasn't hinting—" she began, then laughed. "But I can't deny that I'm delighted with your help. Now, we'll begin by putting it over there...."

They moved the couch three times before Adrienne was satisfied, then arranged the rest of the furniture and hung her pictures. At that point Jared slumped down on the sofa, which had ended up along one wall, and said plaintively, "Are we finished yet?" His narrowed eyes surveyed Adrienne as she stood in the center of the room and observed the changes they had wrought with a smug air of satisfaction.

"Yup," she said firmly, "we sure are. Want a drink?"

"A beer," he breathed, closing his eyes as he laid his head back against the cushions. "A cold beer."

"That I can't provide," she announced blithely, heading for the kitchen. He watched her graceful movements through long black lashes.

"I do have spirits, though," she tossed back casually, looking over her shoulder. She felt a flash of compassion at the fatigued slump of his supine body, the long legs stretched wearily before him. He'd probably spent a restless night and she had proceeded to enlist his aid in lugging around heavy furniture. The twinge of conscience passed quickly. He had offered his help, she hadn't demanded it. "But no mix, I'm afraid," she finished cheerfully.

"Scotch on the rocks, then. You do have ice cubes, I presume?"

She laughed. "In abundance."

As she poured the Scotch for him and some sherry for herself he said lazily, "You're going to have to buy a car, Adrienne."

She brought the drinks over, watched him open his eyes and straighten, then handed the short, heavy glass to him. "I know," she said, curling up on the chair and sipping the sherry.

He took a long gulp of the Scotch, sighed, then said, "We'll go shopping for one next weekend. It's better to do it in the daylight. Know how to drive a stick shift?"

Adrienne felt a warm glow that had nothing to do with the liquor she was drinking. It was the first time Jared had made reference to seeing her again, and she felt a heady sense of excitement and success.

He caught her expression and put his glass on the table. In a husky, almost possessive voice, he said, "Come here."

Adrienne unfolded her legs and walked haltingly across the short distance to him, still clutching the glass in her hands. He took it and put it beside his own, then gently tugged her down beside him. There was no evidence now of the earlier fatigue. As he pulled her against him and began to kiss her, Adrienne snuggled closer in his arms, knowing that that was exactly where she wanted to be.

Monday she miscalculated the length of time it would take to get from her apartment to the office and was late, thereby missing Emery's now-habitual eight o'clock call. He wasn't inclined to accept her explanation of buses, missed and slow, as an excuse and gave her a sharp, pointed lecture on not sinking into bad habits.

That put Adrienne in a temper and thoroughly ruined her day. For three weeks she had slaved long hours to reduce the chaos in this branch. One day, one day out of the past fifteen, she was ten minutes late, and Emery had the nerve to accuse her of acquiring bad habits! There were moments when she wanted to throw her job in Emery's teeth and tell him just how small and petty she thought he was.

But, of course she didn't. She swallowed her anger, telling herself she was a professional and emotions had no place in business. Though Emery irritated her more and more frequently these days, she couldn't let that hamper her efficiency.

The next two days passed with what she had come to believe was the normal quota of problems. As usual she worked well beyond four-thirty and it was after seven when she reached home. On Wednesday telephone service to her apartment was activated, which picked up spirits flagging from a hectic week. Having a phone again made her feel more secure somehow. It was nice to know that her family could get hold of her in an emergency.

Thinking of her parents made her check her watch and decide to call home to give them the new number. They had been pleased by her promotion, especially Morgan, and supportive during the move. She knew, though, that they would worry about her getting settled in a new city and would be glad to hear all her news.

The conversation left her feeling light-hearted. When the phone rang a few minutes later her voice lilted charmingly as she answered.

"Hi there, sunshine," said Jared. "You sound on top of the world."

"My telephone was connected today so I just called home," she explained happily. "We talked for a half an hour. It'll probably cost a fortune."

"I see," he said softly. "Picking up threads, were you?"

"Yes," she agreed slowly, because she hadn't thought of it that way, "I suppose that's it. Making sure no one's forgotten me, I guess."

"No one would forget you, beautiful," he drawled huskily. Adrienne felt the deep voice wrap seductively around her, caressing like his eyes and hands. "In fact, you make quite an impact."

She laughed, rather shakily. "So do you."

"Good," he murmured. "That's what I had in mind." Adrienne felt her heart pounding in a thumping, headlong rhythm. She closed her eyes and breathed deeply to calm herself. There was a short pause, almost as if he was aware of her reaction. A teasing note entered his voice when he continued, "I'm calling because of certain complaints I've received."

Baffled, Adrienne repeated cautiously, "Complaints?"

"Hmmm. From this gorgeous dark-haired lady with soft blue eyes and principles. She seems to think I never make a proper date with a girl so I'm calling her to ask her out to dinner on Friday."

Elation bubbled in Adrienne's throat. "Okay," she said happily. "What time?"

"That was simple. Seven-thirty. Now, if only you were as easy to get along with all the time..."

She giggled. "Wretched man."

He sighed mournfully. "I can tell time hasn't softened you any. I'll see you Friday."

It felt good to relax with Jared at the end of a tiring week. Instead of feeling the lethargy that usually claimed her on Friday evening, she was charged with energy, and their dinner and the dancing that followed it flashed by. Too soon it was after midnight, and Jared was teasingly telling her she had worn him to a frazzle.

At her door, he kissed her deeply, leaving her shaken, then told her he would pick her up at ten sharp the next morning. Adrienne was ready on time, her stomach fluttering with excitement at the thought of a day with Jared and the purchase she was about to make. Having a car of her own in New York had never seemed important to her, and she wasn't much of a driver, but here in Seattle she knew she would be lost without one.

The first showroom they went to specialized in vehicles manufactured in the States. They wandered through the lot, looking over different models until one of the salesmen noticed them and strode briskly over. He introduced himself, then spoke exclusively to Jared, while Adrienne bristled with irritation. Though Jared mentioned that she was the one buying the car, the man continued to direct his comments to the male in the party. They did not buy Adrienne's car from that particular dealership.

Nor the second one they inspected. At the third Adrienne muttered acerbically, "I can see that this is not an equal-opportunity industry," as yet another male salesman strode importantly toward them. Jared shouted with laughter, the approaching salesman looked interested and Adrienne found herself grinning like a kid playing a particularly mischievous practical joke.

They finally settled on a small Japanese import with an automatic transmission, after one bumpy and nerve-racking ride when Adrienne tried her hand at using a manual one. Jared teased her about being a menace on the road, and Adrienne wrinkled her nose at him in mock indignation. She really did enjoy his company—his sense of humor, his thoughtfulness and the underlying desire that smoldered in his eyes.

They spoke once during the week, when Jared told her he was heading into the mountains to ski on Saturday and invited her along. She agreed blithely, as though entrusting her fragile body to two slats of fiberglass and two slender poles in order to career down a gigantic mountain was something she'd always wanted to do.

Jared was an excellent teacher, patient with her inexperience, joking her out out of her barely suppressed terror. She fell more than she was on her feet, bruising herself all over, but was otherwise unhurt. Throughout the day her confidence grew. By the time they left the ski resort she had lost her fear and was demanding to know if they could return on Sunday.

Jared laughed, shot her a wicked look and told her not to be too hasty.

The next day she discovered why. Her whole body felt black and blue, and her muscles had seized up into knotted instruments of torture. Skiing was out of the question. In fact, so was anything except soaking in a hot tub and feeling sorry for herself.

But when the next weekend rolled around she was ready to try again. She did a little better this time, but still fell more times than she wanted to count. Her reward was Jared's quiet approval. For the rest of the season she was quite happy to join him on the slopes at least once a weekend until the snows melted.

Skiing wasn't their only occupation on the winter weekends. Jared seemed determined to make her like living in Seattle. They went shopping at Pike Place Market, a turn-of-the-century farmer's market that was a great tourist attraction as well as a terrific source for produce, meats and seafood.

Fortunately the market was covered, since it was pouring rain the day they visited it. They were wandering through the aisles when Adrienne stopped abruptly at a counter. "Look at the size of the shrimp," she muttered, more to herself than Jared or the observant owner of the stall.

"They're prawns, lady," said the thickset man. He named a price per pound. "How much do you want?"

Adrienne looked at him, a little dazed. "Just a pound."

The man shoveled about a dozen into a bag. Adrienne's eyes grew wide. Jared lounged to one side, watching her face, his expression amused.

"Are they already cooked?" she asked, as she and the proprietor exchanged money and prawns.

"Sure."

Her eyes narrowed. She stole a quick look at Jared, who was grinning now, dipped into the bag and pulled out one of the giant shrimp. Gingerly she bit into it. Her eyes widened. "Oh, heaven," she breathed.

Jared chuckled and accepted the prawn she offered him, then told her she had a one-track mind. Laughing, she agreed.

Another time they went down to Pioneer Square, the old section of Seattle, and enjoyed a romantic candlelit dinner at the end of the day. Adrienne had fun poking through the shops and boutiques in the restored area, perhaps all the more so because she was with Jared.

Their time together was restricted to the weekends. Even if Adrienne hadn't been frantically busy and working several evenings a week, she would not have allowed herself to date him more often. She enjoyed being with him too much already. If she saw him daily she risked losing her heart.

She was shocked into an awareness of just how deeply she had fallen under Jared's spell when he took a ten-day business trip at the end of April. She spent the week deliberately working herself into exhaustion so she wouldn't think about his absence, allowing thoughts of him to invade her mind only in those few minutes before she slipped into the oblivion of sleep.

By the weekend she was miserable, missing him more than she had ever believed possible. Nothing had any savor for her and she spent Saturday cleaning her apartment.

The telephone ringing that evening made her mood swing mercurially from blazing hope that it might be Jared calling, to black despondency when she learned it was a wrong number. The intensity of her disappointment made her wonder—could it be that she was falling in love with him? Somewhere deep inside of her a fire began to burn as pleasure, anticipation and desire came to life. How she wished Jared was here so she could test out this wonderful new feeling! She thought about him, letting her mind rove over the months they had spent together, pondering just when the physical attraction and intellectual respect had begun to slip into something much more special.

It was impossible to pinpoint a date. She couldn't say it was the day they met, when he helped her to move in, the day he coaxed her onto skis and showed her a world she hadn't known existed. No, it was more a combination of things. It was the way he had only to look at her to set her heart pumping wildly, his respect for her "principles" even though she knew it cost him dearly to draw away before his mental control broke under the weight of physical desire. Those moments when she was very tired from a hectic week and she saw concern flicker in his eyes. The thoughtfulness that kept him from nagging her about the long hours she worked, which she knew very well that he disapproved of.

The euphoria of believing herself in love made the rest of the weekend slip by with painless ease. On Monday morning she hummed along with the radio as she drove in to work, her mood still high and carefree. Emery's eight-o'clock call contained its usual quota of petty complaints, but even that couldn't get her down. She tolerantly laughed off his spitefulness and settled down to do the business at hand.

Knowing she had to share the wonderful feelings bubbling through her, Adrienne called Elaine Trent to see if she was free for lunch. Unfortunately Elaine had a doctor's appointment that day and couldn't make it, but she did suggest they meet after work and have coffee. That suited Adrienne just fine. She didn't feel like staying late anyway.

"I'm sorry we'll be rushed," Elaine said, when they met at a a small restaurant that specialized in exotic coffees and teas. They had their choice of tables at this hour and Elaine unhesitatingly selected one near the window. "Jon's picking me up earlier than I expected," she explained. "He was supposed to be tied up in meetings until six, but just before I left he called to say one had been canceled and he would be leaving soon. He should be here in twenty minutes or so."

"That's okay," said Adrienne, hiding her disappointment. She brightened. "I was just feeling really happy and wanted to share it with someone."

Elaine cocked her head inquisitively. "Oh? Did you get another promotion or something?"

"No, nothing like that. It's more—personal."

"Come on," Elaine prompted. "Don't leave me in suspense. Give!"

"I think I'm in love with Jared," said Adrienne, smiling rather bashfully at her confession.

Elaine gasped, then cried, "Adrienne, that's wonderful! I'm delighted for you. Jared's a wonderful guy! Oh, this is great!" There was a honk from a car horn and both women looked out the window. "Oh no!" Elaine groaned. "That's Jon, even earlier than I expected. Adrienne, I've got to run. Look, let's get together again soon so we can talk more." She rose to her feet, full of energy, despite her thickening waistline. Hugging Adrienne, she concluded, "I'm so happy for you, and for me too! Now you'll stay in Seattle and I won't lose a friend at the whim of that awful grump, Emery Thorpe! Gotta go. I'll call you!''

She was gone in a whirlwind of good feelings, completely unaware that her parting words had shattered Adrienne's fragile bubble of happiness. After her departure, Adrienne remained in the café, sipping blueberry tea and wondering how she could have been such a naive fool.

In January she had bragged carelessly that she was a career woman, no ties to interfere with her pursuit of her job. But if she allowed herself to fall in love with Jared she would bind herself securely to him and to Seattle. She knew that he would never consider relocating in New York. Even if she ignored the very successful company he owned, which did all its business in the West and Midwest, there was his firmly held opinion of New York City. It was a place, he'd once told her, for inside people—those who prefer art galleries, museums and theaters to swimming, skiing and hiking. If you didn't participate in those sports then New York was a wonderful city, but it wasn't for him. He needed the outdoors as well as nightlife, galleries and theaters. Seattle could provide both.

Since she was only a transient member of the Seattle community could she afford to put down roots? The answer, of course, was no.

One day, a year and a half from now, maybe two years, even three, she would leave Jared. It was as inevitable as the pain that eventual separation would bring. The more fully they became involved with each other the more intense that pain would be. There seemed to be only one logical path to follow. Break up with Jared now, before they were both too deeply hurt to recover.

Chapter Seven

She had the rest of the week to think about how she would tell Jared that their relationship was doomed and that they should end it. The extra time didn't do her any good. She spent most of it worrying about how he was going to react and how unhappy they were going to be when it was over. Having convinced herself that the breakup was necessary, she stoically accepted this initial hurt as being the only way to avoid even greater pain and refused to alter her course.

Jared was returning to Seattle on Thursday. Before he left, they'd made arrangements to get together for dinner, but in her overwrought state of mind Adrienne didn't think she could handle seeing him. First thing Thursday morning she phoned his office and left a message for him, saying she couldn't make dinner, then made sure she wasn't available in case he called.

The next day she did talk to him and agreed to see him. She knew he was wondering what was going on because she kept her tone impersonal throughout the entire conversation. By the evening he would probably have guessed what her motives were. Jared was an intelligent man. It wouldn't take him long to figure it all out.

When he arrived that evening, she was waiting in the lobby clad in a tailored dress of soft, champagne-colored wool. Her dark chestnut hair was caught in a tight chignon and her expression was one of detached, courteous interest. Inside her nerves throbbed and hammered as they had done since she put down the phone that morning.

When she saw his lithe figure striding up the walk she almost abandoned her resolutions. Her heart skipped a beat and she felt a surge of happiness at the sight of his powerful shoulders, lean hips and angular, good-looking face. He looked, she thought, superb.

While he was unaware of her scrutiny his expression was somber, perhaps a little grim. Her throat tightened with emotion. He'd caught on exactly as she'd predicted. He might not know the details of what she planned to say, but he had guessed the rough outline. Taking a deep breath to steady herself, she pushed open the glass door and stepped outside.

"Hello, Adrienne," he said warily, his eyes narrowing as he took in her cool, closed expression.

Was he seeing the despair beneath? she wondered fleetingly. Probably not. She had mastered the art of showing nothing years ago. "Hello, Jared. How was the trip?"

"Hectic," he replied, taking her hand as she came down the steps to meet him.

She let it lie limply in his, keeping her gaze locked austerely forward. She knew that he looked sharply at her because she could feel her skin prickle with awareness, but she could not meet his eyes. If she did he would see the pain that was eating her up and know the only way to soothe it. She could very easily grow dependent on him and she couldn't allow that.

They talked fitfully as Jared drove skillfully toward their destination. He seemed to want to postpone their inevitable confrontation and Adrienne was willing to follow his lead. She was dreading the moment when she would have to tell him of her decision. It had taken all of her courage to actually face him tonight. When he parked on a side street downtown and led her into an elegant cocktail lounge, she realized he'd only been biding his time until they were settled in a spot where they could talk without interruption. She ought to have known he wouldn't put off an unpleasant discussion without a good reason.

Guiding her to a table tucked away in a corner, he ordered her a margarita, with a Scotch for himself. He waited until they were served, then shot her a probing glance and began.

"Okay. Out with it."

"What? I don't know what you mean." There was a defensive note in her voice, but she couldn't help it.

"No?" he questioned softly. "Adrienne, you avoided me yesterday and today you've been skittish and nervous. Something happened while I was away. What was it?"

This was her chance to tell him that their romance should end now, in a calm, logical way that would leave them friends. She hated the idea of never seeing Jared again. If only this were a perfect world where career and love didn't collide. But in the back of her mind she knew it wouldn't be that easy. The words she had to say stuck in her throat. All she could get out was a little whispered sound of pain.

He watched her intently. "Has New York been after you?"

"New York?" she faltered, off balance.

The gray eyes probed her face, seeking an answer. His voice gentled slightly, tempting her to confide. "Did your boss get wind of me and decide it was time to remind you that you're not here permanently?"

A direct hit, she thought wryly, even though the angle was wrong. She wondered if she should use the excuse he offered. She didn't feel much charity for Emery Thorpe these days. Since she had come to Seattle he had ridden her hard, picking everything she did to pieces, demanding perfection, refusing to give her the autonomy she needed for optimum performance. His daily phone calls were an affront to both her capabilities and her independence.

"Something like that," she mumbled at last, staring at her drink as if it were a crystal ball holding all the answers to her murky future.

"So," he said with deceptive calm, "what are you going to do about it?"

She bit her lip, feeling miserable. "I guess this is the end between us."

He made a soft, not very polite sound in his throat. "That precious company of yours has only to hint and you jump, don't you, Adrienne?" He sat back in his chair, watching her narrowly as he sipped his Scotch.

Adrienne felt a fine trembling begin in her fingertips as she waited for him to continue.

After a moment, he shook his head, saying reflectively, "I'm sorry. I seem to have made a mistake."

Adrienne stared at him. "Mistake?" she repeated vaguely.

Nodding, he explained softly, "I thought that you were ready to cut the ties that bind you so firmly to that company."

"Good heavens, whatever gave you that idea?" Genuine surprise made her forget, for the moment, the aching confusion in her heart.

He laughed sardonically, "You need to ask? You've been complaining about your boss, Thorpe, for the past couple of months."

"Emery has been a pain," she agreed cautiously.

"I assumed you'd finally come to your senses," Jared continued. Adrienne felt her hackles rise.

"Just because I've been complaining about Emery doesn't mean my views or goals have changed."

"APP is using you," he said flatly, his mouth hardening.

"Don't be absurd, Jared!" Her scorn was quite real and quite evident.

He drew in a quick, hissing breath. "Adrienne, I want us to be more than just friends. I want to make love to you, but I also want you to care for me."

I do, Jared, she wanted to cry out. *I love you, can't you tell?*

He continued inexorably, "The chemistry that's between us can't be denied, Adrienne." His voice lowered, became husky with need.

A desperate responsive yearning overcame her. "Jared, I..."

"Adrienne, you have so much to give. Such warmth, such passion. Don't channel it all into your job. It's not worth it."

"My career—" she muttered.

"Forget APP," he ordered. Leaning across the little table he began methodically to drag the pins from her tightly coiled chignon. In the dim light she could see that his eyes had darkened smokily. She didn't, couldn't move as his long fingers did their work, brushing sensuously against her skin, then tangling in her thick hair as it tumbled free of restraint.

"That's better," he said thickly. "Don't wear it in that prim little bun again. Not when you're with me."

"But I won't be with you," she denied shrilly.

His eyes narrowed, the dark lashes effectively screening them from her. She had no idea what he was thinking. She only knew that she wished this dreadful conversation was over.

"So," he said finally, after a long, tense silence. "Good old APP wins, after all. They've got you so tightly blinkered you don't even know how blind you are."

"That's not fair!"

"Nothing's fair," he said bitterly. "If life was fair you'd be trembling in my arms right now, begging me to kiss you. Don't talk to me about fair!"

"Stop it, Jared! I told you in the beginning where I stood. You've got nothing to complain about."

The fine mouth curled humorlessly. "You're right. I should have listened to you. But I sensed something deeper in you. I thought the cold, icy career woman was all an act to protect the sweet, caring woman inside."

His words cut to the quick. For the first time she realized that with Jared she revealed a part of herself that she hid from the rest of the world. An image of herself laughing uproariously after doing a nosedive into a snowbank and then pulling Jared down with her when he came to help her up, flashed into her mind. And another, when he took her to Mount Baker, one of the tallest peaks in the Cascade chain. The road weaved precariously up the side of the mountain and provided awesome views of the surrounding sea of snow-covered crags. Her delight, her excitement in the breathtaking sight had been perfectly natural, unlike her carefully gauged responses at the office. Jared was right. She did put on a disguise when she was at work.

"Looks like I was wrong," he concluded dangerously. "There isn't a deeper Adrienne Denton, there's only the cold creature who masquerades as a woman."

"Jared," she said through the agony that was tearing her apart, "you're wrong."

He shrugged. "It doesn't really matter, though, does it? You've got your precious career. That's all that matters in your life." He stood up. "Come on, I'll take you home."

She looked at him, knowing he would make no further effort to persuade her, hating the despair she had seen in his eyes before he veiled it from her with long black lashes. She wished it didn't have to end this way. "Can't we be friends?" she asked in a small voice.

"You've got to be kidding," he replied derisively, before he strode away, his back straight, unbending.

Adrienne followed slowly. It was best this way, she told herself. If he thought badly of her he would be free to forget her, and whatever pain he felt would be short-lived. How can you be hurt by someone you despise? And after tonight she was sure that was exactly what he felt for her.

At the door of the restaurant he paused, waiting for her. By now she had her emotionless mask firmly in place. "Please don't bother driving me home," she said formally. "I'll take a cab."

He shrugged, the tiny gesture expressive of his uncaring disdain. "If that's what you want."

They waited in silence until he was able to flag down a passing taxi. As Adrienne slipped in the back seat he leaned into the front to tell the driver her address, giving him a couple of bills at the same time.

"That's not necessary," she said quietly as he turned back to her.

"Goodbye, Adrienne," was his only response as he slammed the car door.

During the next week Adrienne's emotions shifted from the hurt understanding to a simmering resentment as she brooded over the details of her last meeting with Jared.

The weekend came and went. It was a lonely two days. The weather was partly sunny, meaning the overcast clouds shifted for an hour or two to let some sun reach the city. Adrienne spent a miserable time, her mood much darker than the sky above. There was no sunshine in her life. The brooding anger that had sustained her gave way to an aching sense of loss and need. During the week she had rarely even seen Jared anyway, so on the surface her normal life style was hardly ruffled by his absence. But the weekend was their time together, and she was tormented by visions of him in her apartment, on the ski slopes, in her little car—serious, aroused, laughing, teasing.

YOURS ABSOLUTELY FREE.

Did you know that Silhouette Romances are not available from the shops in the U.K?

Read on to discover how you could receive four brand new Silhouette Romances FREE and without obligation, as your introductory offer to Silhouette Reader Service.

As thousands of women who have read these books know — Silhouette Romances sweep you away into an exciting love filled world of fascination between men and women. A world filled with age old conflicts — love and money, ambition and guilt, jealousy and pride. Silhouette Romances are the latest stories written by the world's best romance writers and they are only available from Reader Service. As a regular reader you could enjoy 6 brand new titles every month delivered direct to your door, post and packing free, plus an exclusive Newsletter bringing you all the latest information on the top Silhouette authors as well as recipes, competitions, and extra bargain offers.

And by way of introduction we will send you four specially selected Silhouette Romance novels plus an exclusive Silhouette TOTE BAG FREE when you complete and return this card.

FREE TOTE BAG as your introduction to **Silhouette Romances**

Dear Jane,

Your special introductory offer of 4 Free books is too good to miss. I understand that they are mine to keep with the FREE tote bag.

Please also reserve a Silhouette Romance subscription for me. If I decide to subscribe I shall receive six new books each month for £5.70 post and packing Free. If I decide not to subscribe I shall write and tell you within 10 days. The Free books and tote bag will be mine to keep in either case.

I understand that I may cancel my subscription at any time simply by writing to you. I am over 18 years of age.

Name _____

Address _____

_____

Postcode _____ Signature _____

6S6S

Remember Postcodes speed delivery. Offer applies to UK only and is not valid to present subscribers. The publisher reserves the right to exercise discretion in granting membership. If price changes are necessary you will be notified.
Offer expires — December 31st 1986.

YOURS FREE!
Here's the stylish shopper for the real Romantic. A smart Tote Bag in white canvas emblazoned with the Silhouette motif in navy and red. Remember, it's yours to keep whether or not you become a subscriber.

Please note, readers in South Africa write to: **Independent Book Services P.T.Y. Postbag X3010, Randburg, 2125 South Africa.**
Silhouette is an imprint of Mills & Boon Ltd.

Jane Nicholls
Silhouette Reader Service
FREEPOST
PO Box 236
Croydon
Surrey
CR9 9EL

NO STAMP NEEDED

She did her best to keep these haunting thoughts from her mind by leaving the apartment early and spending the days in busy activity. The Saturday she spent downtown, haunting the elegant, underground shopping complex of Rainier Square, then browsing through the big department stores. She bought nothing because she couldn't stop wondering how Jared would like each garment she tried on, and she would feel a shaft of pain that was so sharp and bitter she wanted to weep.

She returned to the apartment for dinner. That was a mistake. Memories of meals they had shared spoiled her appetite. She ended up going out to a movie, sitting through it twice and filling up on popcorn.

At eleven o'clock the film was over and she had to return to her apartment. As she sat in the car Jared had helped her to choose, she considered booking into a motel for the night, just to avoid the glaring emptiness of the home he had helped her find. It would be, she knew, an admission of weakness and she almost gave into it. Right now she didn't feel particularly strong. But the unacknowledged hope that Jared might call and think the worst if she wasn't there to answer drove her back to the apartment.

There was no phone call that night or the next day. By Sunday evening she had to accept he was through with her, for good.

She did a lot of serious thinking over the next week, pushing aside maudlin sentiment, trying to see herself clearly. She didn't like the picture. She'd decided she loved Jared Hawkes, but what had she done? Hurt him deliberately because she knew that one day in the future she would leave him. Were the accusations he had flung at her true? Was she cold? Had the Adrienne who sat in the standard eight-by-ten office, with the regulation furniture, never a hair out of place, efficient and emotionless, completely absorbed the warm, hot-blooded Adrienne of her teen and university years?

With Jared she'd been able to recapture that younger Adrienne and it had been wonderful. He could arouse her with a touch or a kiss, but he also made her laugh without restraint. Yet he didn't treat her like a silly, brainless female. He expected her to think; he let her make her own mistakes and he was willing to follow her lead if she came up with a reasonable idea. He treated her like an equal.

The word burned in her brain for days. An equal. Not a person to be forced or dominated, but one who responds to reason. A partner. He would never pressure her into returning to him. She would have to do that herself.

By Saturday morning she knew it was what she wanted more than anything else. She told herself that the future was a long way off and today was what counted. Her practical reasoning hid a basic emotional truth—she loved Jared and couldn't bear to give him up. She had an unpleasant fear he would tell her flat out that he was no longer interested when she called, but she had to try to explain the twisted thought processes that had led up to her stupid denial of the feelings she had for him. She could only hope he would listen and understand. Even then there was no guarantee he would still want her and perhaps that would be for the best. But he did deserve an explanation and she did need to tell him.

What if she called and he hung up the phone? Or he told her exactly what he thought of her in graphic, cutting terms? Well, it would be embarrassing and it would hurt, but no more so than she hurt now. Besides, Jared was not the kind of man to do that.

Despite these brave thoughts it took most of the day to gather up the nerve to call him. It was nearly dinnertime when she sternly told herself that she must phone or forget about it. As she punched out the numbers she was shaking so badly that she pushed a wrong digit twice. Her hand was sweating against the receiver when she finally managed to dial the correct number and she had to rub it on her jeans or she would have dropped the instrument.

The phone seemed to ring forever. Adrienne sat tensely, wondering ironically if she'd waited too long to call. There was no reason to believe Jared would be in on a Saturday evening. She'd just assumed that he would be in because he wasn't interested in dating someone else. The ringing continued, five times, six times. A hysterical laugh bubbled up in her throat. After all her heart-searching and the concerted effort she'd made to gather up her courage he wasn't even home. It served her right for being conceited enough to think— "Yes?"

The curt, hard tone threw her off balance almost as much as the phone being answered at all. She hesitated, fine speeches going out the window, then said in a small voice, "Jared? This is Adrienne."

"Yes?" he said again, his voice no warmer than before. He wasn't going to make this easy for her. Did she really expect him to?

"I called because I wanted to talk to you, to explain—"

"That's not necessary, Adrienne."

To Adrienne he sounded as if he wanted to hang up the phone and never hear her voice again. Her lower lip trembled and she ran a distracted hand through her loose hair. "It may not be necessary, but I want to do it!"

There was a pause, as if he was debating whether or not to give her a hearing. His next words confirmed it. "Look, Adrienne, you made yourself very clear the other night. What was between us could have been good, but it's over, finished. Why prolong it with self-serving excuses?"

His voice was harsh, the words bitten off sharply. The hope that had lingered in her subconscious shriveled away. There was a catch in her voice as she said, "Jared, I'm sorry. I really am."

"Damn you, don't cry!" he growled.

She sniffed. "I wasn't," and wiped suspiciously damp cheeks with the heel of her hand.

Jared sighed. "Adrienne, I don't know why you called—"

"I'm trying to tell you!"

"—but it won't do any good—"

"I miss you."

This time her interruption stopped him cold. He groaned. "My God, lady! What are you trying to do to me?"

"Apologize. Explain," she whispered, sniffing again.

"Adrienne," he warned roughly, "if this is some kind of con you're pulling I swear I'll..." He broke off, leaving the threat unvoiced. Adrienne wasn't sure whether he couldn't think of anything nasty enough or if he considered an indefinite threat more effective than a definite one.

"No con, Jared," she said softly. "I just want to explain."

"Okay," he said wearily, "shoot. But remember, this better be good."

"It's not good. It's stupid," she responded sharply. "I did some thinking while you were away and it got twisted."

"How?"

"I panicked. I spent the weekend missing you desperately, and I began to realize just how important you were in my life and—"

"Wait a minute," he broke in harshly. "Are you serious, Adrienne?"

She swallowed the lump in her throat and said miserably, "Yes."

"Damn," he muttered softly to himself. "I swore I wasn't going to get involved with you again, Adrienne Denton."

"I knew you were angry," she said sadly, "but I didn't know it was that bad."

He made an indeterminate sound in his throat and said heavily, "Do you know the Japanese garden at the university arboretum?"

"Yes."

"Meet me there in half an hour."

She was on her feet, energy surging through her entire body as she promised, "I'll be there!"

It took her twenty-five minutes to reach the arboretum and it only took that long because she made a wrong turn and got lost when she was almost there. It was well after six and the large parking lot adjacent to the gardens was nearly empty in the cool spring evening. She identified the oyster-white Mercedes immediately, but Jared wasn't in the car or anywhere near it. Sliding out of her little hatchback, she brushed the wrinkles out of her slacks, then hurried toward the entrance.

There was no sign of Jared as she paid the small admission charge. She hesitated, wondering what to do. A gravel path led to a broad ornamental lake filled with goldfish, but it branched several times and Adrienne couldn't shake the terrible fear that she and Jared would pass, separated and invisible to each other, in the glades of pine, cedar and maple.

Slowly, her feet began to move, the gravel crunching in the peaceful quiet. She passed a stream, a trickle of silver gurgling softly over rocks until it reached the lake. The path forked. She kept on the main one, heading to the water.

At another fork the branch to the left led to a low, gray stone bridge that arched over a second delicate stream. Jared stood on the edge of this structure, one foot resting on the low parapet, his hands shoved in the pockets of his jeans. He was wearing the dark leather bomber jacket and the front panels were open, revealing a dark-blue T-shirt that molded his body. He was staring at the stream, his face in profile. There was a brooding quality to his expression and his hair was disheveled, as if he had recently raked impatient fingers through it.

When he turned and saw her his eyes were bleak, his expression carefully blank as he assessed her windblown hair and casual clothes. "You look like you came out in a hurry," he said flatly.

"I did," she replied steadily. "I didn't want to be late and have you think I wasn't coming."

She thought she detected a flicker of some emotion, but it was so quickly masked that she couldn't be sure. He raised one black brow and remarked with apparent casualness, "A bit late to start worrying about my opinions, isn't it?"

She swallowed. "I hope not."

A muscle in his jaw throbbed with nervous life, but he said quietly, "Two weeks ago you had a choice. Me or your career. You chose your career."

"Jared, I was wrong!" she cried.

"What made you change your mind?" he continued in that calm, detached manner. "Has your mentor, Thorpe, let up on the pressure?"

"Jared, I lied to you! There was never any ultimatum from New York. I hid behind your assumption because I was afraid!"

"Of what?" he demanded incredulously.

"Of you! Of us! Of the intensity of what I feel for you!"

"You think more of your career than you do of me." The words sounded cold but behind their flat accusation was a proud torment that cut Adrienne to her very depths.

"No!" she choked. "Jared, that's not true! With you I feel different. I'm free to be Adrienne, not Ms. Denton, career woman!" She turned abruptly away, not willing to let him see the tears that shimmered behind her eyes.

He stepped off the bridge and came over to her. She felt his hands burrow beneath the loose neck of her top to gently massage the tense muscles in her shoulders. "Did some heavy thinking the past couple of weeks, did you?"

"Yes," she muttered, staring fixedly at a bushy rhododendron, a mass of glorious mauve blooms. Wonderful sensations shot through her body. How could she have imagined that she could do without this man? She must have taken temporary leave of her senses.

The kneading stopped. He slipped one arm around her shoulders to pull her firmly against his side. "Now," he began gently, "we'll walk through the gardens and you can explain at your own speed. Okay?"

"Yes," she murmured, resting her head on his shoulder and reveling in the feel of his strength beside her. They ambled slowly over the bridge, then followed the path to the edge of the lake. Willows drooped gracefully along with birch and other Japanese trees. "I missed you when you went away, though now I suppose you'll never believe it."

He made a negative sound in his throat.

She continued with a sigh. "Thanks for that. Anyway, the weekdays weren't bad because I was at work and I didn't expect to see you, but that weekend! I felt lost and restless. Saturday dragged forever."

"Why didn't you go out and do something?" he demanded incredulously.

"I couldn't. I just wanted to sit at home and be miserable."

"Adrienne, that wasn't..."

She finished the phrase for him. "...very smart? No, it wasn't. At that point I didn't know why I felt so low, I just did. It wasn't until the telephone rang and I thought it might be you that I discovered the reason that I had moped around all day. You. I missed you so much even a beautiful sunny day lost its savor. At first I was happy. Ecstatic. I spent the rest of the weekend bouncing around in a daze of joy. Everything was better. Colors brighter, scents sharper, tastes more intense. I didn't even dread Emery's daily phone call when I drove in to work on Monday morning."

His hand tightened on her shoulder. "What happened?"

"I began to think about the future—or the lack of it."

His hold loosened abruptly. "I see."

"No, you don't." She sighed. "Jared, I had the stupid idea that the longer we knew each other, the more painful it would be if we ever had to separate. I was trying to save us both future hurt."

"What the hell!" he muttered, astonished. Halting, he twisted her around to face him. Behind them one of the goldfish jumped in the water. There was a splash, then silence. They were alone in the garden, the soft light of gathering dusk closing around them. He propped his hands on his lean hips as he surveyed her. "Adrienne, you're not making any sense."

She looked down at her rather grubby running shoes, the breeze catching at her hair and blowing it in her face. Absently she reached up to brush the strands away. "No, I'm not, am I?" She lifted her head and was once more in eye contact with him. Stretching out one hand she lightly caressed his cheek. "Jared, my career has dominated my life for years—forever! It's not just how I feel about APP, it's how I was brought up. My father never made an exception of me merely because I was a girl. He drummed the same code of loyalty into me as he did into my brothers. I have responsibilities to the company and one day I will be transferred again and I'll have to go. I can't abandon my career and APP simply because I want to follow my heart."

"Are you telling me you love me?"

She hesitated, her eyes scanning his face for clues indicating what he was thinking. There were none. The gray eyes were hooded, the planes of his face closed, his thoughts hidden. For a moment she wavered, then slowly, her face solemn, she nodded. "Yes."

Joy flared in his eyes as he reached out to grab her shoulders and shake her gently. "You crazy little fool! Have you any idea what you almost did? My God, you deserve a hiding!"

She smiled rather tremulously up at him, taking this explosion as a positive sign. "I know," she said, sighing.

He pulled her roughly against him and kissed her with all the pent-up frustration of two miserable weeks. Adrienne, beset by the same tensions, returned his passion with interest. The kiss went on until they were both weak and shaken. Jared lifted his head and lightly stroked her tousled hair.

"Does this mean," she said in a small voice, "that you don't want to consign me to the nether reaches of the universe and cast away all memories of me?"

He laughed at the plaintive note in her voice and said simply, "It does."

"Oh, good." She sighed, leaning her head against the supple leather jacket. "Because I think I've found exactly where I want to be."

"Where you'll stay," he said firmly.

"Sounds nice," she murmured huskily. "Jared, what about the future?"

"I want you with me, Adrienne, and I'm willing to take my chances with the future," he said emphatically. "But right now I'm going to take you out to dinner and after that—" he paused suggestively, a wicked grin on his lips "—who knows?"

She moved reluctantly out of his arms, a mischievous smile lighting her face. "Are you sure you want to bother going to a restaurant?"

Something flickered in his eyes and Adrienne was certain he hesitated, but when he spoke his response was light. "I refuse to do anything further on an empty stomach, especially since I haven't eaten today." He caught her quick glancing query and grinned. "You aren't the only one who's been missing someone, you know."

Her heart began to race again and a delighted warmth spread through her veins. "Sounds great. But where can we go? We're both dressed like a couple of bums!"

He laughed. "This is Seattle, my dear, not New York. We can go anywhere we please. In case you're worried about the proprieties, how about a pizza? I know a great little place that has the lightest crust imaginable and the hottest tomato sauce. Plus a selection of toppings that includes shrimp." His eyes twinkled as he looked down at her.

"Shrimp?" she said doubtfully, but her eyes gleamed.

"I can see you're hooked. Come on, I'm starved." He slipped his arm around her waist, the tips of his fingers close enough to caress a breast. Adrienne put her arm around his waist and leaned against him. Despite his last words they ambled slowly back to the parking lot, in no hurry at all.

Chapter Eight

Adrienne was chuckling as she pushed the door to her apartment open and flicked on a light. She and Jared had not hurried over dinner, enjoying a bottle of wine and a dish of antipasto before the pizza. While they ate they talked, gradually wearing away the remains of anger, until they once more felt comfortable together.

As the tension between them eased, Adrienne had felt an urge to laugh at the silliest things. It was as if her happiness and relief had to find an outlet or she would explode. Right now she couldn't even remember what it was that had set her giggling, but the warm light in Jared's eyes as he closed the door and threw the lock made the need to know immaterial.

He came over to her, his finely etched lips curling in a knowing smile, his eyes a smoky gray. Slipping his hands around her waist he pulled her gently to him.

Adrienne's arms snaked languorously around his neck and her eyelids drooped provocatively.

"Would you like some coffee?" she murmured.

"No," he replied huskily, "I want you."

"But that's not why we came up," she protested with a small pout.

Jared bent and took her lips with his, teasing away her mock dismay with little nibbling kisses that fueled the core of desire deep within her. Her body arched against his as her hands tangled in his thick black hair. Deep in her throat Adrienne whimpered. The short sound signified a change in the tempo of their lovemaking. Gone was the lazy amusement, the subdued, manageable fire between them. Against his lips Adrienne whispered Jared's name and he deepened the kiss. The flames began to burn with added warmth and sparks crackled between them, blinding them both to anything but the sensations they were creating in each other.

Jared was breathing quickly in short, hard gasps when he wrenched his lips from hers. "Adrienne," he muttered, grazing her shoulder hungrily, "if we're going to stop, it has to be now."

"No!" she gasped, her tongue sinuously lapping the lobe of his ear. Her teeth followed and she nipped lightly. "No. I love you, Jared. I want to be with you."

He shuddered, whether from her ministrations or her words she couldn't be sure. It didn't matter. She wanted to be with him tonight, and tomorrow night and the nights after that.

"You could break the self-control of a saint and that is one thing I'm not," he said shakily, as he picked her up in one fluid motion to carry her into the bedroom. Setting her on her feet beside the bed, he stepped over to the light switch. "I want to see you," he murmured thickly.

The room blossomed with soft illumination. Adrienne stripped off her shirt, then stood before him proudly, her breasts high and firm, the tips already darkened and hard. He drew in his breath sharply, moving closer to rub his fingers against her satiny skin.

Adrienne swallowed and closed her eyes, her tongue moistening dry lips. His hands stroked along her rib cage to her waist where they closed possessively around it. His tongue touched hers and chased it back behind her teeth, letting him soothe her parched lips.

Though their bodies cried out for each other, his kiss remained a light, tantalizing pressure, promising much, but giving nothing away. Adrienne pressed against him greedily, hungrily demanding more. He laughed softly and stepped away. His gray eyes burned with intent, but he wasn't ready yet to take her where she wanted to go.

Adrienne opened desire-heavy eyes, confused. He was watching her, his gaze a caress that trailed hot fire down her jaw to her shoulders, then lingered a moment on her breasts before he bent to capture the rosy tips with his mouth and hands. Adrienne was unbearably moved by the sight of his mouth on her breast, then her eyes drooped closed as sensation swamped her. Her legs buckled and she would have fallen, but he caught her deftly and laid her on the bed.

Almost out of her mind with longing, she reached up and dragged him down beside her. "I want you," she groaned, her hands frantically tugging at his shirt.

He chuckled and kissed the corner of each eye. Adrienne trembled. "But I'm not ready yet," he complained. "I want to explore every inch of you, my love, and I've only just begun."

She whimpered, "Please!"

He kissed the tip of her nose. "Soon," he soothed, shifting away to discard the T-shirt, allowing her feverish hands free access to his body.

She opened her eyes to see him smiling tenderly down at her and a sudden sweetly painful shaft of love for him tore into her. The urgency that had driven her was replaced by a warm, soft current of emotion. Jared must have felt something similar for he positioned himself beside her, not touching, but smiling at her with his lips and his eyes. They lay quietly for a moment, drinking in each other's emotions, then slowly, gently their lips met in an intense, pure kiss that owed nothing to raw desire.

"Sweetheart, you are so beautiful," he said softly.

"I love you, Jared," she replied, touching his face with her fingertips.

He groaned. "I need you. Don't leave me again, Adrienne."

"Never," she promised, her mouth curved in a tender smile.

He kissed her again and their mutual need flared. Adrienne felt his hands at her breasts while hers tugged impatiently at the fastening of his jeans.

The strident shrilling of the telephone on her bedside table brought them both out of their passionate daze. "Ignore it," he growled.

Adrienne tried, but as it continued to ring she stiffened instinctively. Jared groaned and rolled on his back. "You'd better answer it," he said stonily, putting his hands behind his head and staring furiously at the ceiling.

Adrienne shivered and picked up the receiver. "Yes?"

"Is that Miss Adrienne Denton of APP?" demanded a cold, official voice.

She sat up, running her fingers through her hair in an effort to shake herself back to normal. "Yes."

"This is Officer Logan of the Washington State Police—"

She stiffened, her eyes opening wide. "What?"

Behind her Jared abandoned his glowering perusal of the ceiling. "What's the matter?" he snapped.

"This is the state police, Miss Denton," Officer Logan was saying patiently.

"Why are you...I mean, how..." she mumbled, thoroughly confused.

"Adrienne, what is happening?" Jared demanded, sitting up and frowning blackly.

"There's been a robbery, Miss Denton," Logan said calmly. "And someone from APP may be involved."

Adrienne wilted. "A—who?"

Jared took one look at her white face and lunged for the receiver. "Is that an obscene phone call, Adrienne? Give me the telephone and I'll deal with it!" he shouted, deliberately loud to scare off the caller.

Torn between the two conversations Adrienne turned away from the mouthpiece to hiss, "Jared! It's the police!" at the same as Officer Logan said dryly, "Am I interrupting you at a bad moment?"

"What? No. Yes! I—"

"The police! What the hell is going on?"

Adrienne lifted her shoulders and raised her brows in a gesture of ignorance. Jared watched her for a moment, then rolled off the bed, fastened his jeans and strode from the room.

"I'm sorry, Miss Denton," Logan was saying, "but this is an emergency."

"I would appreciate it if you would explain the exact nature of this call, Officer Logan," she said crisply, once more in charge of herself, "so I can get back to my—er—my guest."

"Of course," he replied politely. "A car used as the getaway vehicle in a bank robbery late this afternoon was found abandoned in a suburban parking lot. The registration in the glove compartment was made out to APP, but we've had no report of a vehicle with these plates being stolen." He read out the numbers. "Can you confirm that?"

Adrienne put her palm to her forehead in a distracted way, trying to think back to Friday, but her sluggish brain wouldn't function. Jared padded quietly into the room holding two glasses filled with an amber liquid. He handed her a glass and she gratefully took a sip. Brandy. Good, she needed a stimulant. "I have no recollection of a missing car," she said cautiously, "but my records are not available to me now. They're at my office, I'm afraid."

Jared settled himself on the bed and drew her down into the comforting circle of his arm, the gentle caress of his fingers on her naked shoulder telling her without words that he didn't blame her for this interruption. She leaned her head briefly against his chest, wishing that Officer Logan would go away.

"Then I'll have to ask you to go into your office, ma'am," the obnoxious Logan said placidly.

"Now?" Adrienne cried, stiffening. Jared's arm tightened around her, but he didn't say anything.

"Yes, ma'am. We have to know who that car is issued to."

Though he didn't state it, the corollary was obvious. Once he knew who the car was issued to he wanted to bring the salesman responsible in for questioning. "Dear God," she groaned, taking a sip of the brandy as she imagined the fun the press could have with that. And what would Emery think? It wasn't her fault one of the salesmen had run amok, but that wouldn't stop Emery if he was looking for a body on which to lay blame.

"I see you understand the situation, Miss Denton," said Officer Logan with magisterial calm. "If you would call me at this number when you have the information?"

"Of course," Adrienne agreed, hastily putting down the glass and snatching up a pen and note pad.

Jared watched her as she wrote down the numbers, his eyes narrowed, assessing. When she hung up the phone and turned to him he said quietly, "What was that all about?"

She shook her head helplessly, still amazed by the information she'd just received. "I can hardly believe it, Jared. One of the sales cars has been involved in a robbery. Nothing like this has ever happened before!"

His lips twitched sardonically. He sipped his brandy and swallowed lazily. "You're probably right. APP likes to present a sterling image to the world."

Adrienne was truly shocked. "Are you implying that the company would condone wrongdoing of this sort?"

"No, of course not!" he replied impatiently, sending her a scathing look. He sipped again, then put his glass down on the bedside table. His arm tightened on her shoulder while his other hand settled on her hips to draw her inexorably closer. "Let's not fight over APP, Adrienne. Tonight is ours, alone." His lips gently caressed the tender valley between her breasts.

Her hands found his shoulders and pressed against them. Surprised, he released her. When she moved away, to crouch defensively on the edge of the bed, he sighed and sat up. "I can't just ignore that phone call," she said shakily.

"No, I suppose not." He picked up his glass again and stared moodily at its contents. "So, call Noel and get it over with."

"Noel?"

"Sure. He's the sales manager. It's his job to deal with problems like this."

She stared at Jared, her eyes wide with astonishment. "That cop, Logan, phoned me! It's my job to keep the records for all of the company cars updated. I'm responsible for this. Jared, I was so upset and worried on Friday a report of a stolen car could have come over my desk and I'd never have known it! My mind was on you, not my job! I have to go in and check those files!"

At her admission, his gaze softened. He drained the spirits and abandoned the empty glass. "Listen, sweetheart," he said gently, shifting onto his knees and catching her shoulders in the warm clasp of his hands. "You're in over your head. Noel is the senior person, the sales force is his responsibility. If anything comes of this he should be the one to take the flak."

"But he won't be!" she cried.

"What do you mean?" he demanded, his eyes narrowing as they probed her face.

Adrienne frowned, her mind racing ahead. "If the company gets into trouble because of this I'm the one who'll be blamed."

"By whom?" he challenged implacably.

"Emery." She nibbled her bottom lip. "This could do immeasurable damage to my career."

"For God's sake, Adrienne! Is that all you care about?" he bellowed, his hands clenching with sudden anger and pinching her soft skin.

"You're hurting me," she responded, puzzled by his violent reaction.

"Sorry," he said curtly, dropping his hands. He added flatly, "You insist on going into the office?"

Confused, Adrienne felt an irrational desire to cry. He had slipped away from her again, into the unemotional calm she'd faced that afternoon. Only his eyes, glittering like polished metal, gave any evidence of his feelings. She wanted desperately to call Noel as Jared had suggested, and place the whole sorry mess in his lap, but her sense of responsibility rebelled at the thought. To bail out simply because she wanted to stay with Jared and see their lovemaking to its natural conclusion would be contrary to everything she'd ever been taught. In a crisis she owed her loyalty to the company first. "Yes," she affirmed, her voice trembling.

"Right," he said, a muscle twitching in his jaw. "Get dressed and I'll drive you down."

Shaken by the cold inflection in his voice and the curt way he spoke, she said hastily, "That's sweet, Jared, but you don't have to. It's late and—"

"Exactly," he broke in firmly. "Seattle is a nice town, but no city is safe at this hour for a woman alone."

Desperation made her reach out and touch his cheek. "Jared, I didn't mean for this to happen. You understand that, don't you? But I just can't ignore my obligations, no matter what the alternative is."

The hard, cutting expression in his eyes clouded as the anger drained out of his body. "Sure," he said softly. "I understand." He moved backward and her hand trailed down his cheek until her palm rested against his lips. He kissed it slowly, lingeringly, then raised both hands to take hers and lift it away from his face. He cradled it between them for a moment, his eyes lowered, the lashes hiding their expression from Adrienne. Then he kissed her knuckles and abruptly slid off the bed.

Adrienne's heart was pounding in a fast, excited rhythm. The moment had been achingly tender, but was it a farewell or an acceptance? She watched him reach for the blue shirt and pull it over his head in one lithe motion. He looked over at where she still crouched on the bed and shot her a crooked smile. "Come on, get dressed or I might forget my good intentions and bring the law's wrath down on your head."

She laughed, reassured by the mocking smile, and scuttled off the bed to drag on the clothes she had so hastily discarded.

There was an eerie quiet about the empty office building that grated on Adrienne's nerves. She had noticed it before, of course, when she quit the office late in the evening. But somehow it didn't seem quite so ominous when she was leaving after a long day as it did now, when she was facing potential disaster. The only thing that kept her from jumping skittishly was Jared's hand holding hers in a warm, familiar clasp and the knowledge that he was here beside her, that she was not alone.

Her key grated harshly in the silence as she unlocked the door, blinking slightly in the darkened interior as she fumbled for the light switch. Moments later the suite was bathed in a cold glow from the fluorescent lighting, showing up worn spots in the carpet where the tread of feet had beaten the fibers down, the practical metal desks, their pale paint chipped here and there, the empty sterility of an office with every paper, every pen locked securely away. Adrienne hurried to her office while Jared looked around with casual interest.

She was seated at her desk, pulling the automobile file from her drawer when he wandered into her office and slouched in one of her less-than-comfortable visitors' chairs.

"The place doesn't change much," he remarked dryly.

She looked up, smiling with faint mischief. "If you'd taken the time to come into the reception area instead of dumping a gigantic teddy bear on an unsuspecting female on her first day in a new job..."

He ignored her teasing inflection, replying vaguely, "At least I made an impression."

Adrienne felt a little shiver of apprehension. There had been several times in the almost silent drive here that she'd fought off the same nagging dismay. There was nothing different about Jared that she could pinpoint precisely, just that he seemed to lack enthusiasm for this little venture. Which was perfectly reasonable, she berated herself silently. Their tender reunion had been hideously distorted by that phone call. He had every right to be grouchy over it.

Deciding to ignore the dark undercurrent in his voice she said lightly, "You sure did," sending him a suggestive look before going back to her perusal of the file.

"The last time I was actually in this room Harry Wynn was the manager. Is he still with the company?"

"Harry Wynn?" she repeated absently, her fingers busy flipping through the file. "I think so. In fact, yes he is. He's down in Atlanta now."

"No kidding. Atlanta. Well, he should be happy about that. He always used to complain that he hated the cold winters up here."

Adrienne laughed shortly. "Atlanta would certainly be great for him then. Can't say I'd want to live there. When I leave here I'll be glad to get back to head office where the real decisions are made."

"Are you sure?" he demanded softly, watching her through narrowed eyes.

She looked up in surprise, her attention caught. "Yes," she said in disgust. "I have to check every little detail with Emery before I can act. I've got an enormous budget I'm supposed to administer, but I can't touch it without his okay. If I want to change a secretary's workload I practically have to ask permission—"

"No," he said, cutting her off. "I meant, are you sure you'll be transferred back to New York?"

She stared at him, her eyes wide, the emergency that had brought them here momentarily forgotten. "Yes, of course I am!"

"What about Harry Wynn and guys like him?" he demanded, sitting up. "They weren't sent back to headquarters. They were simply assigned to another branch office."

"I know that, Jared. But I've been given a guarantee—" she began impatiently.

"Do you think they weren't?" he shot back.

"Yes," she said firmly. "Look, Jared, why are we talking about this now?"

He sent her an enigmatic look. "Let's say that coming here highlighted certain—facts."

Frowning, she said, "Why? Do you have bitter memories of when you worked for APP?"

His lips twisted wryly, "Not bitter, no. I always thought the company lacked flexibility. They're on top because of their mammoth size and excellent reputation."

"What's wrong with that?"

"Nothing."

His curt refusal to discuss the question made her say sharply, "If you feel so negatively toward APP why did you ever work for the company?"

He shrugged. "It wasn't until I was inside that I discovered that manipulation and office politics made up the better part of my colleagues' workdays."

"So you quit," she said contemptuously, thrusting aside unwelcome thoughts of the past and nebulous, but growing, fears about Emery Thorpe.

"I left APP because I refused to be somebody's stepping-stone," he replied steadily, a message in his gray eyes.

"Are you implying that I'm a stepping-stone?" she cried indignantly.

His brows rose. "Are you?"

"No!" Her emphatic disagreement was a defense against shameful memories of Ted, using her until she'd unwittingly discovered the truth. These months with Jared had almost wiped that time from her mind.

Shaken, she stared down at the file, afraid to continue the conversation, but unable to read the printing in front of her.

When words finally began to penetrate she heard herself say slowly, "It's Guy Denby's car, and there's no report of it being stolen."

"Call Noel," said Jared decisively, straightening from the lazy sprawl he had once again assumed, "then let's get out of here."

She shot him an angry look, but couldn't find any fault with his suggestion, beyond the fact that it was after eleven and rather late to phone someone. This, however, wasn't a social call. She dialed the numbers with slightly trembling fingers.

Noel answered on the third ring.

"I hope I'm not dragging you out of bed, Noel," Adrienne began politely.

"Heavens, no! Wendy and I spent a quiet evening at home and we're now watching a rerun of a vintage Bogart film. One of my favorites. But I'm sure you didn't call to hear about my social life," he added, his voice changing from chatty informality to firm authority.

"No. I was notified about an hour ago by the police about a stolen car. It belongs to—"

"Guy Denby," Noel interrupted. "Yes, I know all about it. So the police found it, did they?"

"You might say that," she agreed, hiding mounting dismay under a dry tone.

"Good. The young fool left the car running this afternoon while he went in to a variety store to buy a package of cigarettes. He won't do that again! I gave him a lecture that would curl your toes. Well, I'm glad it's back. There will still be paperwork to be done, of course, but only routine documentation."

"Noel, it's not that simple. The car was not reported stolen and it was used in a robbery."

Adrienne grimaced and held the phone away from her ear as Noel exploded. "He what?" When she replaced the receiver, he was growling, "...stupid young idiot. I told him to report the theft to the police immediately! Why didn't he? When I get hold of him I'll—" He pulled up short and said with a sigh, "But this isn't your problem, Adrienne. Thanks for bringing it to my attention. I'll deal with it now. Do you have a name and number where I can contact the police?"

"Yes."

"Good. Hold on a second while I get a pen and paper to take it down."

In the intervening seconds Adrienne kept her gaze firmly on the scrap of paper bearing Logan's number. Jared had been right all along. There had been no need for her to come in tonight. Noel had been home, he knew whose car it was and how the theft had occurred. Her feeble attempts to stave off disaster had been totally unnecessary.

Noel came back on the line. "Okay. Shoot."

She read off the information, then murmured something polite when Noel again thanked her for running interference for him. She hung up the phone slowly and looked up to find Jared already on his feet.

"Ready?"

She nodded, slapped the file closed and stuffed it in her drawer. A terrible sense of impending doom that had nothing to do with Guy Denby or the stolen vehicle clawed at her insides.

They drove home in silence. Jared parked the car and saw her up to her apartment, but before he even spoke the words Adrienne knew he wasn't coming in. There was a certain wary tension about him that she'd noticed earlier. She hoped it was just ordinary weariness, but she was afraid it presaged deeper problems.

"I think," he said gently at her door, "that we've both lost the mood. It would be best if I leave you here."

"Okay." She reached up to touch his dark hair. He didn't flinch, but he didn't look as if he enjoyed the light caress either. Adrienne's fear increased. She said softly, "If you want to stay the night so we'd both be fresh in the morning..." She let the invitation hang, searching his face for an indication, any indication, that he still harbored a trace of desire for her. Nothing. His gray eyes were dark, blank thunderclouds, the angular lines of his face a grim, expressionless mask.

"No," he said harshly. "Not tonight."

Not any night. The implication echoed in her mind. "Jared," she pleaded softly.

He bent to kiss her lightly on the lips, touching her nowhere else and making no attempt to deepen the kiss. Adrienne felt some of her anxiety retreat. The caress, she decided, was a pledge and a promise. Tonight with all its emotional turmoil was not the right moment to fulfill their relationship. Tomorrow, when they were both rested and relaxed, was a much better time.

When he moved away from her she was smiling. "Good night, Adrienne," he said huskily, emphatically, his eyes heavy-lidded with passion, the long black lashes veiling their expression.

"Night, Jared," she replied warmly, "see you tomorrow."

He turned away without responding.

Chapter Nine

A bright ray of sunlight swept across Adrienne's face, waking her from her shallow, dream-haunted sleep. She groaned and blinked open eyes that felt dry and gritty, as if she had spent the night crying. The sheets were tangled around her and her skin was glossy with a film of sweat. She didn't feel rested in the least.

Turning her head to look at her alarm clock she saw the empty glass Jared had used the night before. She closed her eyes and swallowed a lump in her throat, then forced herself to concentrate on the clock. Seventen, far too early to get up on a Sunday, especially when she had slept so restlessly. She lay quietly, willing herself to go back to sleep, but the events of the night before seemed to take over her mind, winding up her thoughts so they went round and round in circles, as aimless and as vivid as her dreams had been.

At some point she must have dozed for when she looked at the clock again the hands pointed to ten. She dragged herself out of bed and padded into the kitchen to put a pot of coffee on to brew before returning to the bathroom to try to rouse her sleep-numbed mind with a cold shower.

By the time she had washed, drunk a cup of coffee and dressed, she felt more able to tackle the day. She wondered briefly if Jared had tried to call while she was in the shower, then dismissed the worry as immaterial. If he'd missed her then he would call again. Her balcony still caught some of the morning sunlight, coaxing Adrienne outside into the warm, almost summerlike day. Carefully, she placed the phone close to the sliding doors so she could hear it if it rang, then stretched out on a lounger to drink in the warm sunshine and relax.

When she awoke the sun had shifted position and was baking someone else's balcony or backyard. It was into the afternoon now, and there was a little nip in the air with the sun gone. She shivered suddenly, feeling unaccountably let down, and quickly went inside. There she drank another cup of coffee, sliced up a tart, tangy kiwi fruit for a snack, then checked the phone to make sure it was properly connected.

With the monotonous buzz of the dial tone in her ear she was forced to the conclusion she had avoided since last night. Jared had had no intention of calling her today. The tender kiss at her door had been a goodbye, not a promise for the future.

Slowly she put the receiver back on its cradle, then sat down on the sofa. Her mind replayed the events of yesterday. What had gone wrong?

Jared knew she was in love with him. He had extracted the information from her at the Japanese gardens. Then later, before the telephone call, she had whispered the words, putting all the emotion she felt into her voice. Surely he understood that she didn't say those words lightly. Didn't he know that she ached for him, that she needed him? Didn't he appreciate how much it had cost her to call him yesterday?

Of course he did. He was a perceptive, intelligent man. He knew what made her tick, where her priorities were. And that was the problem.

She claimed she loved him, but every time APP called, she jumped. At least, that was how he saw it. It wasn't true, but how could she convince him of that? Her loyalty to APP was one part of her life—a very large part—but she was not so blind that she didn't realize there were other equally important aspects to living. There was no reason why she couldn't have both Jared and her job at APP. Men did it all the time, she thought grimly as she got up to make dinner. Juggling company loyalty and personal satisfaction and winning in both fields.

Jared, she fumed silently, hauling a chicken leg out of the fridge and slapping a thick layer of barbecue sauce over it, simply would not see that. He would not accept that her job, and her loyalty to it, had nothing to do with how she felt about him. She was a woman, for heaven's sake! She didn't love a company, she loved a man! Didn't he understand that? Why was he being so boneheaded? Usually he was such an astute judge of character....

She dumped the chicken in a baking dish, then thrust it into the oven with excessive force. Well it was up to Jared now. She had compromised once, putting her emotional stability in jeopardy, despite her certain knowledge that inevitably their romance must end. She was willing to risk all for him. He had no right to throw what they had away because he didn't agree with her principles. He was the one who had to compromise now.

She shut the oven door with a decided slam.

Their stalemate continued into the week. Adrienne had to fill out stolen car reports, arrange interim transportation for a rather sheepish Guy Denby and explain to innumerable people in head office how such a thing could have happened. She also had to placate Emery Thorpe, who, true to Adrienne's uneasy prediction, seemed to think it was all her fault.

With the week beginning in so much confusion the rest of it followed the pattern that had been set. Adrienne's regular work backed up on her and she stayed late at the office several evenings, rushing home in hopes that Jared might decide to phone that night. By Friday she was frantic with a mixture of disappointment and regret. She hadn't been able to concentrate all week and her desk looked as if a windstorm had swept over it. She was trying to tell herself that she wasn't being irrationally proud by not calling Jared when the telephone rang. It was Elaine Trent.

"Hi there, stranger!" she began cheerfully. "I thought we were going to get together for a long heart-to-heart chat."

"Hi, Elaine," said Adrienne glumly.

"Uh-oh. Something's wrong."

"Yeah, there sure is."

"Do you want to talk about it?"

"Not on the phone." Adrienne laughed shakily. "I need contact with my fellow woman to help boost my flagging spirits."

"Man trouble," Elaine observed sapiently. "Have you and Jared had a fight?"

Adrienne sighed. "You could say that."

Elaine made a disgusted sound in her throat. "I'll meet you at that coffee shop where we last saw each other right after work today."

"What about Jon and your ride home?"

"I'll tell Jon to head home on his own tonight. We'll take all the time we need and then you can drive me or I'll get a taxi. How does that sound?"

"Fine," Adrienne said dully, unable to muster any enthusiasm.

"Boy, it's a good thing my ego isn't a fragile one," Elaine observed dryly. "I'll see you later."

"Sure," Adrienne muttered, feeling like a heel.

Coming to this particular coffee shop was not a good idea, Adrienne decided later as she found a table and waited for Elaine. The warm honey-colored tiles on the floor were the same, the rough-hewn pine tables as immaculately clean, the pale lemon curtains on the window framing the identical street scene of congested rush-hour traffic. Only today Adrienne wasn't floating in a dreamworld of optimistic joy. Today she was weary and despondent.

Elaine, on the other hand, looked radiant. Pregnancy obviously agreed with her. Her face fell when she took the chair opposite Adrienne's and scrutinized her friend's expression.

"That bad," she said sympathetically.

Adrienne nodded. "I ordered you an espresso. I hope that's okay."

"Sure, no problem. You look dreadful, Adrienne."

Adrienne looked down at the pine table and shrugged. "I haven't been sleeping well."

The waitress appeared with the order. Elaine fiddled with her cup while her friend sipped blueberry tea and marshaled her thoughts.

Finally Adrienne sighed and began. "Do you remember when I told you how I felt about Jared?"

"Sure." She cocked her head and shot Adrienne a worried look. "But I don't see how that could have led to trouble. Unless..." She eyed Adrienne alertly. "Did Jared tell you he doesn't care for you? Doesn't he want to see you anymore? Is that it?"

Adrienne shook her head. "No, nothing like that." Idly, her finger traced the edge of the cup. "It was me who did the breaking up."

"Oh, Adrienne! You dolt! Why?"

"Because I was afraid, Elaine. One day I'll be transferred back to New York and I'll have to leave him." Hesitantly Adrienne explained her reasoning and the argument it had caused.

Elaine sighed. "Adrienne, when you do something, you don't believe in half measures, do you?"

A small, sad smile touched Adrienne's lips and was gone. "I've been accused of that before. After I left Jared I thought about what we could have had together and what we would never have if I refused to take a chance. It took awhile, but eventually I decided that the pain I was feeling couldn't be any worse than it would be later on."

"So you called him. Did he tell you to get lost?"

"Almost. But we did meet and talked things over and I thought everything would be great. Then there was an emergency at work."

Elaine put her elbows on the table and propped her chin in her hand in a world-weary gesture. "Let me guess. You concentrated on your crisis and forgot about Jared, right?"

"Close enough. That was a week ago. I haven't heard from him since."

"Adrienne, for a smart person, you're really dumb sometimes. Of course you haven't heard from him. He's probably furious! He's probably wondering what kind of roller coaster you are." Enunciating each word carefully, she concluded, "You can't put work ahead of people."

"Why not?" Adrienne flashed back. "Men do."

"Some men, not all of them," Elaine corrected grimly. She watched Adrienne sip her tea. "Does Jared?"

Adrienne choked. The cup hit the saucer with a clatter. "He went away for ten days," she muttered, after she had caught her breath.

"For heaven's sake," snapped Elaine, thoroughly disgusted. "I'm not talking about the odd business trip. I'm talking about every day. Does he bring his work home from the office? Is he tense all the time? Does he growl at you because something went wrong between nine and five? Does he work late every night? When you see him, is he thinking more about the papers on his desk than you?"

Adrienne swallowed guiltily. "You're talking about me, not Jared."

"Well, what are you going to do about it?"

"About what?" Adrienne demanded, feeling pressured. "About my work habits?"

"That, and Jared."

"I can't do anything about Jared." Adrienne sighed. "It's up to him to come to me. Last time I went to him. That was fair. I said the cruel words. I had to apologize. But this time it was Jared's decision. He's got to come to terms with my goals and my life-style. I can't be other than I am just to please him."

"That's just great. If I were Jared Hawkes I don't think I'd want to take you back." Adrienne froze, teacup halfway to her lips. Elaine pressed on, despite the cold glitter in her friend's eyes. "Look at yourself, Adrienne. You put your job before everything—including your own happiness. You don't have time for fun, only for work. You've told Jared in countless ways that he comes second in your life."

Her chin thrust up rebelliously, Adrienne said frostily, "My job is part of me. It makes me what I am."

"Yes! That's exactly what I mean!"

Adrienne reflected ruefully that she should have seen that comment coming. Elaine was not sparing her today. She felt like a boxer going down for the count.

"Put yourself in Jared's position. Think of how you would feel if he was the one who never had enough time, who put you second, who thought more of his job than you. Wouldn't you be upset? Wouldn't you be hurt?" Elaine demanded, leaning forward to jab her finger emphatically in the air.

Adrienne's eyes clouded as she thought of the past months. Elaine nodded in a satisfied way and sat back in her chair, enjoying the pungent flavor of the espresso. Adrienne pushed her saucer around on the smooth pine surface of the table. "Jared's jealous of my job," she muttered.

"I think it's very likely," Elaine agreed judiciously.

"So what do I do? I can't quit. Not even for him."

Elaine eyed her thoughtfully. "It may be hard, Adrienne, but you're going to have to make some changes in your priorities if you want Jared in your life."

Adrienne lifted her cup and drank to give herself time to formulate a reply. Talking to Elaine hadn't been such a good idea. She felt worse than she had before. "I don't know what to do," she mumbled finally.

Elaine wouldn't let her get away with that. "If Jared calls," she said inexorably, "you've got to be ready. You can't continue to be a working machine and have him back."

Elaine's down-to-earth and upsetting advice followed Adrienne all through the next day. She thought of nothing else. She reviewed every step of her relationship with Jared and finally acknowledged that Elaine was right. As long as APP dominated her life she couldn't expect Jared to stay with her. Yet she couldn't give up the job she loved or the career she had worked so hard for. There had to be room for compromise somewhere.

On Monday she returned to her desk not much rested and still troubled. She worked steadily through the morning, assessing the extent of her duties, analyzing how much was priority work and what could be done when she had the time. As usual she ignored her lunch hour, only reminded of it when her secretary popped her head in to say she was going for her own break.

The telephone rang and she answered it absently.

"This is Jared," his deep voice said curtly, after she had spoken her name.

Her heart gave a leap, then steadied, pounding heavily. A wave of almost delirious happiness caught her, infusing her voice with a gay lilt. "Hi! How have you been?" That wasn't really the question she wanted to ask—where have you been was more like it—but it would do.

"I want to see you tonight," he said roughly.

Some of her enthusiasm evaporated at his tone. "Okay," she agreed hesitantly. "When?"

"Four-thirty. I'll pick you up at your office."

She swallowed, knowing what he was doing. He was forcing her to choose between him and her job. He knew she usually worked late and that she was usually tired in the evenings because of it. She stared bleakly out the plate-glass window at the thin, misty clouds. He was asking her to compromise, to make a concession or lose him. Taking the first faltering step, she said quietly, "All right. I'll be ready at four-thirty. If you're early ask Melissa, the receptionist, to buzz me."

"I'll see you then," he replied and hung up. Was it her imagination or had there been a lightening of the grim tones in his voice? Imagination, she told herself warily. She was looking for any crumb of hope she could find.

He arrived at four twenty-five. Adrienne had been on tenterhooks all afternoon, knowing he was testing her and afraid he might go one step too far. She was willing to make concessions, but she would not give up in abject defeat. He had to know that.

Five minutes early was no problem for Adrienne. She had had her desk cleared for fifteen, and had been fidgeting nervously while she waited for him to arrive. She threw a quick look around to be sure everything was put away, then locked her desk. Straightening her pale tan skirt, she shrugged on the matching jacket and picked up her purse, holding it tightly under her arm as she left her office and said good-night to Carol. Her secretary's eyes widened in surprise, but she didn't comment, merely wishing Adrienne a pleasant evening.

As she crossed the open space between her office and the exit, she saw Jared standing with easy elegance at the edge of the reception area, where he could see the movements of the staff and where they could see him. He was talking to Noel Granger, smiling at something the other man said. His eyes focused on Adrienne as she walked quickly across the room.

He looked, she thought with a hint of irritation, extremely handsome. His black hair was combed close to his head, except for that often unruly lock that fell over his forehead, tanned from several weekends of skiing in the sun. As she drew closer his gaze slid away from her face to run down her body, lingering on her lips, her breasts, the curve of her hips, the long graceful line of her legs. The look was sensual, provocative, possessive, all at once.

Noel turned around to see what he was staring at, shot a quick glance at Jared, then a knowing one at Adrienne, whose normal composure was in tatters now. It came to her suddenly that Jared was branding her with that look. Here, in her own office, he was very clearly telling anyone who was interested that she belonged to him. And by tomorrow, she thought bitterly, it would be all the way back to New York that she had a boyfriend in Seattle. The thought of the lewd remarks and the knowing chuckles caused her to tighten her lips and her eyes to darken.

"Hello, Jared," she said grimly. "Right on time, I see."

There was a spark of mischief in those gray eyes that made her wary. "As always," he replied softly.

Noel, who had been listening with unabashed interest, exclaimed, "I didn't know you two were seeing each other! Isn't that great? Tell me, was it my party that brought you together?"

Adrienne looked away from the intrigued speculation in his eyes, only to encounter an even more avid expression on the face of the receptionist. Melissa was so interested in this turn of events that she forgot her usual busy preparations for departure. Adrienne glared at her. Melissa hastily locked her desk and picked up her purse.

"In a manner of speaking," Jared was saying to Noel. "I heard Adrienne was looking for an apartment and happened to know of one that was available. I took her over to see it since she didn't have a car at the time and..." He shrugged, letting Noel put the connotations he wanted on the rest of the sentence.

Noel beamed. "Well, that's great!" He turned to Adrienne, "You won't find a finer man in Seattle. You'd better keep a good hold on him." Adrienne blushed. Noel laughed.

"If you're ready—" Jared paused, that mischievous glint in his eyes again "—sweetheart, let's go."

Still somewhat incensed, Adrienne looked up into his eyes, planning to give him a sharp answer, but the laughter she saw there made her heart melt and she merely nodded. Jared slipped an arm around her waist. She stiffened. His grip tightened, keeping her by his side as he led her out of the office.

"We must get together for dinner," Noel called to their departing backs. "I'll talk to Wendy and set up a time. She'll be delighted."

The elevator was crowded and not the place for private talk. Jared kept Adrienne as close as possible, but she was able to slip away from his hold. She saw his eyes glint with amusement and resented his calm manipulation of her.

Outside the air was cool. The earlier overcast had given way to partial sun, but they still needed their jackets. On the sidewalk Jared made no further effort to capture her, suggesting they walk in the pleasant weather and talk as they did so.

The sidewalks were congested with workers from the office towers all hurrying to reach some destination a moment or two sooner than the next person. It really wasn't a time to walk and talk over differences. Somewhat impatiently, Jared took her elbow and guided her forcefully to nearby Freeway Park.

The park was an innovative bicentennial project for the citizens of Seattle. A section of the massive interstate freeway that virtually cut the city in half was covered over, pipes were laid, earth was deposited, trees and grass were planted. Concrete was poured into rough wooden forms that gave the stone mixture the look of sawed wood when it dried, to make benches, stairways and retaining walls. Waterfalls were constructed to mask the noise of the highway beneath and give the illusion of pastoral tranquillity in the depths of the city. In front of one of the small waterfalls Jared stopped, sitting on a concrete bench and pulling Adrienne down beside him.

The enforced waiting period had cooled some of Adrienne's wrath over Jared's actions in the office, but she still keenly felt the way his eyes had stripped and branded her in front of all her staff, and it rankled. Before he had a chance to speak she said flatly, "That little drama in the office might have amused you, but it didn't strike me as funny."

There was still a flash of mischief in the dark eyes. "I thought you were angry," he murmured unrepentantly.

"You thought! Jared, do you have any idea how long it's taken me to teach those people to respect my authority even though I'm not a man? Half the staff was in love with my predecessor and saw my arrival as a personal insult to him! I didn't choose to be sent here. I didn't fire the blasted man, though after fixing up his mistakes for four months I know he deserved what he got. For weeks that receptionist made my life miserable, botching messages, giving them to me too late to return, telling people I was out when I was sitting in my office."

"If you are referring to that rather vacant-looking blonde, I suspect it's because she's afraid of you." He leaned on one arm, facing her, his eyes watchful.

"Afraid! Of me? For God's sake, Jared, get serious! No one's afraid of me!"

His eyes lit with amusement at her emphatic tone but he shook his head somberly. "Oh, no, Adrienne, don't underestimate yourself. You are one very formidable lady. It takes a bit of perception and a lot of hard work to see beneath that wall of cool control you build around yourself. And I doubt if your receptionist even knows the meaning of the words."

Adrienne had to admit that mental ability was not Melissa's strong point. She sighed, then added, "I wanted to fire her but Emery refused to okay it. He said she did the job well enough and she was decorative. He also said he didn't want my record marred with a firing within the first six months of my tenure." She stared gloomily at the waterfall, remembering that conversation, one of many angry confrontations she'd had with Emery Thorpe since her arrival in Seattle.

"I saw you glaring at the girl. What was that all about?"

Jared's quiet tones brought her back to the reason for her present annoyance with a snap. "She was gaping at us." Misery engulfed her. "My God, by this time tomorrow the whole company will know about you!"

"So?"

His curt question brought her up short. "You have to ask?" she flared. "You know how the company works. Gossip spreads like a forest fire. First there will be leers and knowing looks, then snide comments."

He broke into her impassioned speech. "Adrienne, you're making more of this than it deserves. So you've met a man in Seattle. What's so strange about that?"

She stared at him a moment, her eyes searching the hard lines of his face. "Nothing," she mumbled. She knew that her need to keep her private life a secret from the people she worked with was excessive, but the months of gossip she had endured after Ted's defection had made her wary and very, very cautious.

"No," he continued. "And if there is gossip and some of it is malicious, well, does it matter what someone in New York thinks when you're here in Seattle?"

"No." Jared was forcing her to face the fears that long years of suppressed memories had generated, though he didn't know it. Slowly Adrienne came to realize that he was right. What the people in head office assumed about her relationship with Jared didn't matter. The damaging innuendos when she broke off with Ted were not about their love affair, but about her ability to function in the corporate world. But speculation here in Seattle was altogether different. She said flatly, "I have to care about my reputation with the staff here. Jared, you were very blatant back there."

"It was after hours, Adrienne. The company pays you for forty hours a week, nothing more, and you had already put in more than an eight-hour day, hadn't you?"

She frowned. "Yes, but how did you know that?"

"You told me weeks ago that you always got in early because Thorpe phoned precisely at eight and hated excuses. Today I called during the lunch hour just to see if you'd be in. You were."

"I might have taken an early lunch or just been leaving," she flashed in self-defense.

"Did you?"

"No," she muttered. She took a deep breath and said, "All right. I work a lot of overtime, but that's because the job demands it. When I arrived here everything was a mess. It's been getting better, slowly. In a few months—"

"I can't wait a few months."

His words, uttered in a calm, unemotional tone, stabbed at her. In her heart she had known that eventually this must be discussed. It was the pivot around which their problems revolved. Jared wasn't prepared to sit back and be second in her life. Adrienne wasn't sure she was ready to put her job aside to focus her life on a man, even if that man was the one she loved.

These thoughts flickered across her face under his watchful gaze. His mouth hardened, turning down grimly at the corners. He said softly, "Adrienne, these past months, seeing you only on weekends, perhaps the odd weeknight, have been difficult. I stood it because, well, let's face it—seeing you more often and not taking you to bed would have been more than my system could cope with." He stopped, his hand shifting to hold her chin firmly so she couldn't look away. "If we become lovers I'll demand more of you than that. I want you to be with me most evenings, even if it's only to have you fall asleep on my shoulder. I want to know that you're not burning yourself out with this crazy schedule you keep."

Beneath his steady gaze she felt her eyes flicker and let her lids droop to hide the longing that must be clearly exposed there. He made it all seem so easy. And the picture he painted of a close, loving relationship sounded wonderful.

The calm voice continued dispassionately, almost as if presenting a case to a hostile board meeting, "What do you get for knocking yourself out, streamlining procedures, fixing your predecessor's errors? A pat on the back? A raise perhaps?"

"Neither. You know that. The company doesn't reward what it sees as normal completion of duty."

He drew in his breath sharply. "Lady, the hours you put in and the dedication you show are not normal, and don't try to pretend to me they are. Remember, I worked for the same company for several years. Half the management people are timekeepers and most of the other half, who make the place run, put in their time and talent for purely cynical reasons. There aren't many like you who add an absurd sense of personal loyalty to the combination."

She flushed and jerked her chin away from the light pressure of his hand. "I know I put in a lot of extra time but I do it for my own selfish reasons."

He raised black brows sardonically, disbelievingly. "Do you indeed?"

"Yes," she snapped. "For the satisfaction of knowing I've done my job well, to the best of my ability. Don't you find pleasure in your job?"

He looked as though he was battling a strong desire to shake her. "Yes," he ground out finally, "but I own the damned company. I can see my efforts turned into positive results. I know when I've succeeded—"

"And you think I don't?" she snapped back.

Having fought themselves to a standstill they stared at one another—two strong, intelligent people anxious to find a point of compromise and stumbling unsuccessfully around it because they were evenly matched. Adrienne knew from the implacable stamp of Jared's mouth, the tense set of his shoulders, that he would carry out the threat that had brought them to this impasse. A lock of black hair fell untidily on his forehead and she felt an almost physical ache urging her to reach out and smooth it back. After a moment she did. A little of the tension eased from his shoulders though his expression remained unyielding.

She looked down at her skirt and said hesitantly, "You know, in New York I never worked these hours. I don't know why I went overboard. Vanity I guess. I wanted to prove I was the best manager Seattle ever had."

"You did it," he responded softly, his eyes watching her intently. "Noel was saying some very complimentary things about you this afternoon."

"He hardly had time!" she protested.

Jared smiled. "He started off by telling me that you had the office ticking like an expensive Swiss watch and went uphill from there."

Adrienne beamed, childishly pleased at this praise. Noel was a man she liked and respected. His words carried weight. Moreover, he was the man who was most directly affected by her work. If he was pleased, then she was indeed doing a good job. Jared sat motionless beside her, his expression filled with tender understanding. It gave her the courage to ask, "Jared, why did you wait until today to see me again?" His gray eyes darkened, with pain she thought wonderingly.

"I didn't plan to call at all. But I thought..." He hesitated, picking his words carefully. "I wanted to try again."

Since she too had faced the dilemma she could understand what he had felt. She said softly, "Jared, are you jealous of my job?"

He sucked in his breath in an audible gasp then slowly released it. "Not of your job, Adrienne, but of the hours you keep, the devotion you lavish on it."

He straightened and turned to stare bleakly at the tumbling water. Adrienne noted inconsequently that the patch of sunshine had disappeared. It didn't matter, she had enough light inside her for both of them. An hour ago he had stood in APP's Seattle office and branded her as his own. Just as he would a male rival, he was putting APP on warning. This one is mine. Hands off. And he hadn't been warning her, he'd been telling her. You're mine, Adrienne.

She lifted one hand to the back of her head and tugged at the pins that kept her hair fastened in its neat bun. "You know," she said deliberately, "all of the extra time I put in should start to pay off. I think I can afford to wind down a bit." Jared looked over at her as her hair tumbled free. "Mind you, I'll still have to do some overtime, but only when it's strictly necessary and that shouldn't be too often." Her lips curled in an enticing smile and she ran her fingers through the thick mane.

His eyes lit with a strange fire, a combination of victory, joy and passion. "No, let me do that," he commanded gruffly. One hand tangled in her hair while the other crept around her ribs to draw her close for a kiss. They clung together for sweet precious moments, oblivious to passersby. When he released her lips Adrienne leaned against him, her head resting on his shoulder.

"Welcome home, my darling," he whispered in her ear. Adrienne reached with one hand to touch his cheek in silent, wordless communication.

A bit later she straightened and said pleadingly, "Jared, next time we have a problem let's talk about it instead of going off on our own and brooding. We'll never survive if we don't."

His face was inscrutable for a moment, then he grinned ruefully. "I'll try. I've never made a habit of complaining."

"I'm not talking about complaints and you know it, but since you brought it up, I've got one." She shot him a provocative glance from under her lashes.

He looked wary. "Already?"

She grinned. "Yes. I'm hungry."

"Is that all?" he said with mock relief. "Okay, where do you fancy tonight?"

Briefly, she considered making a teasing reference to her own cooking to see if he would guess her meaning but she quickly rejected it. "Home," she said flatly, a faint blush painting her cheeks as his eyes widened.

"Are you suggesting..." he hinted delicately.

"Yes." The sun made a short appearance from behind the clouds and touched her hair with gleaming highlights.

He said harshly, "Did you bring your car?"

"Not today," she answered steadily.

"That makes it easier." He stood up and grabbed her hand. "Suddenly I'm starved."

Chapter Ten

They didn't bother with dinner. Adrienne hadn't really expected they would. After the poignant disappointment of the past Saturday night neither of them wanted to take any chances with interruptions. When they reached the apartment, Jared closed and locked the door behind them with a purposeful air. His dark-gray eyes observed Adrienne with the same passionate promise she'd seen earlier that day in her office. Once again she walked toward him, slowly this time, enjoying the way his gaze scorched her, heating her blood through the layers of clothing. Just within touching distance she stopped, a small taunting smile on her lips as she forced him to reach for her to bring her against him.

His hands touched her shoulders, the thumbs running erotically over the charged skin of her neck, sending shivers down her spine. The gentle stroking stopped as he moved fractionally to push the suit jacket from her shoulders. She twisted away letting it fall to the floor. Now Adrienne could feel the heat of his skin through the soft silky fabric of her blouse. Her heart began to pound as his hands shifted to the points of her shoulders and his grasp firmed to bring her close to him.

He leaned down, his teeth grazing gently over the sensitive skin of her throat. A great shudder of feeling caught her and she closed her eyes, moistening dry lips with the tip of her tongue. Suddenly she was aware that there was an impediment between her breasts and the solid strength of his chest and her hands frantically tugged at the lapels of his jacket.

She could feel his breath fanning gently on her heated skin as he blazed a path with his lips and teeth from her throat to her ear. There he stopped, nibbling the lobe with increasing intensity until she groaned. Then he whispered, "I'm not letting you out of this apartment tonight."

"No, Jared," she managed to respond, though her mouth was parched and her lips seemed unable to shape words properly.

"I'm going to take you to your bedroom and make love to you all night. Would you like that?" he growled, thoroughly kissing the tender spot below her ear.

"Yes, Jared," she moaned, knowing that he held her emotions captive and only he could release them. When he chose to do so he would. Meanwhile this delightful teasing was stirring her blood and making her throb with wicked desire.

"Compliant, aren't you?" he murmured on a laugh.

Her reply was translated into a satisfied purr as his hands slid down to her hips and his mouth found hers in a kiss that finally allowed her to express some of the pent-up feelings his light, nibbling caresses had generated.

They parted only briefly to travel the short distance to the bedroom, hand in hand, both afraid that to move any closer would break their fragile control. In the bedroom Adrienne was beset by an unaccountable shyness that she realized impatiently was silly, but at the same time impossible to ignore. She turned away as she hastily began to disrobe.

She had her shoes off and was fumbling with the back zipper of her skirt when Jared put his hands on her shoulders and turned her. "Don't do that," he said quietly, his smoky eyes caressing her. "I want to look at you."

He had taken off his jacket and thrown it casually over the back of a chair and his tie was loosened, the top button of his shirt undone. It gave him a faintly reckless air, less the polished businessman, more than Jared she saw on the long days of the weekend. It also made her appreciate that beneath the desire and need that drove him he was tired, almost as if he had taken off a mask to let her see the real man underneath. She felt a rush of love so great that it crushed her bout of shyness as if it had never been.

She moved into the circle of his arms, pressing herself against him. "Let me help you," she murmured huskily, smiling up at him as her fingers toyed with the knot of the tie. Once it was free she slid it slowly from around his neck and dropped it on the floor beside them.

"Hey," he protested, a glint of amusement in his eyes, "that's my favorite tie."

"I'll buy you another," she whispered, busy with the buttons of his shirt. With the last unfastened she rubbed her palms against the light sprinkling of hair that covered his chest to push the two panels apart, then she kissed the fine-textured skin beneath her hands.

He groaned. "No. Adrienne, for God's sake, if you want me to be gentle..."

She made a hoarse little growl of amusement in her throat and continued her steady assault on his skin, her mouth seeking revenge for the delay he'd put her through earlier. Her lips found and closed over a male nipple and her tongue tenderly lapped at it. He groaned again, but she paid no attention until one hand curled into her hair gently tugging her away from his chest.

Adrienne lifted her blue eyes to his face and for a moment was afraid that she had overstepped some private, unvoiced boundary. His eyes blazed, the skin was stretched tightly over the stark angular planes of his face and his mouth was clamped shut in a hard line. Then his head swooped down and his mouth plundered hers with fiery demand. She realized that what she had seen was a man clinging to the last vestiges of control. Her own unchecked response to the hard demand of his lips broke those few remaining filaments.

Their clothes were discarded with careless haste. Sinking to the bed, they touched and caressed each other until they were both trembling with the force of their need.

With a little purr of pleasure Adrienne whispered, "Take me, Jared. Love me. Now. Please."

He needed no further urging. His lips closed over hers as he made her his, driving her slowly, compellingly up an ever-higher path they could only climb together. Adrienne lost herself in him with a wondering surrender that intensified her love as they reached the peak together.

They lay quietly afterwards, exhausted by the storm of their lovemaking and for a while only the sound of their heavy breathing filled the room. Then Jared kissed her tenderly and moved off her. "I didn't hurt you, did I?" he asked tightly, curling a lock of hair around one finger.

She laughed, a supremely satisfied sound that made him smile in response. "If you did, I didn't notice." She added wickedly, "Now tomorrow I may find I'm a little stiff...."

He drew a harsh breath. "Adrienne, I'm sorry...."

"Idiot," she said softly, putting her fingers over his mouth to quiet him. "I was only teasing. I was as crazy with desire as you were, couldn't you tell?"

He grinned. "I did get the idea." His eyes closed and he relaxed, his hand leaving her hair to stroke lazily over her silky skin.

She sat up and moved away.

His eyes flew open. "Where are you going?"

A wave of love washed over her as she looked down at him, his features softened with the aftermath of passion, his gray eyes tender. She gave in to the urge to touch him as she combed the errant lock of black hair from his forehead. "I'll be back," she whispered softly.

He caught her hand and kissed the palm. "Don't make me come looking for you," he ordered huskily.

She grinned, her eyes lighting with sudden amusement. "I won't."

Her destination was the kitchen where she hastily pulled a bowl of fresh-cooked shrimp out of the fridge as well as a bottle of white wine, which had been chilling for days for just such an occasion as this. She quickly loaded a tray and carried it into the bedroom. Jared was lying on his back, his hands behind his head, looking indolent and supremely at ease.

His eyes opened wide with surprise as she entered the room. "What's this?" he demanded, sitting up.

"Dinner," she replied happily, handing him a corkscrew. "Shrimp cocktail." She dipped a shrimp into the sauce she had hastily dumped into a bowl and popped it into his mouth as he expertly dealt with the wine bottle.

"Very nice," he mumbled, "but shrimp cocktail is just an appetizer."

Adrienne reached over to outline his lips with one slim finger. "Can't you guess what the main course is?" she said throatily.

"I don't think I want to wait," he said his lips curving into a slow smile as he reached for her.

The weeks that followed settled into a satisfying routine for Adrienne and Jared. They spent the weekday evenings in each other's company, often making love, other times, when they were both tired, sitting quietly and talking, just happy to be together. On weekends they spent the two days together, loving with glorious abandon during the night while engaged in some equally strenuous activity during the day.

The career that had once dominated Adrienne began to play less of a role in her life. She still worked late, but with less frequency, and she found that she resented those evenings when the extra time couldn't be avoided. Her more relaxed attitude toward her work, mixed with some suggestions on handling people from Jared, eased much of the tension in her organization, and she was able to begin a program delegating authority to the staff, thus leaving her free for other projects.

On the weekends she put her job completely from her mind. The change of seasons did nothing to check Jared's passion for the outdoors, and she discovered that she too was growing fond of vigorous physical activity. He took her hiking, and from there it was an easy step to weekend camping in the lonely depths of the West Coast rain forest. Adrienne wasn't sure she liked the idea of sleeping in the woods, but she loved Jared and since it pleased him she was willing to try. Another activity she found more to her taste were the days spent at one of the beaches along Puget Sound. Not that she swam in the frigid depths of the North Pacific as Jared liked to, but she could lie on the sand soaking up the sun and watching his lithe, supple movements as he worked off some of his abundant energy in the icy waters.

It was there that she told him, one sunny July afternoon, that she had to return to New York for the department's annual meetings. The sun was hot on her head, firing her hair with burnished lights, its warmth trying to coax the tension from her muscles. She dreaded telling Jared that she had to go away. She was afraid he would be furious.

She watched him beneath her lashes, lying on her side, her head propped up by one bent arm, as he strode up the gray-gold sand. The mere sight of him made the love she felt warm her blood. Sometimes it amazed her to think that this attractive, virile man was hers.

"Jared," she began when he sat down beside her on the blanket and roughly began to towel himself dry.

"Hmmm?" he replied indistinctly from beneath the towel, rubbing the water from his hair.

"I have to go to New York," she said quietly, watching him with worried eyes.

"When?" he asked, emerging from beneath the towel and using it to blot the water from dripping arms and legs.

"Next week. Sunday night really. I have to be at head office at eight o'clock Monday morning."

"How long?"

"A week. I'd fly back Friday, but I should spend some time with my folks." She stared at him, searching for a reaction.

He threw the towel aside and stretched out beside her on the blanket. "Have I ever told you," he asked, smiling, "what great things that bathing suit does for your body?" His lips nibbled gently on hers. "If this weren't a public spot I'd be tempted to make love to you here and now."

Forgetting her problem for a moment, she chuckled and said, "You could, you know. I wouldn't put up a fight."

"I know," he replied softly, deepening the kiss before he drew away. "Tell me the time of your flight and I'll meet you when you get back."

His matter-of-fact response to her news puzzled Adrienne. During the week that followed he made love to her with a reassuringly passionate intensity, but he never complained because her job was taking her away. She wondered if he had conquered the fierce jealousy that had once driven him. She hoped he had. Over the past months she had tried to show him how important he was to her. This was the first time, since the incident of the stolen car, that she was allowing her career demands to take precedence over her private life. Jared's calm response was all that she could ask for, but part of her was troubled by the ease with which he had accepted the news.

Adrienne's arrival in New York was uneventful. However, returning to the office building where she'd worked for six years brought back a lot of memories—all of them curiously stale.

She took a taxi from her parents' house, where she was staying, to the Manhattan office. As she paid the driver she realized with some amusement that she couldn't remember the features of many of the people she had once worked with. She found it easy to identify the utilitarian steel-and-glass exterior of the tower that housed the headquarters of APP on its top dozen floors; in fact she had picked it out as the cab was cruising down the street. It was her former co-workers who were a vague blur, from Emery, who had been her boss for five of her six years here, right through to Boyd Sykes, whom she had been dating when she left for Seattle. It seemed a curious irony.

When she reached the fiftieth floor she hurried to the washroom to check her hair and makeup before she went to Emery's office where the managers were to assemble. She surveyed herself rather grimly in the bank of mirrors.

Today she wanted to reinforce the image that she'd left behind six months ago—that of a cool, collected, hard-nosed career woman with no time for feminine weaknesses. She had worn a cream-colored linen suit tailored on severe lines with a bronze-toned high-necked blouse beneath. The blouse had no ornamentation, no frills, no bow, not even a front closure to draw male eyes. She had no idea if her staff in Seattle had gossiped about Jared to their counterparts here, but she wasn't prepared to risk any lewd comments based on her appearance from envious coworkers. Besides, this was her first meeting at this level, and she wanted to make a good impression.

After a quick glance to make sure that her hair was in place, her makeup understated and unsmudged, she was ready. She took a deep breath to quiet the butterflies in her stomach, slowly let it out, then arranged her features into an expression of serene confidence and left the washroom.

When she reached Emery's office she discovered that he wasn't in yet, nor were any of the other managers. She hovered restlessly by the door of his office thinking about the week to come, the unexpected wait playing on her nerves.

As soon as she saw him striding short-legged across the broad, open space her memory clicked into place. An average-size man with an average middle-age paunch he did nothing about and, she thought rather cynically, of average talents and abilities. A man of vanity though, she decided shrewdly, for he was nearly bald now, but he still combed what few hairs remained to hid his naked scalp. It was amazing the insights that came to a person when she had been away for a period of time.

She followed him into his office, much like hers, except the floor space was slightly larger and the furniture a little more pretentious. She sat down on one of the green leatherette chairs without being asked and crossed her long, slender legs. Emery, she noted, eyed them with a somewhat lascivious gleam in his small eyes. She wondered why she had never noticed that little habit before.

When he realized she was watching him he puffed up his chest and said, "Have a good flight?"

"Excellent," she replied politely, once more in control.

"Good," said Emery, not caring. "All prepared for the meetings?" He went on to explain the agenda to her. The first two days were refreshers with each of the departments logistics liaised with. The next two days were for reports from each of the branch managers on their operations, and the final day, Friday, was a recap and overview of the whole department, with the afternoon held free for traveling.

Adrienne replied that her report on the Seattle office was ready and that she had prepared a number of questions and topics she wanted to discuss with the other departments, which would help to alleviate bottlenecks and streamline procedures.

Emery's eyes glittered at this. "You should have cleared them through me first."

"I thought that was what these meetings were for? A sort of forum for new ideas," she remarked calmly.

"Oh, they are!" Emery's bald head bobbed and the light shone on the pink skin. "But this is your first general meeting, Adrienne, and—" he paused, blinking furiously "—as you're the first woman to reach this management level in our department I want to be sure you acquit yourself well."

Adrienne looked at him thoughtfully and said cautiously, "That is very kind of you, Emery..."

"It's not kind at all!" he interjected harshly. "I stuck my neck out to get you this promotion, Adrienne. If you make a fool of yourself you make a fool of me!" His voice softened. "Now, we have a few minutes. Why don't we go over those ideas of yours?"

Adrienne wasn't averse to discussing her suggestions with Emery. Some of them she had been developing over the past months, carving and polishing them for this moment. Others were fresh and without doubt needed work. Either way, Emery, as head of the department, had a perfect right to hear them before anyone else.

He listened to her keenly, told her to forget one or two of the more outrageous ones as being too controversial and then said the rest were sound and deserved a hearing. He suggested rather hesitantly that she allow him to present some of the better ones, laughing a little when he added that the other departments would give them a less biased hearing if the ideas came from someone higher in the hierarchy than Adrienne.

There was nothing she could do but acquiesce though it annoyed her. The ideas were hers and she knew that she would make a far better presentation of them than Emery ever could. There was no time to argue about it though. The other branch managers had started to arrive and Emery made full use of this to avoid further discussion.

At the end of the full day of meetings the branch managers and Emery went out to dinner. As the evening progressed liquor, wine and brandy flowed. Adrienne found herself becoming more and more disgusted. The managers were all booked into the same hotel, along with Emery, and they clearly intended to use the time away from their families to live a little. Adrienne was glad that she'd remained firm against the pressure Thorpe had placed on her not to stay at her parents' home. She didn't feel part of this sort of activity and didn't want to. When Craig Wilton, the manager of the Denver branch, made a pass at her, she decided she had remained long enough. For the rest of the week she was determined to retire from the dinner meetings early.

She wasn't a prude, she told herself, but she did draw the line at that type of conduct. Her principles at work again, she thought with amusement. A sudden image of Jared made her breath catch in her throat and she had to fight back a wave of longing.

On Tuesday she met Boyd Sykes in the hall between meetings. Boyd looked much the same as he had before she left for Seattle. Regular, good-looking features, a shade below six feet, shoulders perhaps too narrow, a rather long body. He was wearing a well-cut gray suit in a lightweight summer weave, almost a company uniform, and his dark-brown hair was brushed cleanly back from his forehead. A perfect example of the budding corporate executive.

He greeted her as had most of the other people she had once worked with offering a pleased smile and a handshake. Nothing effusive. "Adrienne, it's good to see you! You look well. Western weather must agree with you."

After several months of Jared's warmth and intensity, this bland greeting from a man she had dated for nearly a year seemed incongruous. She knew that however she and Jared parted, whether as friends or enemies, he would never greet her as if she had been a casual acquaintance. "Thanks. Yes. I'm really enjoying Seattle," she said dryly. A mischievous light danced in her eyes. "There's a fantastic range of outdoor sports possible out there; everyone's a health nut. I even learned how to ski this winter!"

Boyd smiled faintly and said, "Ski? You?"

She laughed. "I'm not very good yet, mind you! They get an amazing amount of snow on the mountains in the area, you know."

"No, I didn't," he replied, sounding faintly bored.

His response was so typical of him, Adrienne almost giggled. Over the past months they had talked often on business matters, and gradually the personal parts of the conversations had diminished. They had never been emotionally close enough to sustain a long-distance relationship. Meeting Jared and coming to love him as she had showed Adrienne that she and Boyd could never have progressed beyond friendship. Now she doubted they'd even had that. She smiled pityingly and said, "You never were one for sports, were you, Boyd?"

He smiled at her in his usual restrained way and agreed. "I've never seen the point of sliding down packed snow only to be hauled to the top of the hill by a mechanical device so I can slide down again. I'd prefer to spend the money involved on good seats at a play or a fine dinner."

She looked at him and thought, what a bore he is. A prig too. "Well," she said cheerfully, "you can't know until you've tried it. I must be off, Boyd, or I'll be late for a meeting." She began to walk purposefully away.

"Wait, Adrienne," he commanded, hurrying along beside her. "Can we get together for dinner while you're here? Perhaps make an evening of it. There's a great new musical everyone's been raving about—"

She mustered up a sufficient amount of regretful enthusiasm to say, "I can't, Boyd. I'm afraid Emery's got all our evenings booked. When he brings his managers in for meetings he likes to get full measure of their time!" Once she would have accepted Boyd's invitation with alacrity. Now she was simply glad that she had a reasonable excuse. Having dinner with Boyd would have seemed like a date, and disloyal to Jared.

That evening, after another dinner degenerated into men on the prowl, Adrienne assessed the first half of the week-long meetings. They had been productive in many ways. Her ideas had met with mixed reactions. Those presented by Emery as his own were almost unanimously adopted. The ones she suggested evoked discussion, revision and, in a couple of cases, acceptance. In others they were simply tossed out. The proposals Emery presented had been widely praised, but unless he later gave her the credit she deserved, it looked as if he would get the slap on the back for work she had completed. That reminded her uncomfortably of her treatment at Ted's hands six years ago. She decided to be a little more cautious through the rest of the meetings.

On Wednesday the real work began. Each manager gave a review of the year's activities in his branch, outlined the strengths and weaknesses as he saw them and made proposals for the coming year. After each was finished there was a general discussion as the other managers gave the benefit of their experience. Emery concluded the debate by giving his own opinion and more often than not by tearing a strip off the hapless soul on the hot seat.

No one was exempted from his caustic descriptions, but the manager of the Chicago branch, Miles Abbott, seemed to come in for more than his share of criticism. Adrienne felt sorry for the thin, nervous man whose crimes sounded to her to be hardly worth Emery's outpouring of anger. But she, like the rest, didn't speak up in Miles' defense. Each manager had to be able to hold his own, or he wasn't capable of the strength and independence necessary to run a far-flung branch office. That had been drummed into all of them while they were still learning the ropes in head office.

On Thursday when her turn came, Adrienne felt she made a good presentation of her report. In the discussion that followed, her fellow managers were complimentary on her successes and gave her some excellent suggestions on future plans. Emery, however, was savage in his critique. He claimed that she exaggerated the problems she had faced and therefore the solutions she'd found. He made no mention of her progressive proposals that they'd discussed on Monday and capped his tirade by telling her that her program for the next year lacked ambition. He then added that as the most junior manager she had a lot to learn and she must expect to make mistakes.

Adrienne hid her anger under her cool, reserved exterior. She was completely fed up and would have liked to return home for a quiet dinner with her family, but today was the last complete day of meetings, and a dinner with the full staff of the home office was planned. She couldn't get out of it and she didn't bother trying. She endured.

Friday was rather anticlimactic. Most of the managers had throbbing hangovers, for the dinner had turned into a full-fledged drinking bash that lasted until the small hours of the morning. The final meeting session was unproductive and ended when they broke for lunch at one. Emery, aware that Adrienne was not flying back to Seattle until Sunday, discovered a problem with her operation that kept her busy until after three. She didn't mind since the complaint had been a valid one, but she was annoyed when she found that he had left not long after the branch managers.

With the meetings over she was free to do as she wished. She planned to have dinner with her parents, call a few old friends from her pre-APP days whom she didn't have time to see because of her heavy schedule, and turn in early. On Saturday she and her mother were going shopping, then later that evening her brothers were arriving for a family dinner. And on Sunday she would be flying home to Jared. That alone made the week's end special.

The Denton house was in an uproar, as it always was when all four children were home at once. Kevin, the eldest, was arbitrating a strident debate between Luke, who was a year younger than Adrienne, and Philip, the baby of the family who had just finished his last year at university. Luke's wife Fiona, and Kevin's girlfriend, Andrea, had just finished the dishes and were deep in conversation with Adrienne's mother, Gail, in one corner of the ample living room.

Adrienne and her father, Morgan, talked earnestly a little distance away from the others. Neither of them could forget that in another twenty-four hours she would be back in Seattle. The bond between them was close and they wanted to make the most of the time that remained.

"You haven't said much about your meetings, Adrienne," Morgan probed, watching his daughter shrewdly. "I didn't know they were so confidential."

Adrienne stared down at the coffee cup in her lap. She had only briefly mentioned the meetings because she didn't feel up to describing them to her father. They seemed almost like an admission of personal failure. "They weren't confidential, Dad," she said, looking up. "They were disillusioning."

Morgan raised his eyebrows. "In what way?"

Adrienne shrugged. "There was a lot of back-stabbing." With herself as one of the victims, she thought wryly.

"Come now, Adrienne. I'm sure you're exaggerating," her father said dryly.

She looked him in the eye and shook her head. "Unfortunately, no. Being away has given me the chance to look at things from a different perspective. I don't like what I'm seeing."

"Adrienne," her father said soothingly, "it's been a strenuous week. You're tired and your priorities are a little muddled."

Adrienne squirmed in her chair. "I don't think so, Dad."

"Of course you don't, but you will," he replied complacently.

His words annoyed her. "Dad, my boss was one of the people doing the back-stabbing and I was one of his victims. I can't trust him anymore."

Morgan fixed her with a disapproving gaze. "You're not thinking of becoming one of those young executives who switch from company to company at the blink of an eye, are you?"

Since Adrienne hadn't gotten that far in her vague dissatisfaction, she was quite honestly startled by this accusation. "No, of course not, Dad!"

"Good," he said as the telephone rang in the kitchen. "I didn't think you'd disappointed me, Adrienne." He rose from his leather-covered easy chair to answer it, waving his wife back to her seat on the sofa when she started to rise. "No, Gail, I'll get it. You've done enough for tonight."

After he had been gone over ten minutes Gail said with mild annoyance, "It must be one of his business associates. Sometimes they talk for hours. I hope he's not going to have to go in to the office tomorrow." She smiled at Adrienne. "It's been a while since our daughter's been home and I mean to make the most of it."

Morgan wandered in from the other room. "It's for you, Adrienne." The hubbub suddenly died and everyone stared at her.

"For me?" she exclaimed, jumping to her feet, trying to imagine which of her New York friends would have a fifteen-minute conversation with her father.

Morgan winked as she passed him. "Yes, it's Seattle."

For a moment Adrienne felt suspended, as if all bodily functions had stopped. When they began again she was rushing toward the kitchen, calling, "Thanks, Dad."

As she moved to pick up the phone she discovered that her heart was pounding so hard she had to take a deep breath to recapture some measure of control. "Hi," she said softly, wishing the receiver and three thousand miles weren't between them.

"Hi, beautiful," Jared said in the deep caressing voice that made her spine tingle with desire. "How did the week go?"

Rotten, she wanted to say. "Frantic. We seemed to have every minute programmed. And the weather! Jared, you wouldn't believe how hot it's been!" Beyond the kitchen door there was an ominous silence as her family listened with unabashed curiosity to her end of the conversation.

She heard Jared laugh. "Got an audience, have you?"

She relaxed a little. "How did you guess?"

"When I was talking to your father there was a distinct buzz of voices. It's gone now. Am I creating a sensation?"

Adrienne found herself responding to the amusement in his voice. "Well, they're interested. I expect I'll get the third degree once I'm off the phone."

"Does it worry you?"

"Not much," she replied casually, thinking just the opposite.

He laughed. "You're trying to keep your answers short and ambiguous, aren't you?"

"Yeah," she said and began to giggle.

He sighed in a mock-serious way and observed, "I suppose there's no possibility of your whispering sweet nothings in my ear?"

"Not tonight," she agreed, her voice lilting attractively and hiding underlying meaning.

Jared caught that note and laughed. "Okay, I'll be good. I called to make sure you're still booked on the same flight. How's that as a suitable excuse for your family?"

When she had reaffirmed her flight number, whispered a tender good-night and hung up the phone, Adrienne stood for a moment staring at the kitchen sink without really seeing it. Why had he called? Was it truly to make sure of her flight? If so, why had he talked so long to her father? And what had they talked about for fifteen minutes? That last question drove her back into the living room.

"Who is this guy, Jared?" Philip demanded, a brash twenty-one and oblivious to tact.

"A friend," Adrienne snapped, a slow tide of red creeping into her face.

"What's he do?" asked Kevin, with mild interest.

"He owns a company."

Her oldest brother whistled. "Not bad. Quite a catch, sis."

"Oh, stop it!" she said heatedly.

"So what's up, Adrienne?" Philip demanded, with typical bluntness. "Are you going to marry this guy or something?"

"No!" Adrienne cried, driven into a corner.

"That's enough, Philip," said his mother sternly.

It wasn't easy to stop the youngest Denton once he had his mind set. "But there's got to be some reason a guy would phone Adrienne all the way from Seattle."

"He's picking me up at the airport," she said desperately. "He called about my flight."

"That's pretty weak," observed Philip, who was having a marvelous time.

"Well, that's the reason, whatever you care to believe. Dad, what did you talk to him about for so long?"

Morgan Denton, who had been watching his children squabble good-naturedly for most of their lives, had a policy of letting the kids sort things out for themselves. That didn't mean he had been oblivious to the boys' teasing of their sister. There was a twinkle in his eyes as he said mildly, "He wanted to introduce himself to me and we talked about his background and what he does."

Adrienne's eyes opened to their widest extent. Kevin, her oldest brother, took note of her expression and remarked lazily, "Sounds like he's courting her."

Adrienne blushed scarlet. Seeing her daughter's embarrassment, Mrs. Denton said firmly, "Nonsense. He's simply a well-brought-up young man who is considerate enough to reassure a father that his daughter has someone she can rely on in an emergency. And that is enough of that conversation."

Adrienne slanted a quick look at her father. From the amusement in his eyes he certainly wasn't fooled by her mother's description.

Nor was Philip. He grinned cheekily at her and taunted, "Promise you'll invite us to the wedding, sis?"

"Oh, shut up!" she snapped, hard-pressed.

Chapter Eleven

The quiet droning of the engines in the big-bodied jet underlined the steady flow of miles. Half the flight was over. Soon they would be in Seattle. Adrienne could hardly wait. Being away from Jared for a full week made her miss him deeply and being so close to seeing him again was making her impatient. To help the time pass more quickly, she turned her thoughts back to the week she had just spent.

It had been great to see her family again, of course, but sometimes her brothers went beyond the limit. It had always been like that, the three boys alternately mocking and protecting her. She had learned at a very young age how to hold her own among them and not take them too seriously. Their teasing inquisition about Jared had meant no harm. They were undoubtedly curious about the man she was seeing in Seattle, but they knew she was old enough to live her own life.

The other aspect of her visit, the reason for it in fact, led her to more unsettling thoughts. The departmental meetings had opened her eyes to a number of things that she had been hiding from these past five years. Though she had never liked Emery Thorpe, she had trusted him. It was now clear that she had placed her trust in the wrong person.

Adrienne's problem was that she hadn't expected Thorpe's vicious actions. Her failure to foresee them made her squirm internally in silent disgust. She, of all people, should have seen them coming. After her experience with Ted she should have been alert to catch any scrap of evidence indicating Emery's plans. Instead she worked until she nearly dropped and watched her boss steal away her best ideas while he downgraded what he couldn't appropriate for himself.

Why had she been so blind? Because of her principles, the ideals she had been taught throughout her childhood. Those ideals had served her father well, but the world had changed over the past thirty years and the rules rising young executives played by had changed with it. Few people spent their whole working careers with one company anymore, especially if an opportunity for quicker advancement came from elsewhere.

Adrienne knew also that as a woman she had less flexibility in her career decisions. Women in management were still regarded with caution by their male colleagues and superiors. That was one of the reasons she had been pleased to be hired by APP. The company had a reputation for absolute impartiality in its promotion practices. There were women in important management positions throughout APP and even one in the executive committee that made decisions affecting every aspect of the company. Once Adrienne had aspired to that important level, and once she had believed that through hard work and her natural talent she would succeed. After this set of meetings she was not so sure.

How had Jared phrased it when she asked him why he'd worked for APP if he felt so hostile toward the company? He had said that like everyone else he had been fooled by the image. It wasn't until he was inside and saw the real workings of the company that disillusionment set in. Adrienne now knew how he felt. This week Emery had stolen her ideas, then had the gall to imply he had done her a favor in securing her the Seattle position. The hell he had. She was given Seattle because it was a mess and she was the only one in the department who had the brains and the dedication to straighten it out. She was the one doing the favors—not Emery.

This week was a turning point in her thoughts, Adrienne realized. She was still ambitious, she was still career-oriented, but she was no longer blindly loyal to the company. Her father passed Emery and his schemes off as an aberration. But he wasn't. There were more people like Emery and Ted at APP than there were loyal, dedicated Adriennes.

She was not about to discard all of her old beliefs. Loyalty was an admirable trait, as were dedication and determination. But they didn't have to be aimed solely in one direction. She had no intention of abandoning her career at APP, but she would look at it a little more objectively. There were other, equally important factors in her life now. It was time to accept that her career was only one aspect of a more complete whole.

As the jet began its descent into Seattle Adrienne waited impatiently, concentrating on the one important thing at the moment. Somewhere in the massive airport Jared was waiting for her.

When she saw him, he was standing at the base of a bank of escalators that led from the secured area of the terminal to the floor above, his hands thrust into the pockets of his jeans and blue short-sleeved shirt hugging his shoulders and chest. She picked out his tall well-proportioned frame and dark head easily as she made her way through the milling crowd of passengers and those waiting to greet them. There was a frowning, intense expression on his angular features as he scanned the throng. She saw it dissolve into a delighted grin when he caught sight of her. She was in his arms moments later, her long silky hair brushing his shoulders, the heat from his bare arms burning through her sundress. The bone-crushing hug gave way to a passionate, demanding kiss that made her light-headed.

When at last he let her move shakily away she twitched her lips into a beguiling smile and demanded, "Miss me?"

He laughed, but avoided answering directly. "What do you think?"

After the force of that kiss Adrienne could quite happily believe that he had. Still, she would have liked to hear him say it. "I missed you," she whispered, not quite able to look into his eyes.

She was rewarded by another kiss, gentler this time, almost tender in its sweet communication. "Come on," said Jared, his voice suddenly thick. "Let's pick up your suitcase and get out of here."

She was quite happy to let him carry her luggage, which he did with infuriating ease, and to follow his sure footsteps to where the car was parked.

"It's raining," she exclaimed happily once they were out of the covered parking area. Sure enough it was. Not a downpour, but the gentle drizzle that so often constituted rain in the Pacific Northwest. Jared shot her a sharp look then relaxed as he noted her wistful smile. "It's good to be home," she added, half to herself. She shook off the suddenly introspective mood, turning in her seat to face him. "It was awful in New York. Hot! It must have been nearly a hundred degrees and not a cloud in the sky, not even white fluffy ones. I thought I was going to melt!"

"You only do that with me," he said huskily.

Adrienne felt a blush creep up under her skin. "I do, don't I?" she muttered.

He shot her a suggestive glance, then turned his attention back to the road to concentrate on his driving. Adrienne watched him with a warm sense of loving pride as he maneuvered through the traffic with easy panache. It was wonderful to be back with him again, to know that their brief separation was over. She relaxed into the soft white leather seat and gave a little sigh of contentment.

Jared drove directly to his home, which was situated on one of Seattle's many ridges. Hidden behind masses of greenery it faced west. The view from its living-room windows was a marvelous one of Puget Sound and the Olympic Mountains beyond.

Adrienne had been there before, of course, but she was a little surprised he had brought her there instead of to her own apartment. As he parked the car she raised her eyebrows quizzically.

"I wanted to spend some time with you," he said roughly, his gray eyes hungry. "I'll make sure you get back to your apartment sometime tonight, or early enough tomorrow morning for you to change and not be late for work."

She smiled and shifted closer. "There's no need," she whispered against his mouth. "My mother very kindly did all my laundry on Friday morning when I wasn't around to stop her. All I have to do is iron out the travel creases. Do you have an iron?"

"I don't know!" he ground out. "We'll worry about that later."

Adrienne agreed with a small contented sigh and promptly forgot about it as he kissed her.

Adrienne must have slept. They had hurried up to the house through the light drizzle. The moist air felt cool on her skin after the intense heat of New York. She was shivering by the time they entered the house and was glad to be inside. She had laughed and said something silly about goose bumps and getting acclimatized again and then she was in Jared's arms being kissed and caressed until her body was not simply warm it was hot, throbbing with a pent-up desire that caught her unaware. They made love quickly, roughly. At the culmination, they both cried out, then lay entwined. It was then that Adrienne slipped into a contented doze.

She moved and stretched, feeling wonderfully relaxed and complete. The heat from Jared's warm body beside her beckoned, and she snuggled against him. There was a rumble of satisfied male laughter then his hands moved to draw her closer to him. His lips caressed the smooth skin on her shoulder as her breasts made sensual contact with the soft, teasing hair on his chest.

"Hey," he complained softly, "do you plan to sleep through the night?"

Her answer was to free one hand and run it along the hard ridges of bone and muscle on his side down to the curve of his hip, the top of one muscular thigh, then back up again. She felt desire quicken as his body stiffened against her.

"I thought you were asleep," he said thickly, shifting so he could see her face.

She smiled languidly. "I was."

He moved his lips closer to taste hers. "I'm hungry," he breathed.

"You're insatiable," she said in a throaty little growl.

His tongue touched her lower lip and traced its soft shape, then tentatively touched the sensitive corners. Adrienne felt the last of her sleepy contentment fade away and met the tip of his tongue with her own. His mouth left hers to nibble her ear. "For food," he whispered.

"Pardon?" she said hazily, not sure she had heard him right.

"I'm starved, Adrienne," he said plaintively. "I thought I'd wait and have dinner with you, then I remembered you probably would eat on the plane. By that time it was too late."

She blinked, disentangled herself and sat up. Jared propped himself on one elbow and smiled appealingly up at her. "I suppose you want me to cook your dinner," she said, faintly exasperated.

"No," he replied gently, catching her wrist and pulling her back down beside him. "Have I ever told you that your eyes sparkle a beautiful blue when you're indignant?"

"No, but..."

He had abandoned his indolent position and was now leaning over her, still holding on to her wrist. "You don't have to cook," he muttered, dropping light kisses over her eyelids, the tip of her nose, along the line of her cheekbones. "I have a cold dinner all ready. I could have eaten any time. The truth is, I wasn't all that hungry until you came home."

Their mouths met, each nibbling and tasting the other. Adrienne let the fingers of her free hand run through the light mat of hair on his chest. As his lips moved to graze at the tip of her chin and along her jawline she murmured, "Do you want to eat now or wait until later?"

"Later," he replied gruffly. "Definitely later."

"Ummm, that was delicious." Adrienne couldn't remember when she had felt so completely sated. Her body still tingled from Jared's lovemaking and she'd just finished a generous sampling of the cold dinner he had assembled. It consisted of large quantities of shrimp, Adrienne's favorite seafood, and crab, a tangy cucumber salad, plus a regular tossed salad.

When he'd produced this feast, Adrienne had planned only to nibble on the shrimp. After two bites she was hooked. By the time she was finished she'd eaten almost as much as Jared had.

After dinner they retired to the living room and finished off a bottle of wine. Drapes covered the wide windows that looked out over the stupendous view, for it was night and the mountains and the Sound were masked by darkness. Adrienne curled contentedly on the sofa, leaning against Jared.

"How did the meetings go?" he asked lazily. They had talked about New York, the changes she had noticed, the things she had done, while they ate. So far though, he had stayed away from asking about the company or how she'd felt about it. Adrienne didn't like that. She didn't want there to be any taboo subjects between them.

"Useless," she said after taking a sip of wine. "That's pretty all-encompassing, isn't it? There were some valuable suggestions made and adopted." *Mine*, she thought sourly, *not that anyone gave me credit for them*. She wasn't going to talk about that particular aspect of the meetings, not now. She didn't want to spoil the contented mood of her homecoming. "There was a lot of fat. We could have done the whole thing in three days."

"I know what you mean," he said, idly stroking her breast. "I hated the departmental meetings when I was with APP. The boys thought of it as a chance to escape from the security of their own domestic niches and prowl. Since there's safety in numbers it gave most of them a courage they'd lack on their own."

She sighed. "It's still the same."

He casually lifted the wineglass to his lips and drank, but Adrienne wasn't fooled. There was nothing casual about the sudden tension in his muscles or the harsh note to his voice. "Did they give you a hard time?"

She twisted her body around to reach up and touch his cheek. Beneath her fingers she could feel the prickly growth of new beard. "Jealous?" she taunted softly.

"Damn you!" he said savagely, moving roughly under her.

"Jared!" she soothed, pushing him back against the cushions. "I was roped into one very boring evening, which I didn't repeat. I couldn't get out of the business dinners, but they weren't bad because we did discuss the day's meetings. Right after the meal I always left and went home. They called me a spoilsport. I didn't care."

He relaxed, but his eyes still flickered with a hard light. "I should have known you could handle them."

"Jared!" She didn't know whether to feel hurt or pleased.

He laughed and cuffed her cheek in a rough caress. "That was a compliment, sweetheart." He held up the bottle. "It's the dregs, but we might as well kill it."

"Sure, why not?" she agreed, relaxing once more.

"How did your report go? Did your boss heap praise on you for all the work you've done out here?"

"Emery Thorpe does not understand the meaning of the word praise," she said tartly. "I wish he'd hurry up and retire so I wouldn't have to put up with him."

Jared laughed sardonically. "Guys like him never retire. They linger on and on and on, outlasting better men who began before and after them."

She sighed. "Maybe he'll get a nice fat promotion then and I'll get rid of him that way."

He observed softly, without bitterness, "They don't get promotions either, beautiful. They're cogs. Useful plodders who keep the machinery of a large corporation running. They can't make that machinery, they just know how to keep it functioning smoothly."

Adrienne thought about her stolen ideas and Emery's effort to downplay her six months in Seattle, and sighed. Jared had summed up Emery Thorpe beautifully. "Let's not talk about my boss or the company anymore. I've had a week of nothing but and I'm sick of it."

"Suits me," he agreed huskily. "I can think of far more interesting topics."

The summer, with its high quota of beautiful sunny days, drifted inexorably into fall and the weather changed, the rains coming more frequently with whole weeks going by without a break in the inclement skies. Adrienne looked objectively at the operation of the Seattle branch and decided that even with the goals Emery had insisted she set for the coming year she could handle the workload without the massive injections of overtime she had once done. In fact, she eased out of overtime altogether, except for her routine of coming in early. In her own mind she was doing only half a job, for she knew she was capable of much more, but she also knew that she would get no recognition or appreciation for that extra effort.

With Adrienne conforming to a strict schedule of hours it was inevitable that one day Jared would be the one to call and cancel a date because some unforeseen emergency had come up. The first time it happened Adrienne cheerfully told him it didn't matter, for to her mind he had been forced to accept her heavy workload far too long. The second time she reacted the same way. Each time she heard relief in his voice and a kind of embarrassed dismay at what he was doing.

The third time, in early October, her sense of humor got the better of her. "Oh, but Jared!" she whimpered, "I was looking forward to dinner tonight!"

"I know, sweetheart," he soothed, "but this problem with the joint venture in San Francisco came up suddenly and I've got to sort it out." He added heavily, "I'll probably be tied up tomorrow as well."

"Tomorrow too?" she cried in mock dismay.

"Look, I'm sorry but..." he began in a harassed tone.

"You never have time for me anymore!" She started on a wail and ended in a giggle.

There was a momentary pause, then he said softly, "You wretch! When you least expect it I'll pay you back for this."

She laughed, not particularly worried by the threat. "Honestly, Jared, it's okay. Give me a call when you can."

"You know where I'd prefer to be, Adrienne. Hell, I'll try and wind this down early tomorrow. If I can I'll drop by, but don't expect me."

As she put down the phone she decided that Jared sounded worried and tired. She hoped this San Francisco business wasn't going to develop into a major problem. For a minute or two she sat at ease in her chair, making no attempt to get back to her work. Outside her window the sky was bleak, the heavy cloud-cover black. It had been raining steadily all day. She reflected that the balmy days of summer were truly gone, lost in the mists and drizzle of October.

Chapter Twelve

"I never knew it could rain so much for so long," Adrienne remarked to her secretary, Carol, as she took off her raincoat and shook it lightly before hanging it up on the discreetly camouflaged coatrack behind her office door.

Carol, who was standing in the open doorway, replied cheerfully. "There have been reports of flooding in low-lying areas, and houses built too close to unstable hillsides have had yards of earth dumped on them when the rain has caused slides."

"You're very ghoulish! How can you be so bright and casual about it?" Adrienne demanded in considerable amazement.

Carol shrugged. "You get used to it. It's like the roads in the mountains. There are rock slides on them all the time. You don't let it stop you from getting to your destination. You just hope the rocks don't fall on you."

Adrienne shook her head and looked out at the bleak gray sky through rain-wet windows. With a little sigh she said, "Nature sure makes itself felt out here, doesn't it?"

Her secretary laughed. "Whether you like it or not."

Adrienne glanced at her watch. "Yes. Well, I'd better get to work so I'll be ready for my eight-o'clock call. Put Emery through as soon as he phones, okay, Carol?"

"Sure, boss," she agreed with her usual lack of formality. At one point Adrienne had noted the habit with a feeling of faint irritation, but due to Carol's unquestioned abilities she had ignored it. Now it didn't even register as she nodded absently and sat down at her desk. Carol silently withdrew, leaving Adrienne to get on with the first tasks of the day.

At eight-ten Adrienne surfaced from her absorption, stretched lazily and picked up her coffee cup. She was halfway to the door of her office before she glanced at her watch. "Carol," she said as she came through the door, "why didn't you put New York through to me as I told you?"

The secretary swiveled around in her chair at the first sound of Adrienne's voice. Now she frowned. "Because there hasn't been any call from New York yet, Adrienne. I checked with Melissa to find out if any messages were left with the answering service but there were none."

"Oh, well," Adrienne dismissed, "it doesn't matter. Emery's probably in a meeting or something. I'm going to get a cup of coffee. I'll be back in a few minutes." Carol nodded, turning back to her work.

Adrienne walked slowly toward the lunchroom. What she had told her secretary was probably true, but it was still definitely odd. Emery's practice over the—what was it? Nine? no, ten—months she had been in Seattle had been a steady pattern of eight-o'clock phone calls, once a day, every working day. He used the fifteen-minute call to cajole, criticize, occasionally praise, but always to hammer through the message that it was New York that made the ultimate decisions, not her. The calls had always been an imposition, but since the July meetings they had become a nagging irritant, like a burr under the saddle of a horse. Adrienne knew exactly how far she could go without head-office approval. There was no need for Emery Thorpe to reinforce the matter each and every day. But, annoying as the calls were, they were reliable. Emery was a creature of habit. There had to be a reason he hadn't phoned. Not knowing that reason made her edgy.

She poured the coffee and stirred in sugar and powdered cream, still thinking deeply about the problem. Finally she shrugged. Undoubtedly an explanation would soon present itself. Until then there was no sense worrying about it.

She was on her way back to her office when the solution arrived in the shape of Emery Thorpe in person, standing in the reception area having a nice cozy chat with Melissa. Adrienne stopped short, listening to the sound of his light, reedy voice and Melissa's higher one giggling at something he'd said. As she cynically heard Emery flirting with the receptionist, she thought of the time months earlier when he had refused to let her fire Melissa. The girl's performance as switchboard operator and receptionist had been poor and continued to be unreliable, but Emery liked her looks so she stayed.

Suddenly aware that she was the focal point of the eyes of her staff, she shook herself out of her reverie, forcing herself to walk unhurriedly to the reception area. It would not do to let them think that she was disconcerted by her boss's surprise visit.

"Good morning, Emery," she said dryly, watching him straighten slowly from his bent position over the receptionist's desk, his face too close to Melissa's. As he turned to Adrienne a mischievous devil impelled her to add, "Office hours are eight to four-thirty." She looked pointedly at her watch, which now read eight-twenty.

Emery's eyes narrowed and he puffed out his cheeks. "Do you know how difficult it is to get a cab in this town?"

"From a hotel?" she queried gently, her brows raised in polite disbelief.

Emery glanced at her. "Yes. The porter claimed it was because of the rain."

"Of course," she agreed soothingly, smiling without remorse. "Where are you staying?"

He named the most luxurious hotel in town, much more expensive than the one she had stayed in when she first arrived. It didn't surprise her. If she commented Emery would undoubtedly tell her it was all a matter of rank and the privileges due to it.

"This damned rain," he was saying now. "Every time I come to Seattle it rains. What a terrible place to live!"

Adrienne smiled serenely. "You must always come at the wrong time, Emery. August was a beautiful month and in February and March the flowers bloom and the colors spill out over the entire city. Why don't you come into my office? I'm sure you've got a great deal to tell me."

Emery frowned unblinkingly, then nodded.

As they walked across the big open area to the offices Adrienne was thinking rapidly. This was one of what Emery liked to call his flying visits—quick, unannounced inspection tours. Emery had a fond notion that if he visited a branch without warning he would discover the true state of the office. His theory was based on the assumption that the manager, if warned of his superior's imminent arrival, would do a thorough housecleaning and hide all the daily shortcomings under a thick carpet of platitudes.

For whatever reason, Emery had decided that it was her turn to be inspected. She ran her thoughts over a mental list of the most recent problems she had faced. Anything among them still waiting to be completely resolved? No. Good. Now what about personnel—

"Here we are, Emery." She put her cup on the desk. "Let me take your coat." He shrugged it off and allowed her to hang it up without protest. "Would you care for coffee before we begin?"

"Please," said Emery. "Two sugar, no cream."

Adrienne went to the door. "Carol, coffee for Mr. Thorpe, please. Two sugar, no cream. After you bring it, I won't be taking any calls. See that we are not disturbed."

Carol nodded and disappeared. Adrienne turned back to the office to see Emery comfortably seated in her chair, behind her desk. She suppressed a sharp pang of annoyance, smiling coldly to cover it. She knew that Emery was doing this deliberately. It was one of his tricks to prove that wherever he went he was still in charge. Knowing his motives didn't help much. His actions rankled all the same.

She walked to the desk, picked up her now lukewarm coffee and settled in one of the guest chairs. Crossing her legs in a slow, smooth movement she said calmly, "You won't find any holes in my operation, Emery. And if I have anything pending it's only because the solution is not available at the present. I like to keep business current."

"I'm sure you do," Emery replied with a large smile that exposed crooked teeth. "But if I didn't make these little visits of mine my managers might not keep their organizations running as efficiently as they do now."

"You make us sound like little children who can't be trusted to do their homework without mother's supervision," she observed caustically.

Again Thorpe's eyes narrowed and he frowned. "You've changed, Adrienne...."

Carol saved Adrienne from whatever observation Emery had been about to make. She entered the office holding two mugs. One she handed to Emery with a pretty smile. "Two sugar, no cream, Mr. Thorpe," she repeated, then turned to Adrienne. "I thought you might like another cup, Adrienne," she said, putting the mug on the desk.

Bless you, Adrienne thought. I'm going to need that. She passed the now cold cup in her hand to her secretary. "Thanks, Carol. You're a lifesaver."

"No problem." Carol quietly left the room, closing the door behind her.

"Shall we get right down to business?" Adrienne suggested coolly, not giving Emery a chance to return to his earlier comment.

He sipped his coffee then nodded, deciding to let her off the hook this one time.

Two hours later Adrienne said doubtfully, "I don't know if Noel's in the office today."

Thorpe nodded decisively. "He is. I had his schedule checked before I came out."

As they were speaking, Adrienne recalled that Emery always made a habit of having a long, detailed conversation with the sales manager on these flying visits of his. Since the logistics department and the sales department were so interdependent, Thorpe felt that the sales manager for the division knew better than anyone how well the branch and its manager were performing. If Noel was available he and Emery would talk for what remained of the morning and probably extend the conversation over a business lunch.

She had Carol check with Lilith to see if Granger was free. When it turned out he was, she arranged the meeting, then said to Emery, "What about this afternoon?"

"The warehouse," he replied decisively. "The contract is coming up for renewal and there have been so many problems over the past two years I want some firm guarantees before I'm willing to commit our business there in the future. I want to talk to the owner—not the manager. Got that? Make the arrangements while I'm with Granger."

"Very well," she agreed smoothly, not by the flicker of an eyelid exposing the distaste she felt for that particular task. The president of the company that owned the warehouse rarely saw representatives of his clients.

He left that to his hard-working, very charming general manager, Chad Ferris, who spoke easily and knowledgeably on every subject and could never be pinned down. Emery was right, the president was the man to talk to, but setting up the meeting would be difficult.

"You'll see the staff tomorrow?" she asked. That was another of Emery's habits. After talking to the branch and sales managers, he then interviewed each of the staff members personally. It was time-consuming and Adrienne couldn't believe that any of them ever told him the truth about their feelings for their job or their real desires for the future. However, Emery seemed to think it an excellent tool to be used in his evaluations so the interviews continued.

"Tomorrow morning," he said evenly. "I leave in the afternoon. We'll have lunch and we can have an in-depth discussion of my findings."

She nodded and he left her to the wearing task of trying to pin down the president of the warehouse company. She was in the middle of a long explanatory conversation with Chad Ferris when Carol poked her head around the door frame, observed Adrienne's intent expression and retreated to her desk. Adrienne noticed her do this but didn't have the time to wonder why. She was too busy trying to persuade Ferris that arranging the meeting with the president was in the best interests of his company.

After another fifteen minutes Adrienne finally convinced him, and an appointment was set up for that afternoon. She was sitting with her elbows on her desk, her chin on cupped palms, feeling drained but triumphant when Carol reappeared, holding several pink slips.

"I noticed that your light had gone out," she said, referring to the extension button on her phone that indicated when Adrienne's line was in use. "Are you free to return some calls?"

Adrienne grimaced. "I suppose so. Anyone important?"

"I don't think..." Carol began, leafing through the call-back slips. "There was one. Jared Hawkes called while you were on the line just now."

"Jared! Did he mention why he phoned?" She reached for the scraps of paper.

Carol handed them to her, shaking her head. "No, but he did say he would like you to get back to him as soon as possible."

"Thanks, Carol," Adrienne muttered, picking up the receiver. When she looked up her secretary was gone and she was alone.

There was a slight delay while Adrienne identified herself to Jared's secretary, then she heard his deep voice say, "Hawkes."

"Hi there, Mr. Hawkes," she drawled. "You called me?"

She could sense him relaxing despite the distance that separated them. "Hi, sweetheart." He seemed to hesitate, then said flatly, "I've got bad news."

"You have to work late tonight. That's okay—"

"I have to go out of town," he interjected softly.

There was a moment's silence, then she said, "Oh," on a long, drawn-out breath. "How come?"

"That San Francisco problem. Remember a couple of weeks ago when I had that emergency?"

"Yes, but I thought you fixed everything."

"So did I. Hell, it's blown up even bigger. This time I'll have to go down there myself. I'll be away three days, maybe four."

She sighed. "In a way it's a good thing."

It was his turn to say, "Oh," a wealth of meaning in the tiny syllable.

"Now don't start imagining crises that don't exist! I've already got a very real one on my hands."

"What's that?" She was pleased to hear that his voice was edged in concern, nothing more.

"Emery Thorpe has arrived from New York without warning. It means I'll have to go out to dinner with him tonight and entertain him." She wasn't looking forward to that and it showed in her weary, frustrated tone.

"Is he making a nuisance of himself?" demanded Jared curtly, very much the protective male.

His instant championing did a great deal to revive her normally positive outlook. "No more than usual and not in the way you mean. It's just a bother having him here, poking into everything. Right now he's with Noel Granger trying to discover my hidden secrets."

Jared laughed. "He's out of luck if he thinks he'll drag any dirt out of Noel." He hesitated, then said forcefully, "Look, Adrienne, are you sure you'll be okay?"

"Yes, of course! Annoying as Emery Thorpe is he's still my boss, and he does have the right to check into my work. I can cope with him, though. I've been doing it for years."

"Yes." Though Jared was agreeing, Adrienne didn't think he sounded completely convinced. He changed the subject quickly. "I have to be at the airport by two.

Do you think you can escape from Thorpe's clutches long enough to have lunch with me?''

A refusal hovered on Adrienne's tongue, then her features hardened with determination. "You bet," she replied huskily. "When and where?"

Having lunch with Jared helped her through the rest of the long day. She took more than her usual hour, secure in the knowledge that Emery was tied up with Noel Granger, but not really caring whether he found out or not. She returned to the office at one-thirty, in plenty of time to make the appointment at the warehouse, which was located in an industrial area in the southern end of the city.

Emery was already back and waiting for her at her desk. He was pensively writing something on a lined white pad. She was sure they were notes of his conversation with Noel. No doubt she was the main focus of them. She wondered cynically how many of Noel's opinions Emery would allow to seep through. Only those that added to his own luster, she decided. The rest would be lost in the confines of Emery's selective brain.

Though she half expected him to chastise her for keeping him waiting, Emery said nothing on the subject. She discovered that he and Noel had returned half an hour earlier and Emery, in his own phrase, had made himself comfortable in her office. And gone through her desk, she was willing to bet, to see for himself the status of various projects and problems. Well, he would have found nothing out of order; she had no secrets to hide.

They spent three grueling hours at the warehouse. The meeting was a four-way one, Thorpe and Adrienne for APP and the president and his general manager for the warehouse company. Adrienne and Ferris were largely silent bystanders at what started as a heated argument then gradually escalated into a shouting match. In the end Emery seemed quite pleased by the terms that had been hammered out. As far as Adrienne could see they were little better than the previous ones and had the same potential for problems.

For dinner that evening she chose the restaurant Jared had taken her to after he helped her find her apartment. They had returned many times since, and Adrienne knew it was one of the finest seafood restaurants in the city, despite its unpretentious facade. Emery, she was not surprised to find out, was not impressed by the fishing-shack exterior. He did mellow, though, when he saw the inside.

After they were seated and their drinks, a vodka martini for Emery and a margarita for Adrienne, had been brought and sipped, Emery opened the menu and took a quick perusal of its contents. "Not much selection," he grunted.

Adrienne's eyes opened wide in shock and she checked her own menu to be sure no drastic changes had taken place. It was as she remembered it, nearly two dozen seafood entrées, all of them mouthwateringly tasty. When she looked up, Emery had raised his hand to signal a refill of his drink. She said coolly, "How can you say that?"

Thorpe pointed at the menu. "I don't like crab—horrible crawling things. Clams and oysters don't agree with my stomach and mussels—well, I've never had any, but I dare say I wouldn't care for them. Same family as clams, aren't they?" He continued on, not even noticing Adrienne's nod. "Snapper is a fish I've never tasted. The sole might be okay. Or the salmon. My God! Look at this! Squid! Can you imagine anyone eating that?"

"I am," Adrienne stated, considerably annoyed that one of her favorite places was being so ruthlessly criticized.

"What?" For once she had Emery at a standstill. He stared at her with his mouth open. The waiter arrived with his refill and he took a large gulp.

"I like squid," Adrienne announced recklessly, never having tried it.

"How can you?" Thorpe demanded, shocked right to the bottom of his thoroughly conventional soul.

"Because it's delicious." She added for good measure, "They cook it beautifully here, in fresh tomatoes and onions and spices." That, at least, was true. She'd watched Jared eat and enjoy it, apparently without disastrous side effects.

"Squid," Emery muttered. "My God." He rubbed the half a dozen hairs that covered his bald head. "I guess I'll have the salmon. Is it fresh?"

Adrienne did her best to contain her amazement, but didn't succeed very well. "Of course it's fresh! This is Seattle!"

"I know where I am, thank you," said Emery with great dignity. "Even in Seattle restaurants can serve frozen meats and fish."

Adrienne felt herself squirm, but covered her reaction under a cool mask of hauteur. "This is not that sort of establishment."

Thorpe accepted that and ordered another drink along with the salmon and an appetizer of shrimp cocktail. Adrienne chose the cocktail as well and made the request for the squid. Soon Emery was supplied with another martini, his third drink to Adrienne's first, and he began to talk about some of the changes that had occurred in head office since her visit in July.

The meal passed very well. Emery was pleased with the salmon, which was indeed fresh. Adrienne pretended to enjoy her squid, then discovered to her surprise that she really liked the light rather bland flavor, spiced up by the sauce in which it had been cooked. Conversation revolved around safe business topics that left no room for confrontation.

They were at the coffee and dessert stage, Adrienne having refused the sweet but accepted the beverage. Emery swallowed a mouthful of rich mocha torte and said, "This is delicious. You don't know what you're missing. Have you heard about Miles Abbott?"

Adrienne ignored the reference to the dessert and focused on the question. "No, I don't think so. Has something happened to him?"

Emery took another forkful of torte and savored it. Adrienne realized he was teasing her, so she sipped her coffee and waited calmly. When he was finally ready he said, "He's being transferred out of the logistics department."

Adrienne watched him take another bite. "Who's going to replace him?" she asked coolly, her voice faintly bored. She refused to let Emery see her surprise or her curiosity about who would be elevated to the manager's level. She could think of several who deserved it and two who certainly did not.

"Hasn't been decided," Thorpe admitted at last. "Abbott made a mess of things in Chicago. He got involved with one of the secretaries. His marriage is falling apart. He's being allowed to claim that the switch to the finance department was his own request. That is not strictly true. He was given the choice of the transfer or being let go. He chose the transfer."

"Finance is an important division," said Adrienne doubtfully. "I can't see them accepting a person another department doesn't want."

Emery waved that aside, one hand moving graphically, his mouth full of the last of his delicious dessert. When he had swallowed he said with a satisfied sigh, "That alone was worth coming here for." He sipped his coffee, then said very seriously, "Don't make any mistakes, Adrienne, this is a demotion for Miles. He's lost all his responsibility, he has no major budget to work with, his autonomy has been removed. The company is indicating they have lost faith in him."

Adrienne stared very coolly at Thorpe. "Did he ever have those things, Emery? Or were they merely an illusion?"

Thorpe's lips thinned. He didn't pretend not to understand. "Abbott was subject to head office, just as you are, Adrienne. But," he added deliberately, "like you, he had far more authority than his counterpart in New York."

Adrienne shrugged, not willing to pursue the subject. Whether Miles Abbott was being demoted or given a career-building opportunity, Emery would persist in believing what he wanted. Partly because he couldn't imagine life outside the logistics department and also to save face. If Abbott wasn't good enough for logistics he wasn't good enough for any department.

"In my opinion the company should fire him and have done with it." Emery glowered, unwittingly confirming Adrienne's assessment.

Poor Emery, she thought mockingly. Though he might not think highly of Miles Abbott's talents, men in other departments did. Emery was suffering from pique because his view had not carried the day.

"He's been very loyal over the years," she said gently.

"Loyalty doesn't mean a damn thing," Thorpe scoffed, "if a man hasn't got the skills the company needs."

Once Adrienne might have cringed at a comment like this from her direct superior, but the July meetings had made her considerably wiser. She wasn't even surprised by the admission. "Perhaps other executives feel differently."

"There are always a few bleeding hearts around," Emery groused. "I'm not one of them."

Adrienne looked down at her coffee cup and decided it was time to change the subject. "If Miles has left such a mess you'll need someone very capable to straighten it out."

"Yes," said Thorpe slowly, staring thoughtfully at her. "My opinion exactly."

"And I guess you'll want that person to start as soon as possible," she continued, sipping her coffee as she ran the names and backgrounds of various head-office personnel through her mind.

"Not immediately. No, no more coffee," said Emery, waving away a hovering waiter carrying a coffee beaker.

"I'll have a refill," Adrienne stated, pushing her cup toward the center of the table. The waiter poured. Emery looked annoyed.

"As I was saying, Abbott's appointment isn't until the new year. January first. It gives me time to make the necessary arrangements." He blinked rapidly.

Adrienne didn't notice. She was sipping her fresh, hot coffee and thinking that she was glad it wasn't a decision she would have to make. "Yes, it does, doesn't it?" she agreed, only mildly interested.

"All in all, I am very pleased with you, Adrienne," announced Emery as they sat in the sumptuous dining room at Sea-Tac Airport. Adrienne had suggested they eat in the nondescript cafeteria down the hall, but Thorpe balked at that, telling her they needed a quieter, more intimate setting if they were to discuss business. "You have done an excellent job here in Seattle. Better than I ever hoped for," he concluded firmly.

Once this approval would have made Adrienne flush with pleasure. Now it only made her wary. "That is very kind, Emery. Thank you."

He nodded, taking her words at face value. "I'm glad to say I'll be able to give you an excellent report. This will mean great things for you, Adrienne."

She watched him consume the well-done steak he had ordered with a growing sense of disquiet. Her own veal cordon bleu lay virtually untasted on the plate. She knew she deserved the praise, for she had long since eliminated any false modesty in her own ability. However, Emery was not a man to offer compliments, whether they were deserved or not, unless he had a very specific reason. From his tone it was clear that he was softening her up for an unpleasant blow. That had her worried.

It wasn't until the blow came that she realized just how dreadful it was.

"Chicago?" she said on a whisper, because her throat had closed with horror.

"That's right. I have great faith in you, Adrienne. I know you will do an excellent job there." Emery beamed. He was pleased he had finally cracked the shell of cool indifference that cloaked Adrienne Denton.

She reached for a glass of water and slowly swallowed, both to soothe her choking throat and to give herself a moment to think. "Emery," she said, her voice still scratchy, "you told me I was to be here in Seattle for two years, possibly more. There are still any number of projects I have in mind to increase the efficiency of the office. I can't just abandon it all!"

Emery blinked furiously. "Of course you can. Leave your successor detailed memoranda on what you've done so far and what your plans are. He merely has to put your ideas into effect."

"Before I came out here you promised me two years or more in Seattle. You also guaranteed that I would be returning to head office after this assignment was over. Are you telling me now that all I will ever be is a branch manager shuttled from city to city at your whim?"

Thorpe's chest puffed pretentiously. "APP is a publicly owned corporation. It does not exist to cater to our whims—yours or mine. If the needs of the business call for a strong, diligent manager in Chicago then I'll assign the person with the best qualifications for the position. There are no personalities involved. I'm simply doing my job as thoroughly as I can."

"And you think I'm that perfect person," Adrienne said flatly, hiding her emotions from Emery's manipulative gaze.

He sat back in his chair and eyed her for several strained seconds. "Young and inexperienced as you are, Adrienne, you have an intuitive grasp of business and people. When I sent you out here I thought you would be capable of sorting out the paperwork, but I never imagined you would bring the staff around the way you have."

"That's Jared," she muttered under her breath. They had spent hours talking about how to handle people. He was very successful with his own staff and he had generously passed on many of his secrets to her.

"What did you say?" Thorpe demanded sharply.

With a sudden splintering pain Adrienne thought, *Jared! Oh my God! I'll have to leave Jared!*

She sipped some more water and said dully, "When does all this take place?"

"You leave Seattle in six weeks. Your successor arrives in two, you have one month to train him and then a month to train with Miles before he returns to New York to his new position."

"This is why you came to Seattle, isn't it? It wasn't an inspection tour at all." She was amazed that her voice remained so calm when inside she felt empty and dead. "The plans had already been made."

"If the branch had been mishandled in any way I would have scratched your name from my list," he said cautiously. "But I will admit that I didn't expect to find any unwelcome surprises, and I didn't. As I said, Adrienne, you are an excellent administrator."

"Do I have any choice?" she asked evenly, her expression cool and composed, the words apparently only a light, curious query.

Thorpe's voice hardened all the same. "No. If you don't take the Chicago assignment you no longer work for the company."

"I see," Adrienne said sadly.

Emery seemed to accept this as her acquiescence to the move. For the half hour that remained until he had to board his flight he heaped her with instructions on the work she would have to do to arrange a smooth transfer of responsibility. Adrienne listened in silence, making no comment, hardly hearing his words.

When he had gone she made her way slowly to the parking lot, her emotions held carefully in check. The twenty-minute drive downtown from the airport through the charging expressway traffic lacked its usual nerve-racking qualities for some reason, perhaps because she had temporarily put all feelings in the deep freeze.

It was pouring rain when she emerged from the indoor parking lot where she left her car. She stood under the beating rain looking at the puddles on the pavement, the shrouded gray sky, the traffic struggling up the steep, slippery streets. Then she began to walk, not caring about her destination as long as it wasn't the offices of APP.

The rain pounded steadily down on her, soaking through her raincoat and saturating her hair until locks of it fell untidily free of her chignon. Her feet squelched in her shoes as she trudged heedlessly through puddles, mud she never noticed dotting her stockings. She was thinking about her months in Seattle, hearing conversations again, remembering incidents, feeling an acute sense of loss.

She knew the reason for that awful emptiness. Jared. Life without Jared. He had once told her that when the time came, she would not want to leave Seattle. Did he realize then he would be the only reason for her hesitation?

She found herself in Freeway Park, the spot where she and Jared had made up their bitter quarrel and she had begun to question her well-plotted future. She stumbled over to the bench they had shared that day and remembered their conversation.

He had talked of loyalty to the company, to herself, where the boundary should lie. She stared at the water rushing over the square blocks of the waterfall, hearing his deep, caressing voice in her mind. She wished passionately that he could tell her what was right. But he couldn't, even if he were here in person and not just in her memory. The decision she had not expected to make for another two years had been thrust ruthlessly on her today. Should she stay with the company and go where she was sent? Or should she quit and take her chances here in Seattle? Today Emery had outlined her future with APP and it was one she had never expected. One problem-filled branch office after another, cleaning up her predecessor's mistakes, watching her successors reap the rewards of her hard work.

There would be no office in the executive suite, no ultimate authority for many years, if ever. She wondered, though, if that was what she really wanted. APP was huge and impersonal. Perhaps she would find satisfaction in a smaller, more results-oriented company, where survival depended on each individual contributing his utmost. If she refused the transfer and stayed here in Seattle she could combine just such a career shift with her life with Jared. It was a soothing, uplifting idea.

Straining against this, keeping her from an easy decision, was her deeply ingrained loyalty to APP. It fed a creeping guilt that she would be abandoning all of her responsibilities if she left the company. It also produced a sense of shame. Adrienne had never been a quitter. She had always faced her problems and worked through them. Refusing the transfer and leaving APP smacked of running away, no matter how she rationalized the move.

She knew she would have to make a choice within the next few hours. It was a hard decision. She had never felt so torn.

Chapter Thirteen

The overhead sign read Parking. Adrienne followed the directions into the dark interior of the massive seven-story covered garage that faced the air terminal. She found a spot near the elevators, then slid out of the car. As she walked through the raised steel-and-glass passage that joined the terminal and the parking lot she debated where best to meet Jared. He didn't expect to see her and she didn't want to miss him.

She considered waiting at the baggage claim area, then thrust the thought aside. His only luggage had been a leather briefcase and a suit bag, both of which he would probably carry onto the plane. The best spot was where he had met her in July, the gate where passengers left the secured area.

She was in plenty of time to greet the plane from San Francisco that Jared's secretary had assured her he would be on. In fact she was early. She amused herself by watching the passing parade of people, trying to guess which of them lived in Seattle, which were visitors, which were seasoned travelers, which novices.

A mob of people rushing for the exit indicated the arrival of another jet. Adrienne spotted Jared in the crowd at once. He was wearing one of his beautifully cut suits, a midnight-blue pinstripe slightly rumpled from the hours he had been sitting on the plane. In one hand was the black leather briefcase while the other was holding the suit bag slung over his shoulder. The hard angles of his cheekbones and jaw seemed more prominent than usual, and his lips were a firm, grim line, as if the worry and tension of the past few days had taken their toll on him. The gray eyes were shadowed, too, but his posture was erect and his step firm. It took more than a little fatigue to drive away his natural vitality.

Once through security he strode directly to the escalator, not noticing Adrienne, who leaned casually against a wall out of direct view. She smiled faintly to herself and launched her body into motion.

I love you, Jared Hawkes, she thought, feeling rather misty-eyed as she followed him. *I hope I'm doing the right thing for both of us.*

She caught up with him at the top of the moving steps. "Looking for a cab, mister?" she demanded in a husky, faintly mocking voice.

He turned sharply. "Adrienne! What are you doing here?" After the start of surprise his eyes narrowed, taking in her thick hair falling in tousled abandon over her shoulders, the cherry-red, figure-hugging angora sweater she wore, the casual jeans and her grubby running shoes. "What *are* you doing here?" he repeated, emphasis on the second word.

"Offering you a lift home," she answered lightly, looking away to hide the shadow in her eyes. "Care to take me up on it?"

"Eventually," he said roughly, dropping the briefcase to pull her against him for a quick, hard kiss. Someone brushed past them and he looked up irritably, once more aware of their location. "We can't talk here," he growled impatiently.

Overwrought, Adrienne misinterpreted Jared's actions. "My car's in the lot," she said tightly. Striving for a measure of normality she pointed to the briefcase. "Let me carry something."

He shot her one of those derisive looks that said women didn't carry his bags. "I can manage, thanks," he said dryly, bending to pick it up.

"Why are you being so pigheaded?" she demanded passionately. "I'm perfectly capable of carrying the damned briefcase. I use one myself, you know!"

He frowned at the shrill note that had crept into her voice. She caught the look and felt ashamed.

She ran her fingers through her loose hair, tugging it back from her forehead. "Sorry. I didn't sleep too well last night and I'm taking it out on you."

"I thought it was something like that. You look pretty drained."

"You don't look so great yourself," she shot back flippantly, anxious to shift the topic away from her pale skin and the heavy shadows under her eyes. "Now that we've got the amenities out of the way, why don't we head off to the car?" she added, as they were once again jostled.

"Good idea," he agreed.

They moved through the shifting crowd, Jared adapting his long stride to fit Adrienne's shorter one. She walked hunched over, her fists in her pockets, her eyes lowered. She had an awful feeling that she had made a mistake, that Jared was not going to accept her decision easily, that he would not be pleased. He was acting as if he wasn't happy to see her, as if he would rather have taken a taxi back to the city. She told herself fiercely that there must be a reason for that. Perhaps he had to go into his office instead of home. Maybe he was still preoccupied by the problem he had gone down to San Francisco to solve.

"There's something troubling you, Adrienne," he observed flatly, breaking into her thoughts. "What is it?"

She jumped, her nerves so tense and raw that she was startled by the least thing, and shot him a sliding glance. He was frowning, concern in his eyes. A little of her fear fell away. She smiled faintly, replying truthfully, "Yes, there is, but I don't want to talk about it just yet. Do you have to go back to work?"

"No. I'd planned to go to my place."

She nodded. "I'd rather wait until we're there before we talk, if you don't mind. The car's over that way." She pointed and they changed direction.

"This has something to do with that guy Thorpe, doesn't it?" he demanded roughly.

She sighed and said again, "Yes."

"And it's the reason you've taken the afternoon off to meet me?" he continued inexorably.

"In a way," she agreed wearily. They reached the car. She turned to him and put her fingers over his lips in an effort to keep him silent. "No, Jared, please!

Wait. Wait until we're at your house where we can talk without interruptions."

"Very well," he said grimly, when she had moved her hand away. "But I can guess what this is all about."

"Don't," she pleaded softly. "Don't even think about it until we're home."

His jaw clenched. "That won't be easy."

"Please try."

"Damn it, Adrienne!" he snapped. "You've got me tied up in knots over this! What the hell is going on?" He had dropped his briefcase and thrown the suit bag over the roof of the car in order to grasp her shoulders and give her a shake.

Adrienne wrenched herself roughly away and stepped backward, crying, "Stop! I can tell you here if you'd prefer, in bits and pieces and all confused, but I'd rather explain clearly somewhere where we are both comfortable!"

"Damn!" he muttered savagely, reacting to the agony that fueled her voice. "Sweetheart, I'm sorry. Look, is the trunk unlocked? I'll toss my stuff in and we can get going."

She nodded, using the excuse of opening the hatchback to step away. From there she left him to stow his gear while she settled behind the wheel and started the car. She had herself well under control when he slipped into the passenger seat, folding his length with smooth grace. "How was California?" she asked conversationally, reversing the car out of the spot.

He talked lightly about his trip on the drive home. Only once, when Adrienne charged past a tractor trailer, then suddenly had to break through two lines of traffic when she noticed she was almost past the exit she wanted, did he mention the problem that was obviously tearing at her. "Whatever it is that's bothering you," he said dryly, "it's not worth killing us both."

Her eyes widened and she caught her lower lip between her teeth. "You're right. I wasn't even aware how fast I was going until I saw that exit sign. I'd better keep my mind on my driving." She slowed to a more respectable pace for the rest of the journey to his house, parking the car in his driveway.

Before she could slip out of the seat he caught her wrist, holding her steady beside him. His gray eyes were tender as he scanned her troubled features. "We can work it out, sweetheart."

She took a deep breath, blinking rapidly to hold back tears. "I hope you're right," she replied bleakly.

When they were in the house Adrienne wandered into the spacious living room with its banks of windows and the breathtaking view of the Olympic Mountains, while Jared dropped his case in the bedroom. The mountains were hidden today, shrouded by the heavy clouds. She turned abruptly away from the windows. The view was too evocative of her own gloomy feelings. She stood uncertainly until Jared reappeared a short time later.

"Would you like a drink?" he asked, shooting her an astute look. "I have a feeling I'm going to need one."

Adrienne swallowed a lump in her throat and said in a low voice. "Please. White..."

"I know. White wine." He moved over to the liquor cabinet as he was speaking.

Adrienne winced at the faint jeer in his voice, knowing she deserved it. After all these months he knew her habits well enough. She had added the specific in order to distance herself from him. A deliberate ploy to make this easier and he had caught it right away.

He handed her the drink and said gently, "Why don't you sit down?" as he propelled her toward the sofa.

She let him lead her there without resistance, then slumped wearily onto it. "I had some unpleasant news on Tuesday," she began miserably, staring at the glass in her hands.

"I gathered that," he returned dryly.

She looked up. He was standing by the wide windows, his back to the light, his face in shadow. She had no doubt that he could see her own expression very clearly. He must have deliberately guided her to the sofa for just that reason. She felt a spurt of annoyance that gave her the strength to continue.

"I found out why Emery Thorpe came out here so suddenly. It wasn't just one of his surprise inspection visits. There was more to it than that. It was me specifically he came to see." She paused, sipping the wine, giving Jared a chance to speak. He remained silent, watching her steadily, his body tense, his expression unreadable. She continued bleakly, "He came to tell me what a great job I'd done here in Seattle and that because of it I've been transferred." She laughed viciously. "Your boss always tells you news like that in person, you know, not on the telephone, not by memo. You aren't given any choice in the matter. You can't say—hey, I don't want the job, I'm staying here. Your future's already been decided for you. They know you'll agree, but I guess it's the individual touch.

Bad news is always so much easier to accept if it is given personally.''

"You consider this bad news?" Jared asked carefully.

She laughed again. "Bad news? It's worse than that, it's a disaster! When I think of all the plans I had for the office. The projects I was turning over in my mind. I was going to make the Seattle branch, my branch, the most modern, efficient office in the organization by the time I left this city." She swallowed a slug of the wine. "But that was not part of the future Emery Thorpe planned for me. Oh, no. Giving me time to stamp my imprint on a branch was not at all what he had in mind."

There was a clink of ice as Jared sipped his Scotch. "You sound very bitter," he remarked. "Isn't this what you wanted?"

"No! How can you think that?" she cried, feeling tears prick at the back of her eyelids. My God, she thought, what have I done?

He shrugged, then said coolly, "You've never made a secret of the fact you want to return to New York."

"New York, yes!" she bit out emphatically. "Chicago, no!"

"Chicago? What the devil are you talking about?"

"My transfer!" she all but screamed. "I'm sorry, Jared. I didn't mean to shriek at you. I've been agonizing over this damned order for the past forty-eight hours and I'm rather emotional about it."

"Let's get this straight, shall we?" he suggested grimly, shifting away from the window. "You're being moved to Chicago, not New York." He dragged a chair to face her and sat down.

"Yes," she replied almost inaudibly.

"I don't understand, Adrienne. Explain it to me." His tone was gentle, but his body was stiff and his face lined with a frown.

She sighed and ran her fingers through her hair, leaving it disheveled. "The day you left for San Francisco, remember I mentioned that I would have to have dinner with Emery?"

He nodded. "I wasn't particularly impressed with the idea at the time. I worried about it all the way to California."

She smiled faintly. "Emery didn't mention the transfer then. He waited until the next day when he had done a thorough job of softening me up. Anyway, at dinner he told me the Chicago office was in a mess and that the manager was being transferred to a new department as of January first."

"January first! He's not giving you much time, is he?" Jared bit out angrily.

Adrienne laughed sourly, rubbing the side of her glass. "It's worse than that. I was supposed to leave here in six weeks, at the end of November."

She watched him shift uneasily in the chair. "Was?" he demanded harshly.

The rough tone and the wary movement confirmed the fears that had surfaced at the airport. She took a sip of wine and said bleakly, "I'll try and explain this in sequence. I think that's the easiest way." He didn't nod or speak, made no effort to agree or disagree. She continued wearily, "The next day he heaped praises on me, then informed me I was being sent to Chicago, for the good of the company and needs of the business and all that."

"What about New York?" Jared asked slowly.

"New York," she said dully, lying back against the cushions, "is a dreamworld away. When I told him that he'd led me to believe my assignment after Seattle would be New York, he simply said I was needed more in the field than I was in head office." She lifted the glass to her lips, found it empty and put it on the table beside the couch.

"Would you like another?" Jared asked politely, picking up the glass.

She thought about it, then sighed. "Yes, please."

With his back to her as he stood at the liquor cabinet he said, "I think I know how you feel, Adrienne. APP transferred me out here from New York as well. To tell you the truth, I was glad to get away. But once I'd decided I wanted to remain in Seattle I started looking around for some other option. I didn't wait for them to decide that I'd be more valuable in Atlanta or New Orleans or," he added, turning around smiling faintly, "Chicago."

"I thought I had lots of time," she remarked resentfully, accepting the glass from him. For a moment their fingers touched and she felt his warm strength. Tears gathered in her throat as the brief contact was broken. She swallowed some of the wine and continued roughly, "I believed Emery when he told me I had two, perhaps more, years here. I don't know why. I've never really liked him. I just assumed he wouldn't lie to me."

"Perhaps he didn't lie," Jared suggested dispassionately. He was seated comfortably in the chair again, holding the glass of Scotch casually in one hand. "It is quite possible no one expected you to do the excellent job you have. Thorpe must have thought it would take you that long to correct the damages caused by your predecessor."

"You're probably right," she agreed slowly. "I got the impression at the meetings in July that Emery was not at all pleased I'd done as well as I have."

Jared shrugged. "It works for Thorpe either way. If you had needed the two years he could have claimed you were living up to expectations. Now he can say that he knew you had it in you all along and that he was testing you. He might not phrase it quite so bluntly, of course, but he'll still reap the benefits of your labor."

"And then transfer me from one trouble spot to another for the rest of my days," she concluded savagely. "And every time he'll claim, once I straightened things out, that when I was sent the situation was bad—but not that bad." She shrugged off the thought. It didn't matter now. "Anyway, having told me I was being transferred to Chicago before Thanksgiving and that my successor would be arriving in two weeks, Emery hopped on his plane and flew happily home to New York, content in the knowledge that his personal charm had smoothed any anger or sense of injustice I might feel at this turn of events. I went out to my car and drove back to work.

"It was a rotten day," she continued dreamily, "pouring rain and damply cold. I parked the car and headed toward the office but walked right past the building. I wandered around—I don't know how long—until I ended up in Freeway Park. I sat on a bench for a long time, getting soaked to the skin and making people who were scuttling from shelter to shelter stare at me as if I were crazy. Maybe I was. Maybe I am."

She stared down at the glass in her hand, one finger idly tracing the pattern etched in the fine crystal. "I thought all afternoon and that evening and through the night. I thought about you, Seattle, and the opportunities I would have if I chose to stay here. And I thought about my future with APP. Once I believed I was on a route to the executive suite. I'm good at my job, I'm creative, I'm dedicated. What could stop me? Office politics, that's what. A department manager who thinks he can manipulate me so he can take the credit for my accomplishments. Instead of a brilliant future with a steady succession of promotions my career will slowly grind to a standstill as I'm sent from one branch to another.

"APP needs people like me, people who give their best because something inside motivates them. For a long time I believed that ultimately my loyalty would be rewarded. Now I know it won't. I've been giving to APP what I should have been saving for myself and I never even realized it."

"What happened, Adrienne? You used to be so certain of your future." Jared's voice was gentle.

She sighed, staring down into the wine because she couldn't look him in the eye. "A lot of things, Jared. I've told you about some of them, Emery's constant interference, his carping—but I guess the July meetings made the most impact." She told him briefly about Thorpe's actions, her voice gradually growing more strident, then she continued furiously, "That's how he acts in public. In private he gives me glowing praise and tells me I'm terrific. I can just imagine the meetings next summer, after I have replaced Miles Abbott. Suddenly Miles will be a good manager who was promoted to another department, leaving a smoothly running operation behind him, which I, of course, will have inherited. And my successor here in Seattle will get the benefit of all my hard work and be the one who looks like a superstar." Her cheeks were flushed and her eyes sparkling with anger. "Do you know what Emery had the nerve to tell me to do?" She didn't wait for an answer but forged impetuously ahead. "He told me to write up all the plans and proposals I had for the office, laying out what I'd done and what needed to be done in the future, so my successor could carry out the work I'd begun!"

"Adrienne, you don't have to go to Chicago—" Jared began firmly.

"You're right, I don't!" she snapped, putting the glass on the table with a little thump. She stood up and began to restlessly prowl the room. "By yesterday morning I'd decided. I went into the office, wrote up a letter of resignation and sent it off by courier to New York. Emery got it this morning. When I went in at eight o'clock, he had already set the wheels in motion. Noel was there to take my office and desk keys, I was given a letter accepting my resignation and informed that my last paycheck would be sent to my home address. Poor Noel," she added reflectively. "He looked shattered."

"You—quit?" Jared demanded, coming up behind her and spinning her around. There was something in his voice she couldn't define. His eyes, the dark gray of thunderclouds, bored into her. "Does that mean you plan to stay in Seattle?"

"Yes."

"You wretch! Why didn't you say so in the beginning? I've spent the past two hours feeling like part of me was being torn away!"

"This doesn't change anything," she said frantically.

"Damn right it does!"

"No!" she cried, putting her hands against his chest as a barrier. "Look, Jared, you don't have to feel responsible for me. I can take care of myself—"

"Oh, no, you're not doing that to me again," he interrupted furiously.

"Do what?" She searched her mind for his meaning, but she honestly could not imagine what it was.

"Break up with me because of some screwball notion you have that I can't hope to fathom!"

His hands were biting into her shoulders. She looked up into the hard, beloved contours of his face and said softly, "I don't want to break up with you, Jared. That is the last thing I want. Nothing need change between us. That's all I was trying to say."

He said very quietly, "I want to marry you."

The words pierced her heart like a hot shaft of steel. This was her worst fear confirmed. "No. I can't, Jared."

A look of bewilderment entered his face and he shook her slightly. "I love you, Adrienne. You love me. Doesn't that matter?"

She shook her head. "No."

His features twisted in hurt rage and he thrust her savagely away. When Adrienne regained her balance he was standing staring out the window, one hand resting on the frame, the other shoved in the pocket of his slacks. As she stared at his slightly bent head, the black hair falling thickly to his collar, she wondered if she had lost him despite her decision to remain in Seattle.

"I think," he said in a low, gravelly voice, "that I deserve more of an explanation than your simple no."

"Yes," she agreed, "you do." Outside the sky was darkening, throwing the room in shadow. In winter the sun set early, deepening the already dim light from the overcast sky.

He turned. "Well?"

"In New York my career totally absorbed my life. I was hungry, determined to succeed, anxious to live down a stupid indiscretion I'd made in my first year with the company. I was slowly turning into an emotional block of ice, without even being aware of it. Coming to Seattle changed that. Suddenly I began to look at myself and at APP through different eyes. You had a lot to do with that, Jared."

"I'm glad," he said simply, "but I still don't understand the problem."

She shot him a quick glance, but once again his features were in shadow. He was standing tensely now, watching her, both hands thrust in his pockets. Even though she couldn't see his face his stance was expressive. He had no intention of letting her off easily.

She shook her head and spread out her hands in a gesture of helplessness. "Jared, all my life I've been reaching for a goal. When I was in high school it was the chance to go to university. In university it was good grades so I'd get a job in a top-rated company. At APP it was always the next promotion. I believed that hard work and dedication led to success. Now I don't have that anymore!"

"Of course you do," he shot back, moving away from the window, his long, lean body coming to tower over her. "There are always goals, Adrienne, all you have to do is look for them and they're there. Okay, so

APP didn't work out. There are other companies, other jobs, other promotions!"

"But I've never worked for any other company! I started at APP right out of college. I put everything I had into making a success there. I feel like I've given up. As if I've failed."

"That will pass," he said gently. He gripped her shoulders, his shapely fingers rubbing her flesh soothingly. "None of this explains why you won't marry me."

"I think it does," she replied sadly, looking up into his face. "You never spoke of marriage, Jared. Until now. You never even said you loved me, until now. Now, when I've quit my job and my career is gone. I realize you're only trying to help, but there's no need."

His hands stilled on her shoulders. "You think I proposed out of some misguided chivalrous impulse? The big strong male protecting his woman from the dangers of the outside world?"

"It sounds pretty silly when you put it that way," she muttered, looking at her feet.

"Yes, it does," he agreed dryly. As he spoke he moved to flick on a lamp, flooding the room with artificial light, bright after the evening dusk. "Do you think I'm that sort of man?" he demanded inflexibly, coming over to her and lifting her chin with one strong finger.

"Jared, I..."

He read the confusion in her eyes. "The type of man who expects his wife to sit at home, minding the house or minding the kids or both?"

"You were jealous of my job, you admitted it!" she flung out, wrenching her head to one side.

"*That* job, yes! Not your talent or the fact that you were putting your very real skills to work." He slid his hands slowly along her shoulders until they cupped her neck, his thumbs stroking her soft skin in a smooth hypnotic rhythm. "I thought your Emery Thorpe was using you, Adrienne. I was trying to warn you, to prepare you for exactly what happened."

She drew a rueful breath. "Stepping-stones."

He laughed shortly. "Not very subtle, I'm afraid. I wanted you to wake up and take a good, hard look at your position. Until you did I thought there was no hope for us. That's why I left you that night."

"And yet," she said softly, "you let me go off to the meetings in July without a murmur of complaint."

He groaned and rested his forehead against hers. "When you went back to New York I spent the whole week in a kind of living hell. I was terrified you'd come back more dedicated to APP than ever. I hoped you would see the company for what it was and decide that your future was here with me, rather than back in head office. But it was a risk—one I had to take and one I desperately wanted to avoid."

"I thought you didn't care," she said with a sigh, leaning against him and letting her head fall against his shoulder. His hands moved to wrap around her in a close embrace.

"Not care! Sweetheart, I couldn't sleep the whole week, I missed you so." A wry note crept into his voice. "I already knew I wanted to marry you, but I wasn't sure how you felt."

She pulled away, looking up into his face, her eyes surprised. "Jared, I love you. I told you so dozens of times!"

"But you also told me your career meant more to you than anything else, including marriage," he said slowly, some of the worry he had felt then still in his eyes.

A sudden cleansing understanding eased the last of her fears. Jared would never force her into marriage by revealing his own needs and desires. She had to come to him of her own volition. She reached up and silently touched his cheek.

His arms tightened, then his hands moved to her shoulders, thrusting her away so he could see her face. "Will you marry me?"

His voice was urgent, emphatic, questioning. She smiled mistily. "Yes."

He drew her back into his arms to kiss her soundly, possessively. Her body molded itself to his in a promise as old as time. When at last he released her, she asked softly, "Jared, why did you never tell me you loved me?"

He stroked the hair back from her face with gentle fingers, while his other arm strengthened its hold on her. "But I have, my love. I've told you with my eyes and my lips and my hands and my body."

"But you never said the words."

He sighed. "I thought you knew. You seemed to. I couldn't believe you would respond so freely to me if you didn't believe that I felt strongly for you. If it makes it any better I'll say it now. I love you, Adrienne Denton, with every cell in my body. I need you with me now and forever."

His head bent. She cuddled close and willingly met his descending lips. Their kiss was long and deep, a reaffirmation of the love they were pledging to each other.

"And I love you," she said at last, her voice thick. "I want you, I need you, I love you, forever. Now."

"Hmm," he agreed, nibbling her lips. "First I have to decide where I'd like to go for dinner and dancing. The most expensive place in Seattle, I think. Shall I make the reservation in your name?"

"Why?" she demanded, perplexed.

"A little matter of a bet we made at Noel Granger's barbecue. Remember?"

For a moment she frowned, then her brow cleared. "And I lost."

"When the time came to leave Seattle, you couldn't. I intend to make the most of that transfer of loyalties both now and in the future."

"No complaints from me," she breathed, reaching up to bring his head down for a kiss.

Silhouette Special Edition

JUNE TITLES

AS TIME GOES BY
Brooke Hastings

SURPRISE OFFENSE
Carole Halston

MY HEART'S UNDOING
Phyllis Halldorson

TRANSFER OF LOYALTIES
Roslyn MacDonald

LOVE'S HAUNTING REFRAIN
Ada Steward

BIRD IN FLIGHT
Sondra Stanford

Silhouette Special Edition

COMING NEXT MONTH

DIAMOND IN THE SKY
Natalie Bishop

Maybe she *was* crazy to think she could help Jason Garrett. But Taylor Michaelson owed him her career. Tragedy had struck and Jason had now become a recluse. What could Taylor do that others hadn't already tried?

HEATSTROKE
Jillian Blake

Tony Miles had been a rock star. Cary Davidson had been a cheerleader. And in one evening they had shared something Cary had never forgotten. Now, a decade later, she finally had a chance to see if the longing she felt that night was really love.

BITTERSWEET SACRIFICE
Bay Matthews

When Lindy Scott had agreed to become a surrogate mother she really had believed she could give up the baby. Zade Wakefield had no idea it was she who carried his child. He only knew that the unknown woman had changed her mind. And that he was determined to fight — and to win.

Silhouette Special Edition

COMING NEXT MONTH

JESSE'S GIRL
Billie Green

Jesse had never returned Ellie's obsessive love with more than brotherly affection. Except once. And he'd never known the pain he caused. But he was back — and the pain was disappearing. Once Ellie had dreamed of being Jesse's girl. Now she wanted to be his woman.

ZACHARY'S LAW
Lisa Jackson

Unconventional described Zachary Winters to a T. But if he was her last hope of finding her two children, Lauren would ignore the rumours surrounding this roguish lawyer. Perhaps it was just as well Lauren was unaware that the intriguing sadness in her soft green eyes stirred emotions Zachary Winters had long buried.

THIS LONG WINTER PAST
Jeanne Stephens

After watching the disintegration of her parents' marriage, Liann McDowell had vowed never to fall in love with a cop. But when a murder trial threw her together with investigating officer Cody Wakefield he didn't seem content to let their relationship stop at business.

Silhouette Desire

JUNE TITLES

CAUTIOUS LOVER
Stephanie James

WHEN SNOW MEETS FIRE
Christine Flynn

HEAVEN ON EARTH
Sandra Kleinschmit

NO MAN'S KISSES
Nora Powers

THE SHADOW BETWEEN
Diana Stuart

NOTHING VENTURED
Suzanne Simms